CRUSHING

LACHAPPELLE/WHITTIER VINEYARDS - BOOK 1

KELLY KAY

Published by Decorated Cast Publishing LLC

Edited by: Erin Young, EY Literary Management

Copy Edit: Holly Jennings, Freelance Editing Services

Cover Design: Tim Hogan

https://www.timhogancreative.com/

❅ Created with Vellum

DEDICATION

For Eric and Charlie because there is nothing else without
you 2

CRUSH
/krəSH/
Verb

Winemakers loosely refer to crush as the entire harvest from picking the grapes in August through November to the time when the wine is in the bottle. As the grapes ripen, the amount of sugar and sweetness in the fruit increases and those sugars will ferment into wine eventually, with time, care, and attention.

CHAPTER ONE

NOELLE

I feel like he's talking only to me. His voice is commanding but not a deep base. It's like a sweet tenor with a slight vibrato. This silver fox of a sommelier is something to behold. There's sixteen people seated at the table, but he's focused on me. His intense hazel eyes seem to be sparking in the candlelight as he's moving around. Each time he looks at me, they change color. Like he could almost be a different person if he chooses.

My fair skin is blushing under his stare and the effects of the red wine. I'm grateful for my high Elie Tahari navy lace collar. I don't need to look. I can feel the heat prickling up to my neck, and I know I'm blushing. I hope it won't creep up to my cheeks. My icy blonde bob blow-out is skimming my shoulders tonight. As I turn my head to chat, I keep getting hair stuck in sticky, deep fuchsia Tom Ford lip lacquer, aptly named *Infatuate*. My wine glass looks a bit like a murder scene. I've never really been to a high-end wine tasting. I thought there would be a series of tiny tastes in little throw-away cups. I look like I've been giving my glassware head.

Everyone in this room is a client, except the handsome

sommelier. Parker & Co., my marketing and branding firm, is celebrating seven years tonight, and these companies were my first big fish. They gambled on me. I have small pieces of these giant companies' marketing budgets, and it's all my company can handle right now. They made my company finally go into the black. My contacts from Xfinity, Apple, and Southwest Airlines are all getting fancy sloshed and hopefully are impressed with what Asher Bernard has to say.

In our first three emails, I called him Bernard Asher. His name seemed backward to me. I thought maybe it was a European thing but turns out he's from Petaluma, California. He's judged wine competitions all over the world and has been featured in *The Wine Spectator*. I'm thoroughly impressed by him. He worked with my caterer to pair the wines then flew to New York to be with us for this dinner. I picked the date on purpose. I threw this Valentine's party for my favorite clients because I have no time for hearts that get broken and flowers that die.

Asher creates custom wine collections for high-end clients. I had no idea he'd be this intriguing. Asher's guiding us on how to taste wine, but not in a lecturing sort of way. He's leaning over me from behind with his lips so close to my ear that there's a tingle on my skin. After this much wine, I let it happen.

"Swirl. Let it reveal its temperament and unleash its aromas to you. The wine is all bottled up, give it some oxygen. Let it breathe. Then sniff. Take it all in."

He puts his hand over mine, and we swirl. My cheeks flush a bit as he touches me. Maybe I've been bottled up too long as well.

"Now sip. Hold it on the tip of your tongue, breathe in, and let it slide back slowly. Now savor. Tip your head and let it flow down your throat. Notice the finish that lingers behind like the wine isn't ready to be done with you yet."

I put my hands on the table to steady myself a bit. I can't help but think about how erotic that felt. Maybe I should ditch my martinis and negronis. Perhaps I should learn wine. It's rather sexy.

THE DINNER WAS A HUGE SUCCESS, and then Asher raises a glass. "This is a delightful evening. Happy Valentine's Day. I want to toast our host, the enthralling and captivating Ms. Noelle Parker." My cheeks flush. It's a constant Irish-skinned battle not to be red, blotchy, or flush pink. I thank everyone for coming, and they begin to leave.

Asher's lingering like the Cabernet on my tongue as I gather my things to leave. It's around ten when he hands me another glass of wine. I feel as if I can't sip anymore, but it smells fruity and light.

"Late Harvest Riesling from Grgich Hills."

"I don't know any of those words, but if you're handing it to me, it must be delicious. Thank you." As he hands me the glass, his fingers reach around and graze the inside of my wrist. He stares at me intensely as I take the wine from him. As he raises his own glass, we never break eye contact.

"To the most charming host."

I sip. It's delicious and sweet. But to be honest, after this much wine, it might as well be tap water for all my uneducated palate can tell. "Thank you for coming all this way, Asher." I tilt my head to the side after I sip. I lick my lips and his eyebrows raise. He's rather smooth. Everything seems effortless, as if he's rehearsed this moment.

"You know, you did pay me a lot of money," he says sweetly, and then he moves a bit closer to me.

I stand up straighter, not sure if I should be leaning in or away from this moment. "I know. That was to pair the wines and give me a write-up. This was beyond."

"As are you." He takes my hand and brushes the knuckles with his lips. My heart speeds up a bit.

His flirting is on point. I've never dated an older man, but the depth of his eyes and the pepper in his silver hair are damned hot. He's wearing a pinstripe grey suit that fits him perfectly with a pink-striped tie and matching pocket square. I'd guess Ralph Lauren. He's not muscular brawny but clearly tight and in shape. He moves behind me, and he's at my ear as he reaches up, holding his phone. "I tend to take selfies." It's an odd habit for his age group, a forty-six-year-old man.

A thirteen-year age difference doesn't seem all that daunting. I assume there's an intriguing story why he's still single. But maybe it's a choice. He's quirky, exceedingly charming, and adorable. I smile, and he instantly posts it to Instagram. I only have a corporate account, my private life is not on display for clients, but he tags me anyway. What's done is done.

"I really must be going."

"No nightcap?"

"More? You want to drink more?" I look at him as if he's crazy. I let loose with a girlish giggle, and he smiles at me.

"Had something else in mind if you'll indulge me. It's a short walk, I promise." He pulls a rose out of the table arrangement and hands it to me. "Happy Valentine's Day."

HOW COULD I say no at this point? Walking around the corner, we end up at the famed ice cream shop Serendipity. It's Valentine-palooza inside. The aroma of rich chocolate surrounds us as he opens the door. The familiar white bent-wood chairs and the old-fashioned stained-glass lamps are the same as in my memory. My parents brought me to this ice cream parlor when we were in town for my dad to attend a conference. I make my home here today because of that one magical trip when I was twelve. New York City was worlds away from Kansas. Now this stranger has ushered me back into my memories without even knowing it.

We share a hot and a cold chocolate. Asher keeps putting whipped cream on his face and pretending it's not there. Then I dutifully tell him to wipe it off, and he gets more on himself as he wipes the wrong spot. He's entertaining. Not fall-on-your-ass funny but amusing. He takes my hand, and I lightly caress the top of his hand with my fingernails. I hear his breath hitch just a moment.

"I can't remember the last time I had a Valentine," I tell him.

"Delighted to fill that void. I'm devastated about my return to California tomorrow."

"Suddenly, so am I."

We stare at each other a little bit. I shift my chair a little closer to him so my hand can stay in his on top of the table. He picks up my spoon and fills it with chocolaty goodness and offers it to me. I let him feed me. I'm sure to others it looks romantic, and it is. It's just not something I'm used to being a part of.

"Did you always see yourself working with wine?"

He nods and hums a bit. It's quirky and cute. "I grew up around wine. It's a perfect fit for a man like me. And did you grow up around wine?" I laugh at his joke. Maybe a little more than I should from the volume of wine and chocolate in my system. I'm on a serotonin overload. His fingers are drifting all over my hands and wrists. I'm having a hard time concentrating. It feels nice.

"Far from it. I grew up small wanting a bigger life."

"And it appears you got it. Do you always get what you want?" He says this in a slightly sexual way.

"It's built into my DNA. I always get what I want eventually. I'm a bit relentless."

"We share that trait." He stands and holds his hand to mine. We've been in a bubble, and I look around and see that the place is empty.

We're the last to leave. We walk hand in hand back uptown a bit. We stop, and he leans toward me and with snow gently falling, like a movie scene. I step towards him, and he wraps his arms around me. He brushes his lips over mine. They're velvety lips. Then he goes back in, and I lean in as well. Our lips join, but the kiss is a little awkward and a touch too juicy. It's not out of control but soft and sweet, just really damp.

"I don't want to say goodnight," he whispers.

"I know what you mean." We can fix the kiss. I want another shot at it.

"Then let me get us a car." He winks, and I realize I've led him on a bit.

"Oh. No. Sorry. I have an early morning. This will just be this for now." He looks crestfallen, but I don't sleep with men the night I meet them.

My dating rules were put in place after I spent a year not being myself. It was a year of way too many men who didn't dull the pain. Now I don't sleep with men I'm not dating. My friends call it controlling, I say it's romantic. As much as I'm enjoying being romanced by Asher, I'm still not going to break my rules. I'm not so sure about him, which is why dating was invented—so you can be sure this is a person you want in your life and bed. I've learned to take care of myself over the years. Lots of little rules around men have kept me sane and my heart safe.

"If that's what you want, sweet Noelle, that's what you'll get. May I call you?"

"I'd like that." He kisses me sweetly again and then hails a cab. "Goodnight." He leaves me standing on a street corner with lightly falling snow, a rose, and rosy cheeks. It really does feel a bit like a movie moment. I want more. I hope he'll call. I'd like to see if he's this rehearsed and perfectly romantic all the time. Like, will dating this man be like a Hallmark Christmas movie or will it fizzle and die because I didn't go to his hotel room?

CHAPTER TWO

NOELLE

THE XFINITY ACCOUNT IS SLIPPING SO IT'S TIME TO FIRE MY junior creative director. Melissa Grady has wildly unpredictable actions and hair. She gets indignant when clients give her suggestions and disregards Evan, my partner and Executive Art Director. Her work is habitually late, and somehow, she always has a guacamole stain on her shirt.

"Thanks so much for coming in. I'll be blunt. I'm going to pay you out for two weeks. Please hand over your laptop to Evan. I'm afraid we're going to go in a different direction with this position."

"Evan is a sycophant! A class-A suck-up. He does what they tell him to do. No creativity! I'm the only flair left in this place."

I loudly exhale as my phone buzzes and flashes Asher's name. I grin.

She says, "Focus up, Noelle, you're firing me. I should take precedence. Just saying."

I quickly answer, "Of course. I'm so sorry. That was rude."

"Forgiven. I can't stay mad atcha."

"I'm not sure why that is. But Melissa, I feel we can be informal now."

"There's just something about you. You feel it too don't you?" She crosses her legs again and I swear crumb fall out of her pants.

I say a bit exasperated, "Perhaps but really I'd like to say, I don't think marketing and advertising are your forte. I think you're more of a free spirit."

"That's exactly why I'm here. To liven up your stuffy environment."

"We're not exactly stuffy. I do feel there's a better fit for you in another career."

"Of course, there is, you nutty perfectionist. I stuck around here because I find you fascinating."

"What?"

"I had to lay low because of my former line of work and I just can't stop coming into this office. I get it. I'll go. But you should know that aside from my wicked crush on you, I feel as if there's something bubbling up in your psyche and I wanted to see if I'd be around when you crack."

"Perhaps your other career held more promise. You could go back to that."

"You know why I like you?"

"No. I don't."

"You're a straight shooter wrapped up like sweet candy."

"If you say so."

"You've got steel in your veins, but the package is wrapped in is all lightness and cotton candy. You look delicious all the time, and you're firing me right now and I don't even mind. In fact, I straight up trust you."

I shift my weight and lean forward on my desk. I just want this over. "Thank you, I guess.

"Can't go back to the old profession. Certain branches of the government have requested that I don't. I'm a hacker."

She crosses her legs in her misshapen and dingy gray leggings.

I squint. "Is that jelly on your pants?"

"Dropped the toast."

"And you just left the stain there? What do you mean, you're a hacker?"

Her gruff voice fills my office as she leans forward. "Look, lady girl." I roll my eyes as she continues, "I do shell sites, dark web, credit card hacks, NASA, SEC, and online gambling rooms. They couldn't prove it was me, I'm that good, but they did know it was me, and after they come knocking on your door—at an address you thought you'd scrubbed from the public record—and warn you. You rethink your career trajectory. I thought I should try something legal for a while. I'm banned from tech and global research companies."

My eyes are wide as this paradox of a woman pulls something out of her teeth and then rearranges her ample breasts in her bra. I blow out a long breath and sit back. She salutes me and says, "And yes, I've read all your emails. Habit. Sorry."

My cheeks instantly blush, as she continues, "Come on. It's not like they're juicy. You barely have friends. Your love life is dull, and you're a cart loader. Just buy the shoes, don't leave them in the cart hanging there like a promise."

This is why we need an actual HR department. And I don't window cart shop too much. Do I? How did this meeting end up like this?

I exclaim, "Hold up! That means you knew I wanted to fire you."

"For like three months. Evan wanted me gone long ago. Not sure if I'm still here because you're too pussy to fire me or you believed I'd turn it around."

"For your information, it was the latter. You're very

creative, you bring good energy to the office, and you don't mind working insane hours." Not a pussy.

The shaggy, russet-colored-haired woman holds her fist up like we're sisters in some kind of club. "That means a lot." Then thumps her heart with the fist like she has heartburn.

"Okay, then. Thanks so much for all your odd dedication. And stay out of my server." I outstretch my hand to indicate that this bizarre meeting is adjourned.

"I'll try, but sometimes I get bored and hacking you is a legal gray area."

I stand, smoothing down my silk Prada wrap skirt. I extend my OPI *Chick Flick Cherry* red manicured hand to her. She stares at me. I need her to go so I can save the account, see what Asher said, and apparently up our cybersecurity.

She points at me and gestures up and down. What she doesn't do is shake my hand and leave. "You just made sure you looked perfect for firing me. And I mean, you seem to be the only person who can pull off chartreuse."

"Cryptic and odd, but thank you."

"Your white flowers in your office never die. Do you secretly replace the wilty ones?" I shoot my eyes to the peonies on my desk.

"How do you not know I have a standing order with a florist?"

"Never hacked your phone. Out of respect." And her fist goes back in the air. I halfheartedly mimic the gesture.

"Thank you. I guess."

"Your bag always matches your shoes but not too matchy. They always go together cleverly. And never a stray hair."

I straighten my frame as I realize she's evaluating me. My hair was stuck in my lipstick last night. I'm not perfect. I'm exact. I am taken aback by this former felon and her assessment of me. "Another reason I kept you was your attention to detail, and I liked how you could instantly read the client.

Not that you'd listen to them and do as they asked, but you're intuitive. Now please stop turning that eye on me and take care." I try again for a handshake. I shift my weight and cock my head to the side waiting.

She continues but doesn't get up. "You're not spontaneous at all. Have you ever thrown a couple of pairs of underwear in a bag and run off for an adventure spur of the moment?"

"To be fair, no one packs a couple of pairs of underwear and just takes off." I cross my arms over my chest.

"I have."

"And that was a good vacation?"

"Terrible, but you never know. Your office is supposed to feel badass bitch, but then there are these hints of girly charm to remind people you're feminine. Your couch is black leather, but your desk is white and scrolly. You have a pink desk chair. Your whimsy is calculated."

I defend my favorite color. "I like pink."

"I think it's because it matches the inside of your bookshelves and that pink makes the green from your eyes pop, and the blonde of your hair feels more sorority girl golden than harsh platinum corporate bitch."

"Slow up there, sister. I don't have to explain any of these things to you."

"Everything's in its place with a twist. You've calculated a wrench in everything to be not perceived as perfect. It's kind of genius. But I look forward to meeting you when it all falls into the shitter."

"You can go now."

"You can only hold on to so much before it slips, and I can't wait to see who you are when it all cracks."

"You don't know me." And now I begin to pace a bit in my office. I'm drumming my fingers on the desk trying to figure out what to do next.

She continues speaking at me in her crazy babble. Mel

leans forward on her knees as if she might get up, but she only places her hands there. She sits in the chair with her legs spread as if she's on her own couch. "You're like the Persian rug makers, purposefully weaving a mistake into their work, so they're not too perfect in the eyes of God because it would be arrogant. I'm your Persian rug flaw so you're not a controlling perfectionist."

I hustle around the back of my desk and grab my phone and purse. I look at her as I step lively towards my own door. "Great feedback. If you're not leaving my office, then I am."

She's leaning backward over the chair, glancing at me and gesturing with one arm. "I'll miss you, you nutty control freak! You're my favorite disaster waiting to happen. If you need anything in the future, I'll be there." And then there's a finger gun. I react as if she means to stalk me.

"Not like that. Just I'll be around if you need some computer help or something. You wanna grab a burrito some time?" I cringe at the thought of salsa and guac spilling from her mouth and onto her shirt. And worse, she would leave it there. I shake my head to indicate that sharing nachos is off the table.

"Thanks for all of that." I circle my open palm at her to indicate everything she just said is rolled into a slice of crazy.

I walk down the stairs of the converted brownstone that I purchased with my parents' money. This was my second foray into owning my own firm, and the one that I did right. The first one was a bust from the beginning.

Evan and I lived on the top floor of this building for three years before we expanded the office. My bedroom became a conference room, and Evan's bedroom became my office. His office used to be two closets and an ironing board cubby that we made into a light-filled art director's dream. It was us against the world.

We did all the historical reno we could. It's on a tree-lined street between Broadway and 6th. South of midtown but just north of the Flatiron Building. I found this far-from-perfect building when no one was buying in Koreatown/Murray Hill.

My dad always said your value is in the land, so I sacrificed everything to possess my own chunk of Manhattan. I own this building and my apartment. Five years after we opened our doors, I refinanced and paid for full renovations. That's when we finally stopped having to put pots out for roof leaks. And yes, some of our wood trim is my favorite shade of pink: Benjamin Moore *Rhododendron*, #2079-50. It's the perfect pink, not too icy and not too warm. It's bright and cheery and makes me happy.

There are modern touches, like water and light fixtures, colors, and furniture, but the rich history of this house built in 1906 was preserved. We exposed the brick where we could and patched and painted the tin ceiling. The character of this house matters more than being perfect. See, I'm not perfect. Things just need a plan.

When our first local client wanted to meet at our office, it sent us into a frenzy of home renovations. When Antique Party and Events arrived, we'd worked nonstop for a week making sure their path to my makeshift conference room, the old dining room, looked perfect. I sanded and stained only the portion of the floor they'd see; it's all I could afford. Evan patched and painted only the walls in their path, hanging floor to ceiling curtains over the parts that were beyond patching. I conned a construction company into loaning me scaffolding. We put it up with draping to hide the rest of the house, pretending the workers were taking a break during our meeting. For the next year, we'd move the scaffolding to mask the untouched parts of the house as our business expanded quickly and the reno moved slowly.

Fake it until you make it was our mantra. Friends and

neighbors sat in on different meetings to round out our fake staff. They'd pretend to take notes, and it worked. We did all the work. We looked like a company. Appearances do matter, dirty underwear vacations do not.

After I convinced Alan Cummings to throw an Antique Event's turn of the century birthday party at the Edison Ballroom, not only did I keep that client but to this day Antique puts on all my events. They were responsible for putting Asher in my life. They threw that dinner for me.

My building is far from perfect, and we have yet to find a plumber or an electrician who can make sense of our systems. Perfect. Fuck off, you ridiculous wild-haired woman. I painted, I grouted the bathrooms, and I sanded my own damn floors. My chair can be any color I fucking choose. I don't usually take that kind of shit from anyone, but I don't want a lawsuit. I just want her gone.

I slam the door as I exit because if you don't, it won't close. The original door is warped, but I don't care. See, there's perfection in the imperfection.

I storm down the block to Birch Coffee, and as I enter, I listen to Asher's message. The baristas wave at me and begin to prepare my half-caf americano with an extra shot of decaf and oat milk. It's the coffee I've learned to drink, not the one I like.

"I've been thinking about you. I'd really like to see you again. I'm judging a competition this weekend in Guerneville, and then I have a dinner in Healdsburg. I'd love for you to join me. Separate hotel rooms, of course. Come and let me show you my Cali."

We spoke last week, and he invited me to Tahoe. I felt that was presumptuous, and I didn't know how to deal with something that spontaneous. He's a gentleman. It's not a text or an email. No one's swiping anything. It's a call, with a message. A voice telling me he was thinking about me. Fuck Melissa for getting in my head. I can be spontaneous.

"Well, hello. That was faster than I thought you'd respond. How are you?"

"Asher, I'm well. Yes."

"Yes! You'll come to visit me? That's wonderful."

"Separate rooms would be lovely. Thank you."

I grin that he wants to be with me enough to withstand my strangeness of not jumping in bed with him. Other than googling him and sharing some frozen hot chocolate, I don't know him.

"I'll fly in on Friday afternoon," I continue. "I'll even leave work early."

His voice is excited and a little squeaky. I think it's charming. "That's the best thing I've ever heard. Do you want to give me your credit card number to book your room? How about adjoining rooms with a living room at the Hotel Healdsburg?"

"I can call." I don't need a man to do this for me.

"You'll need to get a car and drive north. Is that okay? And there's a wonderful dinner just for us on Sunday night, you'll have to go back on Monday."

I never take a day off. I haven't been on vacation in about eight years. So, hell yeah, I can take a Monday off. "Okay! Okay. I'm really doing this. I'm really going away with a stranger. And taking a vacation day."

"I'm not that strange. But I am incredibly happy to see you in four days."

I hyperventilate a bit. I'm doing this. This is something I'm doing. I need to buy shoes. Shopping. I'm good at shopping. "Bye, Asher. Thank you for the invite."

"You're quite welcome, lovely." My stomach turns a little into something like new nervous knots.

CHAPTER THREE

NOELLE

WE'VE TALKED FIVE TIMES THIS WEEK. LONG GETTING-TO-know-you conversations. My lips tingle when I am thinking of kissing him. I'm hoping we can improve upon the first one. It was a bit juicy. I do need a good kiss, and I think with a little coaching he'll improve.

I'm arriving in Northern California just before bud break. Asher explained that it's when all the tight little green buds of future grapes burst open. The leaves are small so it looks almost like the vines are covered in green popcorn. The drive up here is breathtakingly beautiful. Over the Golden Gate and then up into these rolling hills. The vines are covered with tiny little bright green leaves and small flowers that over the next six months will become grapes. The landscape is lush and sensual.

In the elevator up, I think of his sexy speckled hair. We chatted facts this week, he's divorced, no children but is open to the idea. His ex is in Europe, so I won't have to deal with her. He was very upfront about kids. It's refreshing and shocking to entertain those thoughts.

No one discusses having children in New York. Conversations center around: new cocktails, politics, parties you missed, parties you attended, music, theater, new restaurants, bad restaurants, restaurant closings, potholes, streets to avoid and what new exhibits are opening. But having children seems to be a passing thought for when we all inevitably buy something in the Hudson River Valley, not for dating in Manhattan.

It's hard not to anticipate sex when you fly across the country to a luxury hotel, and he continually speaks of your beauty. We have three nights. I would like there to be sex. Oh, god. I hope he wants to have sex with me. This is a second date. We didn't just meet so my rules allow for some fun naked time. Which has been sadly missing from my life lately. He'll be working most of tomorrow afternoon, and I'll explore by myself.

The door's ajar, and he's standing by an open balcony door in a living room area. He's wearing a forest green cashmere sweater and gray creased wool herringbone pants. His Gucci loafers kicked off to the side, and he's wearing socks that match his top. The color is darker than my emerald eyes, but I do love green. He's sipping something ruby in hue. I drink him in before he sees me. I quietly put my coat down and sneak up behind him. I wrap my arms around this man that I've only known for one evening.

"Ah. Now, this is perfect." He places his hand over mine. Then he grabs them and spins within my arms.

"Hi. Whatcha drinking?"

"2014 Hendry Red."

"And it's just red. I thought it had to be a thing?"

"It's a Bordeaux blend, which is the combo—"

I interrupt him. I tend to geek out over research. "A blend of five grapes that grow in that region in France. But it's not a Claret, which just means a red from that region or a Meritage, which must be a blend of at least two Bordeaux grapes with no one varietal being more than ninety percent of the blend. It can be a white wine as long as the grapes line up!"

"Hmmm. If you know all my secrets, how I will impress you? If you know the magic five noble varietals, I'll give you a prize." He leans down, brushing his lips softly to my ear and says, "And trust me, you want this prize."

I don't hesitate. I memorized it an hour ago. "Cabernet Sauvignon, Cabernet Franc, Merlot, Malbec and Petit Verdot, whatever that is."

He backs up. "How did you learn that in a couple of days?"

"It's two *cabs*, two *m's*, and a *pv*."

"Clever."

I lean into him. He looks down to me and tentatively takes my lips. I push forward, hoping to get a more scintillating kiss out of him. My arms get little goosebumps as he runs his hands down my neck and into my hair. He pulls down my messy bun, and I moan a little. It's a problem I have, I moan. My chest and cheeks are flaming flushed. It's my skin's curse, and it's been a while since I was with a man.

I whisper to him, "Do we have anywhere to be?" I'd like to explore this man's mouth a bit more.

"Unfortunately, we need to be at a dinner in thirty minutes, and I need a shower."

"Me too. But not together."

He laughs at how I've flipped back to chaste. I don't like to shower with people, ever. And shower sex is a joke. It's always sexier in movies than reality. I have a particular way I wash my hair and body. Nobody in the shower, it's one of my rules. He points to a door that connects to this suite. I assume that's my room.

He kisses me. He's sensuous and soft, but it's still a sloppy kiss, and his tongue seems to need more direction. Good thing I like making sure everything is just so. His tongue is one big pillow. I've seen him command a room, but so far, he's not like that with intimacy. Perhaps I could use a little soft in my life.

HE'S SITTING in the living room waiting for me. I check and recheck my makeup. I'd like to look perfect. We're dining with one of his clients tonight, and I want to make a good impression. I've pulled my hair into a French twist and am wearing my mother's emerald earrings. They complement the short silk dress I'm wearing. It's a vibrant Persian blue and makes me feel glamorous. I slide on my silver sparkly three-inch Jimmy Choo heels. They pinch but are totally worth it. And now I feel like an Amazon at five-foot-eight.

My blonde hair, peaches-and-cream skin, and my eyes to match the dress all came together perfectly. Sex with this man is a probability, even though it's been something I've avoided in recent history. It's not that I don't like it; I just don't have the time to invest in my heart. The longest and most destructive relationship ended when I found my ex-business partner and ex-fiancée fucking our new assistant on my desk. An image I try to scrub from my mind even after eight years.

I rebuilt my reputation and my company on my own, but as for my heart, it's never quite returned to working order. Just maybe Asher can heal the cracks.

CHAPTER FOUR

SHE APPEARS, AND HER ROYAL BLUE, KNEE-LENGTH DRESS IS lighting up the room. She's perfect for me. She's ideal for my reputation and image. "Stunning. Ravishing. Beyond."

"Thank you."

"More incredibly, you did that in twenty minutes." I hold my arm out to her and say, "Shall we?"

"How long must we stay?" She winks.

And her suggestive nature suits me fine.

SHE DAZZLES IN THE ROOM, and I pick up three new clients because of her allure. Not only am I going to have her tonight, but she might also be of more use than I initially thought. I found her engaging and personable around her own clients, but now she might just be the one to secure the deal I've been waiting a lifetime to make.

She's a force of charming nature, and no one can resist her. I also did a tad bit of research, and she's quite capable and well respected in her field. I've decided to keep her.

At the end of dinner, I'm holding my wine a lot better than she is. We stumble back to the elevator. She gives me a crooked smile, and I kiss her lips. I'm working my best moves, and she's gasping for breath. We make it back to the room, and I arrange the condoms on my nightstand while she heads to the bathroom. As I get my hangers out for my sweater and pants, she emerges sans shoes and her hair torn down.

"So, Asher."

"Yes, Noelle?"

"I think I might just turn in." She shrugs and covers her mouth like she's yawning.

I'm standing there dumbstruck and then she giggles. I launch on her and throw her petite body down on the bed. I'm on top of her in an instant and kissing her neck. I'm feeling her thighs, and she's gasping a bit. Her noises are super distracting, to be honest. Why is she moaning? I haven't done anything yet. I need to be inside her power and beauty. But she needs to be quiet.

She dominates a room without anyone even realizing they've been manipulated. I noticed, but no one else did. I'm not even sure she recognizes her power and potential. She will be my secret weapon.

I stand as she watches. Her eyes are leering at me, and she looks hungry. No real chase here. I tug my shirttails out of my pants then reach for a hanger. Noelle kneels on the edge of the bed. She begins to unbutton my shirt. I lift her dress over her head, then she grabs it and throws it to the floor, which I don't understand. It's a beautiful dress. I pick it up and drape it neatly over the dresser. I'd like to hang it up, but I don't want her to think that I don't want to see her body. Her white bra is glistening and her breasts heaving with each breath. And then this goddess does the most sublime thing. She unbuckles my pants and takes me so quickly, I don't know what's happening. My member grows in her skillful mouth. I push the pause button to remove my pants, fold them, and put them next to my shirt.

Then I return to her mouth. "Surprising. Wow. Noelle. This is…so very good."

CHAPTER FIVE

NOELLE

HUH? DID HE JUST FOLD HIS PANTS? HIS DICK WAS IN MY mouth, and he pulled it out to hang up his dirty shirt. His dick is bobbing in and out of my mouth, and all he can say is it's 'so very good.' Not the best of dirty talkers. Again, coachable. But I'm fucking amazing at this. I love that I alone get to decide whether he gets to come or not. I need to get back into this.

Wine messes you up in a different way than cocktails. I hope Asher's buzzed. It's the only justification for sloppier and goopier kissing. One man with so much saliva. He might be perfect in so many ways, just needs to get that kiss in line. But the juicy mouth could be useful elsewhere.

I cup his balls, and he groans. I have no idea if he's close. He's not saying much. I should be concentrating on the job at hand, but my mind keeps drifting to *why isn't this hotter?* We had good suggestive conversations. He wanted to bed me night one. I'm a little bored. I'm going to stop. Maybe he excels at eating me out. Perhaps that's his deep dark hidden talent. He does make a living with his tongue.

I stop and look at him. He abruptly lays down on the bed spread-eagle and proclaims, "Ride me, my angel."

Angel? He didn't even ask if I was ready. I climb up on top of him, ignoring the soft endearment of *angel*. All the while moving my hips and trying to keep friction on my clit. Now I'm getting a bit wetter. No penetration yet because I'm not afraid to ask for what I want. "I need a little more before we get to that. What if you were to dip down…?" I nod my head in the direction of my crotch, but he doesn't move.

He pulls his face to mine and says, "My precious sweet angel, I'm so sorry. I cannot do as you would desire. My tongue is sacred. You wouldn't ask a concert pianist to move furniture, would you?"

He kisses me hard. I wipe my mouth when he's done. I'm disappointed, but I understand, I guess. I remove my bra, which is still on for some odd reason, and circle my nipples myself to get myself a little wetter. He moves off the bed to grab a condom. I finger myself quickly with his back turned so that I'm ready for him.

He comes back and resumes a starfish position. I straddle him and move back down his body, kissing my way down. He's grunting. Okay. Okay. I can get off like this. Friction is my friend. I take him in and begin moving forward and back. It's about average size so it's fine that I'm not so wet.

He's bucking awkwardly underneath me with his eyes closed and his hands tucked behind his head. I lean forward to brush my tits on his chest, and the feel of his chest hair rubs the nubs of my nipples hard. I gasp at my own work. I reposition for maximum clit friction. He grunts loudly, holds his pelvis up, almost throwing me off him, and I think he finishes. It's been, like, a second. Surely that wasn't it. I begin to move again, but he gently rolls me over and pulls out. A quick kiss to my forehead and he stands up. If you add in the partial blowjob, it was like five minutes.

He gently rubs my arm and says, "You are a goddess."

I hear the shower turn on. I sit up naked and seriously unsatisfied and stare at the bathroom door. Now I'm not sure why I'm here. I feel as if I've overstayed my welcome somehow. It's been so long since I've wanted a man in my life, and now I'm terrified I've made a seriously wrong choice.

Hold up. Do you taste wine with your fingers? I mean something could have been done to help me come. Stunned. I'm stunned and sexually frustrated. Thank god there's a sprayer hose in the bathroom. I'll have to take matters into my own hands. I need to rethink everything.

CHAPTER SIX

ASHER

I WAKE UP WITH MORNING WOOD, AND SHE'S GONE FROM MY bed. She must snore and was being considerate. I'll pop over to her bedroom. She's a bit of a wildcard in bed, and I like it. I don't believe that she had an orgasm. Women rarely do when they're intimidated by a powerful sexually dominant man. Though, she was excessively and distractingly noisy, so maybe she did. I've never had complaints in that department. I look forward to this morning's encounter.

She's the perfect piece to my puzzle. As long as she's loyal and faithful, there's nothing I won't give her. Noelle Parker is vital. My next deal must work out, or my existence will have no meaning. It's the culmination of my life's work. And that means Noelle must remain in wine country.

I scoot to the coffee area and find an empty pot with a note. Noelle has lovely handwriting, but I don't think this is something I want to see.

Asher,

Please forgive the note. I know you wanted to stay in bed this morning, just us. But I went out for a run and exploration. Last night's dinner was wonderful. Thank you for showing me a piece of your world. I'll see you later, I think.

Noelle

No. No. This is not happening. She must be frightened by our connection. This smacks of an excuse to leave. I *will* make this up to her. I cannot lose her.

CHAPTER SEVEN

NOELLE

IT'S ONLY ONCE I'M AT SOME WINERY CALLED SEGHESIO, sweaty from running, and sipping something divine called Venom, that I look at my texts. I haven't run in years but felt the need to clear my head. I felt uncomfortable and nervous. I had to get out of there. Nothing I can put my finger on. He still might be something. Maybe he's a slow burn instead of instant heat. Perhaps his attentive nature and calm demeanor are the exact things I need in my life. The bedroom thing needs to be worked out, though.

ASHER: Noelle. I have called you as well. Listen at your leisure, but please call.

ASHER: Beauty, what is this all about? I am confused. I apologize if there's something I've done.

ASHER: Just let me know you're safe, angel. Even though we have not known each other long, I do care for you.

I'll answer him later. Why does he speak so formally? It's odd. Like maybe he is a throwback to a more formal time. It's a quirk I could deal with if the rest of it can get sorted out. Although, I could do without the 'angel' moniker.

I'm going to finish this tasting, then my run. Then I'll head back to the pool and work from there. I don't know why we suck in bed. I don't know why I feel a tug in the base of my stomach that something's just off. I'm overthinking everything. It's been so long since I dated and now, I've flown across the country and trapped myself here. I'll be like Melissa and just let the guacamole fall where it will.

NOELLE: I'm safe and overwhelmed. The flowers in the room are beautiful.

ASHER: They're not as beautiful as you. May I call you?

I do like his accountability. I call him.

"Noelle."

"Asher."

He says, "I feel as if there's more to the story. Are you okay?"

I respond, "I am. It's been a while since someone cared, and I guess I might have panicked."

"We shared an intimacy, and I don't want you to think I take that lightly."

He's saying all the right things. Except that he knows how to get a woman off. I hedge my bets. "We did share an intimacy..." I stumble over using that ridiculous word for sex. "...But I left feeling as if I missed out on a complete experience."

"My beauty, there's much work to be done. Surely we'll get better at making love."

I shake my doubts away and dive back in despite his use

of the phrase 'making love.' We just met, there's no love yet. He speaks unlike myself or the men I usually date, so I'll give him some leeway. This whole thing is such a reflection on my own hang-ups. "I'd like that."

I hear him sigh on the other end. "That's such a relief, I'm not ready to be without you yet."

The sex thing can be worked out. I just need to show Asher what I want. My lips curl up at the thought of getting a second shot at him. Having even mediocre sex has awakened a part of me I thought was gone. I love sex. I forgot that. Even subpar sex is better than solo sex. Well, almost.

CHAPTER EIGHT

NOELLE

I'M NOT COMPLETELY SOLD ON ASHER, BUT I AM SOLD ON HIS lifestyle. Mine has gotten dreary and predictable in New York. Then Asher winked at me, and I was brought into an entirely new world. Asher reminded me that there is a whole part of life I was ignoring. He wants to share his knowledge with me, not lecture me. Most older men who hit on me want to show me something about the world or mansplain finance or technology to me. It enrages me to be patronized. Asher simply lets me sip and learn how to train my palate.

We're headed to some all-star dinner thing tonight. The only name I recognize is chef Jonathan Waxman. His restaurant used to have the best chicken in New York until fucking developers got rid of Barbuto NYC. The rest of the people are growers, vintners, and chefs from California. The attire is supposed to be Wine Country casual. No clue what that is. I hope that hair down, a denim Josie Natori halter jumpsuit, and red suede Christian Siriano wedges covers it. I top it off with my ruby red cashmere wrap. I've been told that we're eating in a barn. My vision of a barn is probably very different than the Wine Country's version. I still know very little about wine, but barns I got wired.

I am going to commit to Asher for just tonight. I put aside my reservations and jump in without a thought. Be like Melissa. This is super hard for me. But despite what Mel thinks, I can let whatever happen. I am capable of not controlling the moment or the outcome. Dinner with an accomplished man and sex in a gorgeous hotel in the wine country. Another movie moment. I'm ready.

CHAPTER NINE

ASHER

I'm sipping a spicy Bowmore 12-year-old scotch waiting for her in the next room. Her scent is permeating the place, and it's choking me a bit. I don't know if it's perfume or her, but it's screwing with my sense of smell. My nose is more sensitive than most, it's one of the things that makes me in such demand. I carefully choose my own scent, and that's all the olfactory room I have for things not being sipped. I need her to be impressive tonight.

After she accomplishes my goals at dinner, I'll get to see all of her as I take her from behind. That might help her with her orgasm situation. Some women just have lower libidos and are incapable. Perhaps she's one of those that has never experienced the pleasure of a well-timed orgasm.

"Simply stunning." I want to rip off her halter and bend her over the couch and have her instantly, but I'll wait.

I brush my scotch-flavored lips over hers. There's a particular winemaking couple who are key to our future. I need Noelle to charm them. Those bare shapely shoulders have my brain so topsy-turvy that I'm actually planning a future with someone I've known for just a moment.

Tonight, we'll impress and dazzle as a couple. Noelle looks perfect on my arm. She also sucked me off like a fucking Dyson. I could use that around as well. But tonight, I need her marketing mind to impress. I won't let her know all my plans. I'll be patient. I'll have her the way I want, but first too much wine.

CHAPTER TEN

NOELLE

"PLEASE MEET SARAH LACHAPPELLE-WHITTIER AND WILL Whittier of LaChappelle/Whittier Estate Vineyards and Winery from Sonoma." Asher does a grand introduction.

I reach out my hand to the man with kind eyes who stood up to greet me. I joke, "I feel like that was a Game of Thrones name."

Will cocks his head and says, "And what's your Game of Thrones name?"

I don't hesitate, "I am Noelle, of House Parker, first of my name, Khalessi of Kansas, conqueror of Nordstrom's, wearer of lipsticks, breaker of balls." The couple laughs very hard. Asher does not. That was funny. What's wrong with him? Stop judging, Noelle, maybe he didn't hear you. Enjoy the evening. I've been introduced around, but I think I'm sitting next to this couple.

Sarah's hair has gray threaded through her raven locks, and it looks like it's decorated with silver tinsel. She has the most sparkling deep blue eyes. She's put together but still maintains a bohemian thing. Will's hair is a bit wild coppery blond falling over soulful brown eyes that droop just a little. He winks at me, and I'm flattered. His charisma radiates through the room and is complemented by his wife's nurturing vibe. I'm picking up that they're genuinely a yin/yang couple. They seem to be the most earnest and open people I've ever met.

"It's lovely to meet you, Noelle, first of her name." Sarah smiles and shakes my hand.

Will sits back down after pulling out my chair for me between them. Asher disappears to the other side of the table. Will looks directly at me and says in a joking manner, "Nope. I'm not feeling Noelle." They're the age that my parents would've been.

I jab back at him. "Not into me? I can find another seat, or I can sit here and be so dull it's like I'm not here. Your choice."

Sarah's lilting laugh rings through the room.

Will stares at me and rubs his finger and thumb over an imaginary beard. "No. You're fine, but the name is not. You should be Elle, not Noelle. Noelle evokes a frilly, dainty girl with a laugh like a titter or a dark Italian untouchable, unremarkable beauty." I giggle easily and then guffaw loudly, to prove his point. "Anyone call you Elle?"

"My dad used to."

"Then it's settled, only he and I get to call you that."

His charm and openness burn my heart a bit. I'm not sure I've ever felt this open with anyone so instantly before. It's like I've always known them somehow. He's so insistent that we'll be connected it's hard to say no. "It will be only you, though. My parents were killed in a car accident fourteen years ago."

"Then it's just me and whomever I deem worthy enough to use that name. Sarah hasn't earned it yet." His wife places her hand on my arm and hits her husband playfully. I grin at them. He kisses her hand.

She says, "Honestly, Will. Dear, pay no attention to this doofus."

"Oh, but the love of my life, you adore it when I put my foot in my mouth."

CHAPTER ELEVEN

ASHER

I PLACE ONE HAND ON THE BACK OF HER CHAIR AND LEAN down. "How are my two favorite women at this table doing? Sarah, do you know what Noelle does?"

She says, "So rude of us. We've talked for over an hour. Elle, where are you from?"

"Manhattan."

"Kansas?"

I am getting impatient. Noelle is clearly from New York, look at her.

She corrects them, "No. New York. But grew up in Kansas."

"Fancy. You still live there?" Will chimes in.

They need to know what she does. I'm anxious to get this ball rolling. Will gets pulled away just as she speaks.

She speaks only to Sarah, "I own a marketing and branding firm there."

Phew. I hang back as my plan takes shape. If all goes well, I'll be deep into Noelle within the hour.

"Really? What sorts of things do you do? Will! Will, come

here." He's across the room but returns swiftly pulling a chair to join the ladies.

"Elle owns…"

Will interrupts, "Honey, you've not earned that name yet."

"Shut up, my One Perfect Thing. She owns a marketing, branding firm."

Will bellows, "FATE! Tell us specifically about your work."

"Okay, you want my elevator pitch?"

"YES."

"I elevate the visibility of unique brands in a competitive market. We also work with smaller brands within larger corporations. We create awareness, mostly events. We create the tools, launch, and walk away. You don't need us managing your business for more than a couple of years."

Good girl. She can hook anyone. I walk away confident that Noelle is going to be in my life for quite a while.

CHAPTER TWELVE

NOELLE

WILL ASKS, "YOU HAVE A HIGH TURNOVER?"

"It's more like project-based clients. It keeps us fresh and away from falling into old tricks or habits. Everyone pays a retainer, and we've been able to make a profit this way. We've worked with Apple on twenty individual niche projects, but never their overall marketing structure. We handle boutique or luxury brands."

Will grins widely. "We're in the process of looking for a buyer for the winery."

"Really? Why?"

Will and Sarah exchange looks, and she nods. Sarah places her hand on my arm. It's an intimate gesture but doesn't feel odd. "Elle..." She looks to Will. My connection with these people is palpable. And they lighten my soul a bit.

He nods his approval and says, "You may use my nickname for her. You've earned it."

Sarah continues, "I was diagnosed with Parkinson's about three months ago. Please don't say sorry. I'm so utterly sick of pity."

"Then you'll get none from me." I squeeze her hand that's on my arm.

"The diagnosis made us want to step away from the pressures of the winery business and be with each other. See the world, maybe explore alternative treatments."

Will says, "We've been chained to the winery, which we love since we were twenty. Sarah's been there her whole life. And we want a different second act."

"Surely there's someone to take it over for you."

Sarah and Will share a pointed look. He puts his hands on her shoulders as she shakes her head no. I don't push further. They've been so open, this seems like a raw subject, so I let it go.

Will sits back up and shakes his head. He leans into me and lowers his voice a little, "The initial offer was two million."

"Which is total bullshit."

Will's lips flatten into a smirk. "Agreed. We were told if we want a larger number, we need a higher—"

I interrupt, "Profile. There are great San Francisco firms if you want a recommendation."

That offer is pathetic for any company, let alone a winery. I'm sipping their Cab, and it's delicious.

"We, uh…"

Sarah clears her throat to gently interrupt her husband. He takes her hand as she begins to speak. "We know all of the local firms, but they're all winery, all the time. Maybe you could offer a fresh perspective. You're not from the area, and you said that you pick things that excite you. Do we?"

I'm blown away. I break out into a smile, and warmth spreads throughout my body. It's nice to be wanted. "I'm honored you want me to pitch. I don't know anything about winemaking. Except for the five grapes in a Bordeaux blend."

Will slaps me on the back, "That's enough. It's perfect."

I laugh. "What's the timeline of the pitch? And I'll need your RFP."

Sarah responds, "No pitch, dear, no request for proposal needed.

Just tell us your retainer fee and come by the winery as soon as possible to tell us your plan. We'll wire the money right now."

Will hovers his finger over his phone screen, "I'll do it. Don't doubt me. I can get it done right now." They tell me as if they've already discussed all the details. They're so in sync with each other they don't need words apparently. "But our only condition, we don't want an account manager."

Sarah clarifies, "No, Elle. We want you. We can put you up if you need it. But we want you. I feel as if we were meant to meet. That this is fate and I'm done turning up my nose at fate and leaving anything until another day. So right now, we need you."

I feel a strange tug towards these people. My life is upside down. I'm fighting tears of joy. I'm drawn to these people, and they want me as well. "When?"

"When what?"

"When do you want my plan?"

"There's a staff meeting in five days. They'd have to approve of the plan and you. We don't do anything unless our staff is on board. You'll have to win them over too."

Will says, "Mrs. Dotson's going to be your stickler. She does payroll and runs the credit card reports and shit like that. I think. She was old when we took over the winery thirty-two years ago, but she's a battle-ax now."

I look at their faces, smile and take a leap of faith. "That's a tight turnaround."

Will sits back. "Thank god. I fucking hated everyone else."

"Can I call if I have questions?" And I take a Melissa

approved leap of faith. No planning, no control, simply dive into the deep end. Take that, guacamole girl.

Sarah says, "Let's have lunch tomorrow, and we can lay out what we need and what you might not understand. And you can tell me if it's something you want to do for real. How about the girl and the fig restaurant at 1 p.m.? It's in Sonoma, not up here in Healdsburg. Our winery is just at the far end of town. After lunch, we'll go so you can get a sense of the place."

I stand up to go tell Asher, but Will pulls me into an embrace. A true hug. I don't know the last time I had one of those. No random back-patting or half-hug but a giant embrace. My brain is buzzing with ideas and questions, but suddenly, my mind goes still as I hug him back.

CHAPTER THIRTEEN

ASHER

I'm begging, "Noelle. Please stay at my house. You can work here."

Alas, she stayed with me for only two nights. Then moved to the El Dorado hotel forty minutes from my house and on Sonoma's central plaza. In her tenure at my home, we didn't make love. We did have a splendid night after dinner on Saturday night, but it was torture as she dove into her computer rather than me the following days.

"I'm so sorry. The town is helping me see and formulate my plan."

"I miss you."

"Come to dinner. We can eat at EDK and then maybe have dessert upstairs."

That Sunday morning after the dinner where she met Sarah and Will, she disappeared into a vortex of research and plans, her brilliant mind working overtime. She picked my brain for all the information I had on LaChappelle/Whittier Vineyards. I told her just enough.

She met with them each day. Her presentation is tomorrow. She spent time tromping through mucky vineyards and meeting all their employees. She didn't need to do any of that to win the account. I'm the one who got her the job, not those disposable vineyard workers. Tonight will be all about me and us.

SITTING AT THE TABLE, I'm staring at her. She looks exhausted, less than Noelle perfect. I don't care for a casual look. Her hair is in a messy ponytail, and she is without makeup while we eat foie gras. She's stunning when she's showered and coiffed, but she's currently wearing a Sonoma sweatshirt. I'm in a suit, and she looks a bit like a college student. I'll have to picture her beautiful.

CHAPTER FOURTEEN

NOELLE

"I've been researching like a demon. Did you know that the winery is a hundred and forty-seven years old and it's never been out of family control?"

"I do. Do you know how my day was?" He snipes at me. "If we're a couple, I'd like to be part of the conversation."

We have been on dates, but are we really a couple? "Oh. I'm sorry. I'm *so* wound up and nervous about tomorrow. How was your day?"

"Spectacular. I've been asked to judge a competition in Ft. Lauderdale…" I stare while he drones on, and all I can think about is Sarah's father and what I discovered today. He bought land and planted a second vineyard in Lodi with another vintner's family from here in town. No one could see that it would produce enough juice for two mass-market labels. All the winery stuff is clouding everything else. I'm super stressed and afraid I'll forget a detail. I need a release. I'm ready for tomorrow, but I am wound the fuck up.

We'd sort of found a rhythm last Saturday night for about six minutes. I did have the slight beginning of an orgasm. Sadly, I had to finger myself later to release the rest of the tension. Hopefully, it will be a little longer tonight or maybe twice. Or perhaps that's who we are, and I'll get used to it with time. If we're a couple. I don't know.

I did blow him that night, and he stopped me. I do enjoy that activity. I was hoping he'd want to reciprocate, but I got the golden tongue argument again. My goal is to not need my own hand tonight. I can convince people to do almost anything. I'm a salesperson by trade. I move mountains in my job every day, surely, I can make this happen.

He seems to be uninterested in what I have to say, and yet I'm supposed to be completely enraptured by his travel plans. All the details for tomorrow are swimming in my brain. I only wish he were more captivating to take my mind off it.

Sex. Fucking him will get my mind clear. He needs to stop bragging for a minute. I motion for the bill, and we've barely gotten our food. I whisper to the waiter to put it all on my room, and he nods. I grab the bottle and look at him suggestively.

"Do you want to keep talking about your day or do you want to come upstairs and help me forget mine?"

His lips upturn into a tight smile. I can see the slight bulge in his pants instantly, and I lead the way.

On the other side of the door, I whip off my ridiculous tourist hoodie to reveal my absurd local restaurant merchandise, my new Sunflower Caffe t-shirt. I didn't pack for casual, so I Amazoned some leggings and purchased a lot of local swag. He slowly removes his tie and lays it out on the couch. Then carefully removes the rest of his clothes while I throw my jeans in the corner and whip off my shirt. I lunge at him, and he backs away until he's folded his pants and placed them with the rest of the pile. Passion and wrinkled clothes are not his things.

Then he places his hands on either side of my face and squeezes a little too hard. I can already tell we're out of step with each other. I push on. I need to get laid. For real. I'm going to guide him to give me multiple orgasms tonight. I'm wound too tight.

He's kissing me, and his blobby tongue is taking up all the room in my mouth. I push him down on the bed and stroke him through his briefs, and he moves his fingers to my nipples. "They're perfect." He rolls them between his fingers, and I push my body into the side of him, hoping his hands will continue south.

I'm slightly wet and need a little bit of encouragement. The nipples are helping. But Asher doesn't even use his mouth. He removes his underwear, and his dick is still not completely hard. I grab his shaft, and his hands return to my face. No. That's not where I need his hands. He lays me back and gestures for me to pull down my thong. Then he kisses my belly button. That is three inches too high, dude. Lower. Please god, lower. And then I hear a slight squirt of lube, and I sit up abruptly. Hold up! Where does he think he's going with that?

"Hold out your hand. Angel, this will solve your issues."

Huh? Holy shit, he won't even rub lube on me? Maybe if he sees me do it. I rub my own clit with it, close my eyes, and gasp. I open my eyes, and he's picking lint from the lampshade. Okay. We're done here. That's enough. Pack it up, man. You don't have to go home, but you can't stay here. Wow. This sucks, and now I'm sticky. He even bought a shitty lube.

I roll over before he can come at me with his needle dick in a condom, and I grab my phone from the other nightstand. Then stand quickly. He's holding himself and looking at me quizzically.

"Asher. Terrible timing. I'm so sorry. Evan, my business partner, just texted with a time-sensitive marketing emergency. Can we put a pin in this?" Because that's a thing, a marketing emergency. I need him out of here.

"I didn't hear anything."

"I saw it flash. So sorry. Emergency."

He goes limp instantly. I hand him his underwear, which was folded on the edge of the couch.

"Noelle. My angel. My soft moment." I may puke, that's the worst pet name yet. After he puts his underwear on, I wipe off the lube. I grab my only clean panties, and they happen to be my sexiest lingerie.

"My sweet darling, I can't say I'm not disappointed, but I know that we have time and you're so important."

"About that Asher. I'm going to deep dive into work for a while. We should really take a break. I know you're traveling. Bon Voyage! I'll be in touch."

He looks puzzled. "You're still pitching tomorrow to Will and Sarah?"

And now I look puzzled, "Yes. Of course, but why are you worried? Do you know something that I don't?"

"Not at all. I just wanted to be supportive and tell you good luck, my exquisite angel lips."

He kisses me, and the dead slug tongue does its last sweep inside of my mouth. This is the worst kiss I've ever had, and I'm done with Asher.

CHAPTER FIFTEEN

ELLE

HE WON'T STOP TELLING ME I'M EXQUISITE, AND I DON'T KNOW what to say to that. How was I so off about this guy? Also, stop calling me angel. I hate pet names and nicknames, it's one of my rules. I refuse to get myself off again. That entire experience was just ick. I want to wash the taste away with whiskey. I grab my red cashmere poncho wrap and trek down the block to a bar. An actual bar. Not a wine bar but one with beer and cocktails I understand. I need to get my head clear, and drinking wine isn't going to help.

Steiner's Tavern is dark and moody. The neon sign in the window looks as if it's been there forever. There's a series of mirrors running along both sides of the bar. On the left is an odd long shelf that could hold a beverage and the right is a curved old oak bar with shelves of open bottles in front of the mirror. It's perfect. There's a smattering of high-top tables in the middle. I hear pool balls clacking in the well-lit area towards the back. I sit near the door at the wrap-around part of the bar. I turn towards the room with my back to the mirrors. "Basil Hayden, two fingers neat, please."

"Beer back?"

"Sure. Whatever's on tap is fine." I shrug. I don't care. Just bring me something to get the blobby taste out of my mouth.

The bartender is younger than me. His lank blond hair pulled in a ponytail, and his glasses balance on the end of his nose. My hair is out of control. I tuck the strays back behind my ears then shove the rest back into a self-contained messy bun. I genuinely look like Melissa right now, sans food stains. "Tab?"

"I'll cash out."

"I've got it." A red-faced puffy man offers up. Sitting down next to me, he places his hand on my knee. I'm ill-equipped to deal cleverly with this drunk sixty-something letch. I attempt to remove his hand, and he squeezes tighter.

"I can buy my own drink. Thanks."

"Why would you have to? I'm here." He wobbles a bit as he says it. There's a group of his peers calling him back to their table. He's not listening. "You and I are going to have a good time tonight."

I don't want whiskey anymore. I want out. I tug at this random man's hand again, and he pushes further, almost knocking me off the stool. I grab onto the bar and ponytail bartender looks a little scared of this guy. This whole night is shit. A commanding but sexy, raspy voice booms from behind me and it rattles my brain.

"Hey, there, Dr. Johnson. Seems you've made a mistake. Clearly, this lady is taken." A steady hand removes the intruding meaty paw from my knee. My head flips to his face as he puts his hand on my shoulder. I don't usually enjoy being rescued, but tonight I could use a helping hand. Especially this strong and large one.

Then his eyes capture mine, and we stare at each other. They're azure blue and sparkling. His hair is a sandy copper blond and looks like it could get out of control if he didn't tame it with so much product. His worn jeans are tight, and I notice his outline as my eyes skim up his body. He's wearing a tie and certainly knows how to fill out a tailored jacket. He seems completely off. Like he's supposed to be at a different bar, one with more complicated drinks and clientele. He's controlling the moment, and I just want to rip off my clothes.

"Are you alright?" His voice is calm and rich.

"Yes. Yes. Yes." It's like I'm responding to an imaginary sex invitation. I have to say something else, so I don't seem like a moron. I struggle and then find my voice and wits. "Thank you, stranger."

"I'd like to say he means no harm, but I'm not sure."

My breath is gone. I'm momentarily stunned at how masculine he is and how magnetic a pull I feel to this stranger instantly.

There's a sexy heat radiating off him, like wavy lines in a desert. I'm flushed and flustered just being in proximity to him. Fuck, he's hot. I wish I had makeup on or a low cut anything instead of this stupid tourist t-shirt. My nipples are starting to rise against my bra as he holds my gaze.

"I might have a bruise from his fingers, but other than that, I'll be fine."

He moves to face me and crooks an eyebrow. "You bruise that easily?"

I pull my long bang out of my face and tuck it back behind my ear, and his full lips curl up on one side. They're lush and inviting. He licks them. Buckets of adrenaline dump into my system as my nerve endings all fire at once. My stomach twists, and my mind begins to imagine what he tastes like. The whiskey is doing its job. I can feel the flush from my chest starts to creep up to my face. I don't know if I have words, my breath has yet to return. The old man staggers away as my sexy savior turns back to me, removing his hand from my shoulder. Damn, put your hand back on me sexy savior. Forward flirting bursts out of my mouth, I can't stop it. He's too damn hot.

"I don't bruise all that easily. I'm tougher than that."

"I'll file that information away."

He winks and instantly, my panties are soaked. I cannot look away from him. It's as if the rest of the bar just disappeared and we're the only two people alive. His voice is deep and rumbling. His eyes are locked on me. I feel it down through my barstool. His hands look gentle and manicured, but this overall person seems rugged. His body is clearly well taken care of and something I'm becoming more intrigued with by the second.

"Please sit."

He takes his hands and runs them through his overly styled hair and exhales. "We're drinking whiskey?"

"We are. Bourbon. Basil."

"Perfect."

"Isn't it, though?"

He winks again as one appears for him and another for me. He reaches across my body to get his drink and my skin sears where he brushes it. He pauses as if he feels the heat bloom on my skin as well. My confidence increases with every moment he stares at me. Not a creepy stare, but one that is sensual and intriguing. Can't imagine what he sees, but I'll try to work my t-shirt and jeans. I'm mortally embarrassed about my appearance. I realize how little I must have cared for Asher. I didn't even swipe on mascara or concealer tonight. I'm not even wearing lip balm.

I don't go anywhere unless I am show-ready. And here I am, trying to make a connection with this man in what amounts to weekend gardening clothing. Not that I garden, I just imagine this is what gardeners wear. I need to make an excuse to bend over so he can see one of my better assets. He brushes my skin again in search of a cocktail napkin. I involuntarily take in a sharp breath through my teeth while he crooks an eyebrow at me.

He says, "Well, tonight just got more interesting."

CHAPTER SIXTEEN

JOSHUA

Who in the fucking hell is this? And what god did I please that she's here alone and ripe for the taking? Drinking bourbon and not wine. Not a fruity cocktail, but alone sipping expensive bourbon. Perhaps she's my karmic gift for having to fucking come back home to stop shitty business decisions. I fucking hate babysitting. I hate that I have to be in the town at all. I'm irritated by everything and everyone except this gorgeous creature in front of me.

This one who fills out her jeans in all the right places. Her breasts are a perfect size, and I can see her nipples pulling into her bra. I want them. I'm so sick of the silicon set. The overly done faces and buckets of lip gloss. She's so pure and perfect. I want to fucking have her translucent skin under my fingers tonight. Her face is stunning. Her skin and her bone structure are flawless.

Her voice is deeper than I imagined. She looks feminine and petite, but there's a throaty, sexy quality to it. My need to possess this woman is instantaneous and something I've never really felt before. I don't think I can walk away from her, even if she asked. If she's feeling even a portion of what I feel right now, she won't walk away either. I've just been staring at her while we both sip our drinks.

She straightens up, and her golden hair falls back into her gorgeous face. "The first part of my evening was a disaster. You might have to work a little harder to make it up to me."

"I can certainly try." Game on. I swallow down my drink and motion for another. I am compelled to take her hair and tuck it back behind her ear. I am in control of everything in my world outside of this bar. Yet I feel the need to touch her like I need to breathe. What the fuck is this? She's still sipping, and I can't stop staring at her rosy lips and the way they curl into a sly smile. I'm watching her delicate finger bend around the glass, and I am hyper-aware of the way she crosses her ankles. She's wearing red ballet flats. Simple and perfect but she seems anything but.

She cocks her head and turns her body towards mine. She stares at me straight on, and a small and joyful grin springs up on her face.

Holy hell, this woman is fucking gorgeous, quick-witted, and at Steiner's, which is a complete mystery to me. I rarely come in here but just needed a quick drink to settle my night before my annoying meetings tomorrow. But now her tight little ass sitting on that stool in skinny jeans that should be illegal will be my nightcap. I want to pummel the idiot drunk doctor for trying to attack her.

Her eyes are as vivid green as the Tanqueray bottle that's behind her at the bar. Her skin seems to be soft and is reflecting the light. She's pearlescent and luminous except for the bit of blush creeping over her t-shirt neck. She may be local, but I don't think so. Despite the messy mass of sunny blonde hair and lack of makeup, she seems more sophisticated than this town. Her highlights are subtle and expensive. No one in this farm town can do that or would bother spending that kind of money. She's sitting on a ruby cashmere wrap that looks luxe, but she doesn't care. She holds herself regally. I'm drawn in and drawn to her.

I don't want to be me tonight. I don't want her to be a local and know people in common. Hell, I'm only here for the night. I drove up from Santa Barbara today, taking the day off work. I drove up because there's a weasel I need to take care of. And now I lost out on a critical deal because of the drive. It pisses me off, but the volume of all that bullshit has been turned down by her smile.

I want to be whatever she needs me to be. I'm looking forward to peeling down those jeans. I am going to lick her from stem to stern. I'll suck all the places in between. My mouth is watering at the smell of her. If I'm not mistaken, it's lilacs and orange blossoms. She turns to face me again and leans on the bar towards me. Now I want to bend her over the bar right here. She shoots her drink, and I gesture for two more.

"Who are you?" she asks.

I play with her, "No one of consequence."

"Do I call you hero or savior?"

"Lord and savior will be fine." I lay my arm on the bar and just stare right into her eyes.

"Okay." She sits up straight on her stool and without missing a beat says, "So God, what do you do?" I laugh at her joke. She's got a bit of sass. No one in my everyday life talks to me like that. I like it. I want her to scream the word god in another way entirely.

"I'm Joshua. And you are?" She takes a moment to answer like she's trying to decide who she's going to be tonight. Besides mine.

"Elle. Nice to meet you, Joshua. But I think I might just call you Suit."

"Why?"

"Your Kiton blazer seems more Cafe LaHaye than Steiner's."

How is this fucking woman a local? She knows the town. But she is also quite aware that I'm wearing a seven-thousand-dollar Kiton cashmere blazer. I know this town is full of farmers but also incredibly intelligent and accomplished people who escaped major metropolises with fat wallets and dreams of a simpler life. I haven't been here in a while, but surely someone would have told me about a girl like this. I'm not sure I can screw a townie. Who the hell are you, Elle? Why do you know fashion? Men's fashion?

I ask, "Do you work at the Sunflower Cafe?" Looking for a little intel. She also doesn't have a phone on the bar. Is she without technology? My phone is going off in my pocket with updates from tonight's meeting, and I ignore it as I await her answer.

She quickly explains, "No. Just a fan. I found myself without clothes, so I picked up a couple of Sonoma-themed items. I don't live here, just visiting."

Fucking perfect. I can't deal with the aftermath of someone the next day. "No clothes?"

She explains, "Nothing comfy and cozy. Just outfits to impress or make me feel pretty."

I lean forward towards her and say, "You don't need an outfit for that."

"Are you seriously this charming?"

"Are you charmed?"

She draws a quick breath and says, "Apparently so."

I want her to know that I'm dead fucking serious, so I stare into her mesmerizing eyes. "I'm completely serious."

She grins and bites her bottom lip and then looks down at her drink. Her eyes slowly return to me, and I haven't looked away. She says quietly, "Thank you." Then she shifts on the stool and pulls back from me for a second. I lean back as well.

I ask her in a less flirtatious tone, "What is it that brings you to Sonoma and Steiner's in particular?" I don't want to scare her off.

She says quickly, "An opportunity and a disaster."

"Life-changing?"

She bites her bottom lip again, and I want to be the one biting it. I refocus as she answers, "Yes, to the first and no to the second. Turns out the disaster was just an annoying waste of time, good lipstick, and my favorite blue dress."

"I think I prefer the t-shirt and cashmere thing you got going on."

"You haven't seen the blue dress." She flashes a suggestive smile.

My nerves flex. They all spark at once. My brain instantly conjures an image. What the fuck is it about this woman? I've never found a comfy outfit a sexual turn-on, but suddenly it's all I can think about. I imagine this woman curled up on a giant bed, surrounded by pillows and sunlight streaming in through the window reflecting off her sparkling emerald eyes. She's dressed in stretchy pants and one of my old t-shirts. In my fantasy, she's trying to hold onto a cup of coffee. I slowly kiss my way up to her face. Her hand on my knee pulls my attention back to her in reality.

"Are you okay?"

I adjust myself on my stool to try and shake the image. I say, "I am. Was just thinking an extremely uncharacteristic thought."

"Hmm. Care to share?" She just moaned at me like a preview. Her voice reverberates through my balls, and I'm going to need to fuck her to stop them from vibrating.

"Maybe someday, but it's rather dark and disturbing." I'm genuinely rattled by imagining her in a domestic situation. I don't fucking do domestic. And I don't even know this woman.

"Twisty has its place."

Shit. She did not say that. "What do you do, Elle?"

"No jobs, Suit. Let's just do random truths. Random questions. What food would you eat if you could eat anything in the world right now?"

Her. I'd eat her. That's what I'm hungry for. I say instead, "A local carne asada burrito. And you?"

She thinks, and then a melancholy smile overtakes her. "Fresh corn on the cob."

I play her game and ask my own random question. "An intriguing answer. What nonalcoholic beverage would you order right now?"

"Coffee. Or Pamplemousse La Croix."

I laugh at her, "What the hell is Pamplemousse?"

She explains, "Marketing speak for grapefruit. And you?"

I laugh again. "San Pellegrino. And coffee. I don't trust anyone who doesn't like coffee."

She looks down and drains her bourbon. I do the same, and I feel as if we're at a crossroads. Order more, risk getting drunk and ruining this evening, or get on with part two of the night. We've talked about nothing. We've barely talked at all. Kind of flirted, yet I think that's enough for me. I don't need to know anything else about her to want to screw her into submission right now.

She leans over and places her fingers on my hand. My cylinders are firing. I'm seriously like a moth to a flame. My cock twitches, and I struggle to keep it down. I have to have her and in so many different ways. I look down at her long delicate and freshly manicured fingers as they trace my hand and run up my arm then back to her exceptionally beautiful face.

"Um...New girl?" I say wryly.

"Yes?" Her voice is a vamped-up babydoll whisper—and inviting.

"You're playing with a bit of fire." I look down at her hand then up to her face again. As much as I want to devour her, she seems somewhat predatory herself.

"Not afraid." She states with the best lip curl I've ever seen.

In one motion, I yank the back of her head to me and stop just short of my face. Her mouth opens in a sexy as hell gasp, and her whole body leans towards mine.

I emit a guttural whisper, "There's no going back from this."

She runs her hands up my jeans and stops just short of my crease. I'm absolutely hard as she glances down and grins. This sexy little thing has just made my year. It's been a shitty one. She's also made me completely forget about how pissed off I am that I'm up here in Sonoma. Now it may turn out okay. I'm glad there seems to be a bright spot, at least for tonight. What the hell is wrong with me? Why would I think past tonight?

"Promise?" she whispers back.

I lean into her ear. My lips brushing her with each word, "Oh, I promise this. I'm going to fuck you so hard you'll feel me all day tomorrow."

Her lips tug upwards slightly. I wait to see if I pushed too far, too fast or if this is my girl.

Then she sighs and says in that babydoll whisper that going to ruin me, "Promise?"

I crush my mouth to hers, and she responds with a moan that almost makes me come. Her tongue quickly finds mine, and we're bruising our lips further with intense pressure. She pulls back, and I suddenly panic that I misread tonight.

She stands up and raising her arms in the air and

proclaims to the entire bar. "Thank fucking god you're a good kisser. And you know what to do with your tongue."

"Oh, we're just getting started."

I tug her between my legs with my hands on her hips. I take her lips again. I know she can feel me, and she's slightly moving her hips into me. I could seriously spend the next couple of hours kissing her. Her hands end up in my hair and fuck it if it doesn't feel insanely good as she drags those hot pink nails against my scalp. I pull her closer to amp up this kiss. I'm possessed by her as her tongue flicks with mine. I need those nails to scratch down my back. I got her. I know she needs this as much as I do. She pulls back again and says two fucking sexy words, and I'm done. "El Dorado." And I toss a wad of cash on the bar.

CHAPTER SEVENTEEN

ELLE

THIS MAN'S MOUTH IS EVERY FUCKING THING. I AM NEVER this forward, but I can't help myself. And it's just one night. I can be whoever I want. But being around this man, insanely attracted to him, I abandon all of my so-called rules for sex. We've exchanged no real information. His pillow lips and the way his tongue slips in and out of me is my new favorite thing. Nothing sloppy or awkward, only heat.

I'm surprised I didn't slide off the stool. I can have sex, get off, and still get a good night's sleep before tomorrow. It's only 8:30 pm, it's perfect timing. We scurry out of the bar and down the block towards my hotel. A couple doors down, he stops and pulls me to him. He backs me into a closed storefront window and presses forward.

"How did I get this lucky tonight? You're so sexy and beautiful. And funny. Sexy and funny. Where the hell have you been?" He pulls a stray hair and tucks it behind my ear again, and I'm gone, lost in those deep blue eyes.

Then I answer him as earnestly as he spoke to me. "It took me a while to get here, but it seems as is if I'm finally in the right place at the right time." I guess I can thank Asher for that.

He seizes me with his hands on either side of my face, and we kiss long and deep. There are sparks on my tongue, crackling with desire and energy. I dig my nails into his shoulders. I move my body towards him. He nudges my legs apart with one of his, and I end up rocking on his thigh. This is more than I've felt in a while. I'm dry-humping him on the street. Now I need him to lose the jeans. I'm aching for release. I back away from the kiss, both of us with ragged breathing. I grab his hand and run towards El Dorado Hotel, pulling him behind me and bolting upstairs.

The night manager looks strangely at me since I walked Asher out of here a couple hours ago. Whatever. If he looked into this man's eyes and saw the same desire, he'd be running upstairs too.

We're on the other side of the door, and he's yanking me to him as I pull off his jacket. I throw it on the floor. Very different than earlier, a very different man. I just remembered I have on insanely sexy underwear.

I'm so wet for this man that this pair is toast. They're black lace panties with a leather crisscross peekaboo back. My bra matches with leather strips and lace. Hope he likes my ass. He seems to, he is squeezing it with manly intensity.

"Elle. I need you to tell me what you want. That you want what I want too." I kiss him again. "Words. I need you to say it." He looks at me earnestly as if he's looking for consent or a partner in tonight. Not just a conquest. I'm happy to be his co-conspirator.

I pull his head down to me as I go up on my tiptoes and lick his ear while I whisper, "You. I want you. All of you. Anything you want to do to me is okay with me, as long as I can reciprocate."

"Glad to hear it." He undoes the button of my jeans and

reaches his hand into me, and his fingers probe south. I gasp and roll my hips forward. His lips never leave mine. I'm so happy someone else is touching me.

"Fuck. Is that all for me? You're soaked. I fucking love it. I'm so hard for you already." I feel his jeans and begin to unbutton them when he removes my hand from his waist-band. "No. We're just making you come now. Take your jeans and shirt off. Take them off now."

I look at him quizzically.

"New girl. Listen up. I don't plan to leave anytime soon. There are way too many things we're going to do to each other tonight for there to be a time limit. No rushing." I gasp, and he smiles. "First, you're going to come loudly and then there will be some fast and furious fucking. And after that, I'm going to spend the rest of our time savoring every fucking inch of you. So, Elle, beautiful, sexy-as-fuck stranger, I repeat myself. But only once. Take your jeans and shirt off right now."

My mouth is wide open, staring at him and his declaration that just made my whole body tingle. He kisses me deeply and then nods at me. I don't usually do well with being told what to do, but his commanding presence and my anonymity help me comply.

I peel up the hem of my t-shirt, and it gets flung onto the floor. Joshua is instantly on my chest. His hands grip the outside of my bra as his thumbs circle my already rock-hard nipples. They're straining to get out, and he's teasing them. Then he pulls my jeans down, kissing his way down my legs. I step out of my pants and turn around for him.

"Fuck. That's a good outfit. You're fucking stunning. Damn. This ass. Christ. That was underneath your tourist crap all this time. Sexy as fuck." He smacks my ass, and I gasp loudly. "This is mine tonight."

He kneels and kisses all the parts of me in front of him.

He's so tall that this is a proper angle for him. We have almost a foot difference between us, I'd guess. He's so strong and sexy. I tear at his shirt buttons while he worships me, his lips leaving a trail and his hands continuing their excellent work with my tits. Then he stands and reaches around and releases my breasts. He goes right back to pulling, nipping, sucking, and cupping. He takes my nipples and rolls them through his fingers and sucks each one until I moan loudly. He stops and puts his hands on my hips and turns me around.

"Your ass is amazing. They should stop making this panty for anyone but you."

He kisses the top of my ass and then grabs a handful. With a playful slap, he stands back up. "Take them off and go over to the bed. Sit up and spread your legs for me."

"What? Wait, did you just order me to…"

He cuts me off with a finger to my mouth. I grin and open my lips to let it fall onto my tongue then wrap my lips around it to suck. "Don't answer me. Do as I say. Take your panties off. Hand them to me. I've decided to keep them. I don't want anyone else to ever get the pleasure of seeing them on your perfect ass. Now get on the bed."

No one has ever ordered me to do anything like this, but the sudden torrent of wetness between my legs tells me that my body must like it. It's incredibly hot, and I'm just going to see how it plays out.

He throws the duvet onto the floor in a flourish and stands there commandingly staring at me. Then comes over and takes my cheek sweetly. He bends me down to the bed and kisses me gently. I rub my hand on his chest lightly, and his hand covers mine. After a soft and lovely kiss, he takes my hand in his and brushes his lips over the top. He presses a kiss to the top of my hand, and I smile at him.

His shirt is unbuttoned, and I'm glancing at his perfect

chest and commanding shoulders as he stands, leaving me wanting him. I want to touch him, but he keeps his focus on me.

He's broad and lovely. He makes a small production of putting my underwear into his pocket. I giggle, and then he removes his jeans. He's not wearing anything underneath. Holy shit, I am not giggling anymore. I did not know dicks like this existed in real life. His hard, long, and insanely large cock breaks free. Yesterday at LaChappelle/Whittier vineyard, I saw some Old Vine Zinfandel grapevines. They were thick, solid, ropey, and long. He's got a long thick vine, and I'm going to harvest every inch of that.

He smiles that I'm staring at it. He strokes it, and it grows even more. I don't know how it's getting bigger. I'm licking my lips when he comes to the bed, tossing his shirt behind him. My eyes return to his, and he raises an eyebrow, seemingly pleased that I can't stop staring at his cock. It's literally the elephant in the room.

He draws one breast into his mouth like he's trying to suck my orgasm out that way. I arch my back. He swirls his tongue then nips at me. I moan loudly. It's been a while since a man's tongue was on me. He kisses me deeply while his hands keep kneading and pinching my nipples.

Joshua proposes something to me. "That's such a good fucking sound. Here's the deal." I sit up on my elbows as he holds himself up over me, basically planking. His defined and massive biceps caging me in place. The man is insanely sexy while doing a difficult core exercise like a pro. And his abs are definitely pro worthy.

"Will this deal put your mouth back on my body?"

He smiles wickedly at me. "You keep making that sound, and I'll make you come so hard your toes will cramp. You'll beg me to stop making you come. You stop making that sound, and I stop."

I say in a lusty voice that I didn't know I had. "I'll do anything you want."

"Change of plans. I'll eat you out later. Because what I want is to turn you over and fuck the hell out of you right now."

"Good. That's what I want too." I answer.

His hands snake down my stomach and suddenly his fingers are playing with me. I groan as he pushes a finger inside of me. "A little prep work, new girl."

I managed to moan, "Good work." Then he adds a second and third finger stretching and pumping inside of me. I scream his name as I get close to coming.

Then he's gone. I protest and he laughs at me. His hands reach down to his jeans. I hear him grab a condom from his wallet. I help him roll it on, and in that brief contact with his cock, I almost came.

He planks over me again, and I just want to feel the weight of him in and on me. Joshua says, "Perhaps like this at first."

My eyes flash wide as he kneels on the edge of the bed. He pulls me down to him, and I feel his cock nudge at my entrance. I quickly reach down and line him up perfectly. He stays right at the entrance as he pulls my legs around him, pulling my pelvis up and instead of driving into me, he's pulling me down slowly onto him. My breath is gone as he inches in. Our eyes connect, and we're moaning already. I'm stretching to take him, but I'm so wet that the path is smooth for him.

"Fuck, yes," I say to him in a breathy tone.

"Fuck. Shit. Elle. You're so tight. You're the perfect pussy." And then the moment ends as we both begin to move as wildly as we can. We're slamming into each other, and he's filling every crevice of me. He's driving over and over. He moves my hips again with his large, powerful hands. He angles me and begins hitting the most perfect spot. He reaches his thumb for my clit, and I won't last long. I need this so badly. I see his lips curl as I begin breathing quickly.

"I want to feel you come on my dick. Elle. I want to give this to you. Come for me. Come."

"Yes. Yes. I can. I'm coming. I can't stop it." And I'm dancing in that glorious moment where I want to move in and stay. That fleeting moment of being utterly present in the moment. Nothing else matters except pleasure.

"Don't stop yourself. There's always more. Do it. Let me see you come. Let me feel it so I can come."

I contract around his dick as the rest of my body freezes in position for one moment. His thumb pressing down as he speeds up inside of me.

When I moan loudly and shudder, his growl fills the room as he fills the condom.

Both of us are staring with our eyes wide as the last ripple of pleasure glides over us. Then we rhythmically try to catch our breath. Joshua leans over me and kisses me sweetly.

"Sweet fucking Christ." He says as he lays down on the bed to face me. He moves my hair out of my face. I shudder a little at his touch. I'm still so sensitive.

"I know." I gasp out.

"I don't remember coming that hard in forever. Or that quickly. You have one magical cunt." I grin sheepishly. I usually cringe at that word, but I like it from his sexy lips. As manly as he is and every inch is manly, there's a boyish charm to his face. He slowly backs out of me, and we both groan a bit.

CHAPTER EIGHTEEN

JOSHUA

THAT WAS NOT TO BE FORGOTTEN. I NEED SO MUCH MORE OF her tonight. Shit. That was fucking epic. She's a demon in bed. I head to the bathroom and remove my condom. I bring her a towel to clean up. I rinse off. She's grabbed the sheet from the floor and wrapped it around herself in a makeshift coverup. I join her in bed.

I look at her. I kiss her shoulder, and she moans lightly. Her eyes are soft and silky looking. It's like they're liquid gems. She reaches for my head and runs her fingers through my hair as I continue kissing and sucking on her neck and shoulder.

I say to her while still feasting on her perfect pearl skin. "What do you want to do now? Gin Rummy? I mean I'll need a minute until I can ravage you again." And I need an excuse not to leave. It's all fucked up. Leaving is one of the things I do best, and I can't quite make myself do it at this moment.

She giggles, and it's like a soft purring. "Sure." She stands up, she lets the sheet fall to the ground. She's wholly unself-conscious and unaware of what her delicious curves do to me. Women usually cover up with a discarded shirt or disappear into the bathroom instantly. But this one, thoroughly gorgeous and naked, pulls a deck of cards and a bottle of Gelbert Family Winery Cab from the mini-fridge area. She holds them up, and I'm baffled by this sexy stranger. Her nipples are reaching for me, and I'm lost in her tits. How is it she's this comfortable with me already? How is it that I'm comfortable enough with her to stay? I grab a pen and paper from the desk.

She grabs a t-shirt from the floor. I wish I could tell her to put on my shirt, but instead she drapes it and my jacket over a chair. I tell her the truth. "I'm going to kick your ass." She giggles again at me. "You know, you're a fucking Hellcat in bed."

Elle answers me right back with all the sass she can muster. "You know, I'm only playing cards to give your dick a little break before I'm going to need that thing inside of me again." She sits back into the bed and reassembles the sheet around herself, looking like she owns the world. She's so confident, it's like being with myself. Nothing wrong with a little arrogance. She must master her world. She must be in charge of things somewhere. I'm so fucking intrigued.

I lean over and pull her face to mine. I hold her there staring at her deep liquid jade eyes for way too long. Then I kiss her again. Our lips meeting in a gentle way. Then she opens for me, and I lick into her mouth. Our tongues meeting in long sensual strokes rather than totally amped up. The kiss is hot enough that I pull a sweet moan from her. "Hellcat."

She protests. "I am not."

"You have no idea what you're doing to me."

WE ACTUALLY PLAY RUMMY, and she's solidly beating me.

We barely get through the firsthand of our second game when the sheet slips and I see her legs exposed. There's no way I can go on with this charade.

"Is that your strategy? To distract me?" I raise an eyebrow and lick my lips.

She inquires, "Is it working?"

"Fuck, yes. That path to the perfect pussy opening up to me. Daring for me to suck the hell out of it. And you want me to see if I can match my three of spades? Hell no." I tackle her. The cards go flying. She laughs as I dive under her shirt and take her breast into my mouth.

She arches her back and protests in jest. "But the game. I want to finish the game. I was winning." She smiles as she picks a the Jack of Clubs off my ass.

CHAPTER NINETEEN

ELLE

JOSHUA IS CAGING MY BODY AGAIN, AND I'M SO HAPPY WE'RE done with cards.

He says, "Maybe we finish later, but first I need to taste you. I want your pussy so wet for me that I slide right in. In fact, I'm going to suck all of you until you come and crash all over my face. Then I'm going to be buried in you again. But right now, I'm hungry for that clit. I need to hear that perfect noise erupt from those fuckable lips of yours."

No one has ever spoken to me like this, and I am dancing on the edge of coming just from the dirty description of the things he's going to do to me. My lips curl up slightly. "Yes."

"You're not getting this, Elle. I don't want to hear your words anymore. I said your response is that glorious moan. Don't make me punish you." And my eyes widen at the thought of what *that* could be. Shit. I want everything this man wants to do to me.

I moan his name loudly as his fingers trail through my slick slit and down to the rim of my pussy. My clit pulsing and desperate for attention it finally gets as his face disappears. He's nipping below, and I'm tugging at my own breasts trying to mirror his movements. The pain of his teeth mixes with potent pleasure, driving me closer and closer to climax. His head peeks up, and he sees me playing. He sits up and cups me, scooping up slickness with his finger and then pinches and wets down my nipples.

"Oh, good god. Oh. Joshua. Fuck. Yes." I arch my back into him.

He returns to dining on me, and I can't help it. His tongue enters me and slides in and out like he's trying to taste every part of me. I'm grinding into him, trying to increase the pressure on my clit. I feel it build low in my belly. I've been ready and coiled up for days, never finding the electric fucking hot lighting that I need to coarse through me like it's doing right now. It's epic as I release with a giant groan and then quiver as he keeps going. He's relentless, pushing me to come again. I pull his head into me. He won't stop, and I twitch again, riding the wave of a second and possibly a third orgasm. I'm a slave to the moment. I can do nothing but release every bit of tension I've ever had. And shutter all around him, gasping his name. I think I black out for a second.

My eyes pop open as I am stunned. No one has ever found that much in me before. All I want is more.

CHAPTER TWENTY

JOSHUA

I DEVOUR EVERY BIT OF HER, AND SHE DOESN'T DISAPPOINT with her moaning. I feel her crash into me again and again. My dick is so fucking hard it's aching for her.

"Fuck. Elle. Do you know how good you taste?" I wet my fingers down and take them to her lips. I paint her lips with her. She emits a low growl like she's meowing and licks them.

"I've never tasted me before. It's sweet and tart at the same time."

"You should know that it's an honor to sample. Most are not this way. I could eat that sweet pussy of yours all day, but there are other things to explore right now." I'm uncharacteristically honest, not something I'm used to doing on a one-night stand. I also don't remember playing cards during any night of fucking either. But fuck me, she does taste good.

She's got wild eyes like I could fuck her any way I wanted to right now. But I need my cock tended to. I want to fuck her face. Her lips now wet and flushed. I move up the bed. She's quick to sit up and grab me. We're kneeling, and she's kissing me, showing her appreciation for what I just did for her. Her glorious tits smashed up against me with her hands, stroking me. And as if she's a mind reader, she drops her head and licks me from root to tip then takes the tip into her mouth while holding the base of my shaft.

"Fuck. You're good. Fuck. Elle."

She moans in response. And I need to just keep her coming. All night. For the first time in a long time, it's not about me. It's about her. I reach around her fabulous backside to find my way back into her vagina. I thrust a finger in her, and she picks up her pace on my dick.

"Good girl. Just keep moaning. You can take more."

Then I reach down and get two fingers inside of her and pump away as she sucks and flicks. She's taken most of me in her mouth. I can feel her throat welcoming my cock as I rock slowly between her lips. I'm so deep. Her eyes water a little, but there's no gagging, she swallows me down, and I'm close. I can feel the back of her throat. Fuck, no one can do that. I can't take it. I pull my fingers out of her, grab my wallet to find another condom.

She's groping at me, and I spread her legs. I plunge instantly inside of her wet and tight cunt. She moans loudly as I slowly ease out and then back in. I want to do this all night or forever.

"You're so tight. You're so fucking good for my cock."

She's staring at me with her Hellcat look that's going to tip me over the edge. Then I watch her face as her pussy contracts around my cock. I watch her arch her back, and it's a fabulous fucking thing to see, so hot. I must get myself under control, or I'll blow. She bucks harder into me, and then I jam my thumb on top of her clit. She screams loudly again and squeezes even harder. It's too much to take. I wanted to last longer, but she does something to me. I unload inside of her. We both twitch and come for what seems like forever. Both riding wave after wave of ecstasy together. Okay. So that's the hardest I've come since like an hour ago.

I fall next to her. Her soft blonde hair is all around. As we catch our breaths and she recovers from what I gave her, at least four orgasms, she rolls over on top of me. "You have no idea how badly I needed that. I haven't been fucked like that maybe ever."

I smile at her like I'm going to keep her. And that's not something I do. But her pussy is crack, and I just want more. And that face. It's stunning, and I'm lost in trying to figure out what else will make her skin blush other than orgasms.

I jump up to get towels and clean us both up, my dick still twitching at the sight of her creamy skin and slight Irish flush. Not sure how my cock is still working. It's a shame I'll probably never see her again. And I don't even know where she's from. There are many more things I want to do to her.

I try to grab a little more intel on this Hellcat. "Where did you come from again?"

I slide back into bed, and she scolds me like a school teacher. Also hot. "No. No locations. Ask me something else."

I reach over and drape my arm around her. She snuggles into me. I pull her into the crook of my arm. I don't hate this feeling. Her back is to me, and I'm kissing her neck. I move her hair out of the way, so I have better access. I prop myself up on my elbow and trace her body from her bent knees up to her graceful neck. I tickle behind her ear, and she admits a tiny adorable noise.

"I get it, nothing about our present. How about you tell me a memory, Elle?"

"Okay. How about the memory of how a stranger gave me one of the greatest nights of orgasms?"

"One of the greatest? That's certainly nice to hear, and I reciprocate the feeling. But tell me about sixteen-year-old Elle." Who the fuck am I? I can't even recall my ex-fiancée's middle name, but for some reason, I want to know about this one. She's doing odd things to me. I feel like she knows me somehow. That we're connected far beyond what we've physically exchanged tonight.

"Sixteen-year-old Elle. She loved rainbows and driving fast. Her best friend's name was Gemma. And every day when she came home from school, her mother would make her sit down for five minutes to discuss anything she wanted."

"What were some topics?'

"Random stuff. I would update Mom on who got asked to prom or where I wanted to live when I grew up. Hopes and dreams, as well as the mundane. It didn't matter what I said, my mom just wanted to connect with me for a moment before I disappeared into my room. Where I'd listen to music or hang on the phone."

"Did you end up where you dreamed of living?"

"I did."

"And that would be…" I really want to know where the hell she came from.

She turns over and looks at me with a stern cute face. She's not going to tell me where she's from. Then I lean down and kiss her. It's a sweet kiss. It's intriguing.

"Your turn, Joshua. Tell me a memory."

"I was not a good kid at sixteen. I got in fights, mostly with my best friends."

"More than one best friend?"

"We were like a gang growing up. Our allegiances always shifting with the day or who was going after which girl. I'm still close to all of them, but one remains my best friend. But yeah, I had like four or five best friends growing up. It's the closest to cousins I guess I had."

CHAPTER TWENTY-ONE

ELLE

I AM INCREDULOUS OF THIS STATEMENT. I QUICKLY NEED clarification. "Hold up. You don't have any cousins?"

He laughs and says, "No, I don't. And I know. I'm a freak."

I cannot believe this is true. "I can go one step deeper into freakier. I'll bet I can tell you why you don't have cousins. Are you an only child of only children?"

I sit up quickly and knock him on his back. I lean my chest over his. We're still naked, and it feels incredible, but I've never met anyone else like me. I kiss him. Mostly because he looks so freaking cute. There are no wild tongues, just a sensuous kiss.

Then he answers me, "Yes. I am just that. An only/only. How can you know that?"

I interrupt him, "Me too! The only child of only children."

He grins at me and kisses my nose. Then his hand grazes my back lightly as he says, "I used to hate it growing up."

"Me too. But now?"

"Now, I'm cool with it," he says confidently.

"Does it help that you have chosen cousins? This gang of friends you talked about?"

"Maybe. I guess. I mean their parents were like aunts and uncles to me. I don't see them that often anymore though."

Then I tell this stranger some very personal stuff. "Funny. I used to be. I used to think I was unique. But now I'm not cool with it at all. I don't hate it so much as it makes me a little sad. No one else to share your childhood with or anything really. I'm the sole owner of my history. It's a lot of pressure to remember. You're lucky to have your gang."

"I am." He tucks my hair behind my ear, and I put my head on his chest. He continues to stroke my hair, and I attempt to not think about my lack of cousins, uncles, and aunts. Why the hell did I just tell Joshua that? The stranger. I need to flip this script. No more about me.

"Hungry? I can call for food. Mary's is open this late right?" An insane grin overtakes his face as he gets out the bed heading towards the bathroom.

Joshua calls out from the bathroom, "Fuck yeah, but they close super soon. Call now. Might be too late for pizza. Oooh. See if we can get pesto breadsticks. Miss those."

I throw on a t-shirt and brace myself on the bathroom doorframe. "Interesting. You're from here."

He looks at me sheepishly. "Or have I had them before, and they're amazing?"

I let him off the hook and head to the couch. "Yasssss, they are. I'm obsessed with them. Wings?"

He says as he re-enters the room, "Perfect. And more wine."

He moves to his pants to grab his wallet. "I got it. You bought drinks."

Then he heads back to the bathroom and closes the door. I call, and they're making me pick it up. I throw on my jeans and my Sonoma hoodie as he emerges.

"No. NO. NO. I will not allow you to cover up all that perfection. What's happening? I'm the one that's supposed to leave." He jumps into bed and puts his hands behind his head. Himself on full display for me. "But I'm not."

"I have to pick it up. Be right back." I lean over to him, stroke him quickly, and he kisses me. "Don't get dressed."

IT ONLY TAKES a couple of minutes. Mary's is less than a block from the hotel. They give me all kinds of leftover stuff. Unclaimed pizzas, half-open bottles, and mozzarella sticks. I hear the shower as I place our giant bag of food on the desk.

He's fantastic and exactly what I needed. But now I want more. I quickly strip. I wrap a fluffy robe around myself and lean on the doorframe watching him in the shower.

He's running his hands through his hair with his back to me. His high and tight ass flexes as the water goes from cold to hot. His back looks like a sculpture carved out of marble and chiseled to perfection. I watch him for a couple of minutes. It's like my own personal Cinemax softcore porn. He's not doing anything but washing himself and relaxing.

Then he sees me, and his smile widens. He beckons me to him. I get close to the open shower door. Then he yanks the tie of the robe, and I skip forward into his warm and soft lips.

He removes the robe, and I step into the shower. He runs his hands down my back as my hair gets drenched. He holds me as we kiss, and the water falls down on top of us. We're feeling all of each other and hardcore making out. Just exploring the depths of our mouths. It feels innocent and intimate. Somehow one of us has to break this spell. It's too much for one night, it feels far-reaching. This moment is more than fucking.

And then he steps back and gets the shampoo in his hand

and moves behind me. He rubs my head, curling his fingers into my hair. He's washing my hair. It should feel strange, but somehow nothing has really felt strange tonight. He's scrubbing me as I turn around to him. Our bodies touching, our mouths kissing while he rinses my hair.

"Conditioner?"

I turn around and bend my neck back and stick my bottom to him. "Why thank you, yes."

He leans forward as he rubs it in, talking in my ear. I feel how hard he is against my back. "You do realize that it's taking every ounce of self-control not to take you from back here. That ass, Hellcat. That ass is going to destroy me."

I smile and turn around quickly, grabbing his rising marble member. I take hold at the root and then squeeze the conditioner on it. The water rinsing my hair as I stroke him.

"Your hair's not getting finished." He molds me to him again, and his hand is instantly between my legs rubbing as my tits are coated with the remnants of the conditioner. Our bond is slick, and so am I. I moan into his mouth.

His raspy perfect deep voice makes parts of me tremble as he says, "I think I would fucking do just about anything to hear that noise from your perfect lips. You may need to record it for me, so when you're not around anymore, I can hear it. It gets me hard in an instant." I moan in his ear in response. And then he puts his hands on my ass and throws me up against the wall. He growls, "Climb me."

And I do. I hitch my legs around him as he lifts me. I whisper into his ear, "Condom?"

He roars back and my body prickles, "I'm clean, and I don't plan to come inside you right now. I have plans. But for now, I'm desperate to feel you." He raises his left eyebrow at me.

"I'm on the shot and squeaky clean."

I flash a wicked smile at him. I should be going to bed, but I want him again. We're staring at each other as he circles my entrance with the crown of his cock. I move down towards it. He pushes in slowly, and we don't break our gaze while it happens. I gasp and then moan. His dick was good before, but now bare it's even better.

"Uh. So much. Fuck yeah. Your pussy is fucking amazing."

"Christ. You are too. Feels too good. So, fucking good."

"Say it. Tell me."

And he thrusts so deeply as I ride him up and down. With my body pushed up against the wall, I hold on to the top of the shower. My tits are bouncing in his face. One of his hands leaves my ass and finds my super sensitive clit. I will not be able to hold out. He circles but doesn't press down on it.

"Say it. Elle. Tell me. Elle. Oh god. You're so fucking beautiful. What is it you like?"

I'm out of my head, and it explodes out of my mouth. "Your cock. I like feeling all of your cock. Like this. I like your cock. Holy fuck. I need you this deep. I like feeling your balls slap against my ass."

"Good girl. Now you get to come. I'm going to keep fucking you until I come. But, you, I'm going to need to feel you come for me at least three more times tonight. You're gorgeous when you come. Come now, Elle." And with that, he pushes down on my clit, and I tip over the edge.

I'm breathless at the idea that my body could possibly produce that much more pleasure. I don't think I can function, let alone come again. But unbelievably, there it is, ripping through me like a tornado in a trailer park, destroying everything in its wake. I scream his name and then quake all around his dick. He's relentlessly thrusting into me, and I collapse into him.

"I got you, Elle. That was the single sexiest thing I've ever seen. Again?"

I have no breath. Every word comes out separately. I'm insatiable. "I. Dare. You. To. Do. That. Again."

"Don't ever fucking dare me."

CHAPTER TWENTY-TWO

JOSHUA

I PEEL HER OFF THE WALL, TURN OFF THE WATER, AND HOLD her legs around me as I slowly walk through the bathroom, something crashing behind me. She's gasping and staring at me.

"How are you doing this? You're walking and fucking me. You're like a circus act."

"I'm very good at multitasking." It helps that she's like five-foot-five, light as a feather and I'm six-foot-three and work out a lot.

She's moving her sexy hips in small sensuous circles, and I'm still inside of her. When we reach the bed, I lift her off my dick and place her down. She pouts. Then I flash her a wolfish smile, and she strokes me.

She blurts out, "I miss it already. Please don't put that on."

She's fucking perfect. I can't get enough of her. "Flip over. Get on your knees. I need to see that sweet ass of yours." She grins at me and does as she's told. This is going to be freaking monumental. I never ever fuck without a condom. I didn't even trust my fiancé. I never felt her raw.

She crawls up on to the bed and puts her head on the

pillow with her perfect peach ass up air. Her green eyes shine back at me. "Jesus. It's intoxicating. I'm drunk on your ass and your eyes."

I lightly smack it as she reacts with a moan in the best way. Then I rub her ass while I get behind her. I grab her hips and push into her again. By her sounds, I know I've hit my target from this angle, her G-spot. I grab the headboard and begin pounding into her. Nothing delicate about what we're doing now. She's moving back and meeting me thrust for thrust until we hear the headboard crack. She's screaming random words and phrases, but I'm concentrating.

She laughs and goes up on all fours. I reach around to feel her wetness and slide my hand to her clit. "Such a sweet, wet pussy."

"Not usually this much."

That's right, I did that. Elle shivers under me, and that's little number two but holy Christ it's followed quickly by a large one that's clamping down on my dick. And I feel my balls tighten and I roar her name and lighting shoots through me. I wish there were a next time. *"Fuck. Elle. Fuck."*

She flips over, her right leg passing in front of me and wraps her legs around my hips. I shake uncontrollably because we're still attached. No woman has ever swirled her pussy around me while I'm inside. Holy Christ, Hellcat.

She's wide-eyed and lifts her hips towards me. I can't do anything but shake. She's still trying to come again. I watch her roll her hips as my dick is unable to respond. I press down on her clit as she holds her hips up in a bridge position, and she miraculously comes again, groaning my name as loudly as possible. She falls down, and we breathe raggedly, smiling at each other.

"Holy shit, woman."

"I know! I didn't know I could do that. I didn't know

someone could do all that to me. Joshua. You're amazing. I think four more."

"That's not enough. I need you to lose fucking count."

She gasps as I pull out of her and grab the towel on the floor for her. I smash my mouth to hers, and she's weakened, but I need to hear her one more time. I reach down and cup all that left-over wetness and one quick swipe of her clit with my fingers inside, and she throws her heads back and moans loudly collapsing into me. I ride the wave of her multiple, but smaller orgasms until I feel her cunt slow down. She'll feel me for a fucking week.

CHAPTER TWENTY-THREE

ELLE

I LAY IN BED LIKE A SPENT SEA STAR HAVING LOST COUNT OF MY orgasms. Who loses count? I guess anyone fucking this Joshua person. It's like three in the morning. Where the fuck did the time go? The food is cold and untouched, I am not. I'm hot and thoroughly touched. I need to be at LaChappelle/Whittier by ten. We just screwed and talked for like seven hours.

I don't know who he is or where I'll ever find orgasms like that again. He played my body like he memorized the instruction manual. Damn. Focus. Sleep. I do like that we're going to leave it as it is. I feel a scary deep connection to him. One I'm not ready to face. It has to be the overload of serotonin in my system instead of something more cosmic.

Even though I somehow feel more comfortable with this stranger than any man I've ever met, I need him to leave. I don't know what to do with that feeling. We agreed, no last names or phone numbers or social media crap, just let it be orgasms. I need to fall dead asleep, entirely spent, and sated for probably the first time in my life. Maybe it's because there are no consequences. I don't ever have to tell anyone what a fantastic slut I was tonight.

"I'm dead. You killed me. Killed me with pleasure. So much pleasure. So much fun." He's putting his clothes back on and stares at me while he's doing it. He's laughing at me.

"Holy hell, woman. I have nothing left to give you right now. I know you're sleepy, but you're also so fucking gorgeous and smart and hysterical and confident. I'm afraid that if I don't leave now, I won't ever leave. My dick won't let me. That is one enchanting pussy you got there. It's a shame there won't be another moment for us to think up more crazy shit to do to each other."

"It is also a shame that I can't keep my eyes open and be flattered. If I just say 'samesies' back to you, will you be as flattered? Although I do want to add that your torso belongs in some kind of fucking museum."

He leans down and kisses me. It's a soft sensuous kiss. It's a stirring and deep kiss like we're saying all the things we can't face in reality. I have no filter left, and I speak the truth, "That was one of the most amazing nights of my life. Thank you. No one has ever made me come that hard. Strangely, I'll miss you, not just your cock."

"Beautiful, beautiful Elle with those bright green eyes with the golden flecks that see too much of me. I'll dream of you for quite a while, for many reasons, I suspect." Then he winks. "I haven't come that hard either. Maybe ever. Or felt a connection like this, ever."

I whisper, "Agreed."

"Goodnight and goodbye, Hellcat."

I talk with what's left of my voice. It comes out way too sleepy, but I mean it. "No goodbye, that means that there will never be another chance meeting. If the universe needs us to fuck again, it will figure out a way. We owe it to the honor of good sex to not say goodbye but later, Suit. Make it an ellipsis instead of a period at the end of that sentence."

"I wouldn't want to let the universe down. Until later, Hellcat."

He grabs two bottles of water from the mini-fridge. He puts one on the nightstand with some Advil then leans over my limp and sated body. His soft and luscious lips find mine once again. The room is a disaster of pillows and towels everywhere. The sheets have all come up, and I'm curled up on a scrap still covering the mattress. He finds the duvet from the floor and tucks me in. I'm almost asleep before the door even closes. But I do hear him whisper.

"Elle. I will never ever forget that sound. It's mine now."

The insane thing is that I think that too, I can't imagine making it for anyone else.

CHAPTER TWENTY-FOUR

ELLE

I AM REMARKABLY REFRESHED. THANK GOD FOR NERVES AND adrenaline. I drive across the little town with mist rolling off the field and vineyards. As I pull into the winery, I mentally tick off all of my rules I broke last night, like a debauched checklist:

- Kissed two men in one night
- Slept with a stranger
- No last names
- Sex with someone I just met
- Sex without knowing what they do or telling them what I do
- Sex with someone who I talked about my mother with. I don't talk about my mother with anyone.
- Sex with someone I'm not dating
- Sex with someone I met in a bar
- Sex without a condom
- Shower sex
- Sexy hair washing
- Washed my hair with hotel shampoo

- Broke a headboard
- Slept on a strange bare mattress
- Let him tell me what to do
- Said the word cock. A lot.
- Ate cold pesto breadsticks for breakfast
- Liked the stranger WAY too much

Thank god the scenery is so breathtaking to take my mind off my slutty evening and his deep and endless blue eyes. I pull into the winery, its tumbled stone gated entrance leading me up the hill to a lush and verdant vineyard. The sloping hills of northern California are something I didn't really know about. They're feminine in nature. The winery sits just before the Carneros Valley and on the edge of Sonoma.

I pull into Emma Farm, the official name of the land their winery sits on. It's named after the woman who founded the winery. She's a direct ancestor of Sarah's, and I like that they still recognize that it's a farm. There are several large stone and wooden buildings on the property. There's a large and restored building they call the Farmhouse. Will and Sarah live there and have for most of their lives. Just across the parking lot from their house are the admin offices. They reside in a converted old Cooperage that they aptly call, the Cooperage.

Down a hill and about a five-minute walk from the offices are the tasting room and a large welcoming slate patio that overlooks the vines and pond. It's a converted half-barn and half of an old stone warehouse. The tank rooms, destemmer, and crush pad are all connected to the back of the tasting room. The wine is made on the back end of the tasting room building and through the back of the cave. Sitting close and up on a steeper hill, there's a large amphitheater and pavilion. They have concerts and outdoor films in the summer. The cave, which I have yet to see, is across a large patio area from the tasting room.

I enter the Cooperage, and Mrs. Dotson greets me to guide me to the conference room. The entire staff is gathered. The building has some newer built parts, but you can smell the mineral of ancient stone and imagine the history in these walls. I love the smell.

"Elle, where ya been? We had this meeting hours ago. You've been fired." I laugh as Will embraces me. "Come. Can I get you some coffee?"

I'm nervous. I really am. Even though I've spent most of the last five days in Will or Sarah's company, I'm worried they won't like what I thought of. I want to make them proud.

"That would be great, thank you. A little sugar and a little cream, please." I don't get nervous. I can slay any room, but for some reason, I just want this gig more.

Sarah nods, and I follow Will. Coffee is fine, but what I really need is a shit ton of more Advil. I'm walking bowlegged. He did promise me that I'd feel him tomorrow. I hope they don't notice the walk. Or—more importantly— think Asher did this to me.

I need to push down the thought of my filthy gorgeous stranger and get my head back in the game. I have my back to the window out to the open part of the office. Kind of a bullpen of scattered desks and couches with high vaulted ceilings that are gorgeous with the exposed beams.

I greet everyone individually and take my place back at the front of the room. All the departments are present and the vineyard crew. I'm going to give them an overall view of the plan. I'm wearing a bodycon, color-blocked dress. Turquoise, white, and brown. It's a little tight for a business meeting, but I didn't plan on doing business when I came to Sonoma eight days ago. My hair is in a French twist, and I was able to salvage my nails this morning with some buff nail polish that matches my nude sky-high Lagerfeld pumps and nude MAC *Honey Love* lipstick. I have no idea how I chipped a no-chip manicure during sex.

I have delicate silver jewelry on my wrist but bold earrings that dangle just a bit. As I turn the corner, they brush my neck, and my thoughts turn to him again. Eventually, he'll fade for me. I don't have time to keep thinking of Joshua.

I refocus in order to shred this meeting. Time to be the tiger I am. I'm pulled to this project. I don't want it to go away. I'll do the bulk of the creative work with Evan and hold on to this opportunity for myself. I won't pass this account off to my staff to manage.

I like these people. I want to help them sell the place. I'll help them wine and dine buyers if that's what my role becomes. I love that they have their vineyard manager, the tasting room employees as well as the accountant and direct sales manager sitting around this table. Most of whom I've met over the past couple of days. Their sense of community and the family feeling at the winery is exactly my pitch. Others may talk about assets and commodities that are worth something in a sale. I'm going to market the name, the feeling, and the family. The oldest continuously family-owned vineyard in California.

There's always been either a LaChappelle or a Whittier at the helm. Some of them were businessmen, and others were winemakers along the way. The vineyard hasn't been out of family hands for a hundred and forty-seven years. Research is my secret weapon. I could draw their family tree right now if they wanted me to. I'm not bored with wine or the story, I really do have the advantage of a fresh eye.

I smile and stand. I pass out my prospectus to everyone at the table. I gut check the fire in my belly and begin, "Hello everyone, most of you know, I'm Noelle Parker from Parker & Company Marketing. My goal here is to make sure everyone understands that all I want to do is highlight the unique nature of this vineyard to glorify your amazing product. I want to ease the way for people to find you and appreciate what you have to offer, in service, in the product, and in beauty."

Everyone is nodding and smiling. I continue, "I'd like to go through my prop..." My breath catches, my body freezes, and I lose my words. Usually, nothing knocks me off my game, I'm a showman. But he's much more than nothing.

He breezes into the room, leaning up against the wall, crossing his arms then his eyes lock with mine and instantly go wide, and his eyebrows go straight up in the air. He seems as shocked to see me as I am to see him. I look around and begin to babble. "What are you doing here?"

He says in a raspy tone, "How are you here?"

I shoot back to him, "How are *you* here?" He looks sideways and then shakes his head pointedly at me.

Everyone looks at the two of us, and I pull my shit together. Why is he here? My stomach is in knots. My knees knock. How did he find me? What does he want? Oh, god. Is he a stalker? Why is Joshua here? His hair's a little out of control, and I know why. He catches my gaze, and his eyes track to Will and Sarah, then he purses his lips. I guess he doesn't want to do this in front of his bosses. But he does look hot. I grin at him and try to regain my composure.

"Well, sir. Have a seat and I'll continue."

The azure blue of his casual linen shirt mirrors his eyes, and I see that the bottom button has come undone. How the hell am I supposed to concentrate? The open shirt flap frames him in his faded jeans. Unfortunately, I know exactly what's under the jeans, nothing but his giant dick. I struggle to look away. He catches me looking and smirks. Then he nods as I return my gaze, skimming up his impressive figure to his chiseled face.

His eyes take in every piece of me in this dress. Then his facial expression changes. It's not as open as I knew him to be. He stands up a little straighter, and his demeanor flips. I almost feel the chill come over me. Oh, god. Did I imagine our connection? I'm an idiot. I opened up way too much.

Mrs. Dotson pipes up with a quasi-explanation of who I am, "She's from New York. We're here to listen. Can she just get on with telling us how she's going to rebrand and save the winery?"

"Hi."

I'm flustered, and there's a slight redness overtaking my chest and creeping up. I'm grateful for my crew neck dress but hoping I can contain the flush to my chest. FUCK. Get out of here. His eyes harden after Mrs. Dotson speaks.

Everyone's staring at me and then him. Joshua's words come out cutting, "Interesting. By all means, continue. I wasn't aware we needed any of that. Elle, is it?" This is not a tone I've heard from him before. "Please continue. Or are we waiting for Asher? You okay? You look as though you've seen a ghost." I collect myself while he looks like he's pissed.

"Asher Bernard will not be attending today. This has nothing to do with him."

"That's not what I heard, Elle," Joshua says with a look like…

"It's Noelle. The name is Noelle Parker. Elle is a nickname used by very few." Will tosses his arm up to acknowledge that he can use that nickname. He settles me.

Will looks over, "Cop a squat, Josh. It's not what you think also you don't know this woman well enough to call her Elle." He winks at me, and Joshua's eyes flick between the two of us. Again he looks utterly confused.

But he's almost cruel to me. I'm so devastated that the

man I chose to be so vulnerable with might use my softness against me. Also, how does he know about Asher? Fuck. Does he know that Asher and I were a thing? How does he know any of this?

"Please enlighten us, *Noelle*, with how you're going to save us all. Big city New York, Cosmopolitan girl. I wouldn't want to miss your plan on how to make the winery viable and edgy. I'm sure you will use every advantage you can to help us, possibly exploiting people unbeknownst to them."

Fuck. He thinks I knew who he was, that it was planned. I still don't know who the fuck he is or what he does at the winery. He's not been around the last five days when I've basically lived here.

I look around the room to salvage the meeting, and everyone is staring at us like we're on display. I address the room. "I want to remind everyone here that I'm only here because I was asked to be by Will and Sarah."

"Then, by all means, let's get to this fabulous plan that only someone like you could come up with."

I must look like I've been caught stealing. I'm baffled and pissed at this guy now.

"I'm sure you're competent, but right now, you look like a damsel in distress."

"Nice point. I didn't make the first contact." That's not translating to everyone else in the room, but it is a reminder to him that I did not seek out this random surly employee of LC/W. He saved me from the letch. I was just trying to get the taste of Asher out of my mouth.

He nods at me acknowledging that as fact. Now, I need to get back on track. I mean, hold up, asshole. Maybe your eyes aren't that fucking blue.

I fire back because this is my meeting. "I'm sorry, Suit, why don't you take a seat and let me get started." Shit. He rattled me. I need to get back to professional.

He doesn't move, and it's incredibly distracting. What the hell does he do here? I thought I knew everyone and their roles. I'm rolling through the employee roster in my mind for a Joshua. Nothing. The frustration flush of a minute ago is fading into a rage. That red could take over my cheeks at any moment. Curse of Irish skin, everyone always knows exactly what I'm thinking.

"I'll sit when I'm ready. Proceed there, Ms. Cosmopolitan."

Sarah turns to Joshua. "I'm not sure what the hell is going on, but this is incredibly unproductive."

What the hell is that supposed to mean? He can sense that I'm confused.

Joshua looks at Sarah. "One second. I have something to say, and then I'll sit down." It's about time. I'm rapidly losing credibility.

"Fine. But be kind." Sarah glares at her employee.

He speaks in a low raspy tone that pisses me off it's so sexy.

"I'm just not sure someone who spends most of their time in steel, concrete, and glass is going to understand how things are done out here in the terroir, rolling hills, and clean air? Even if they do own jeans and a local cafe t-shirt, this version seems to be the real you. But give it your best shot. Seriously, where the hell did you come from?" Everyone is looking confused at his intense anger. I am baffled. Will seems to be delighted by the whole thing. I will not lose this job.

Sarah speaks again, "Okay. That's quite enough. Sit down. Let Elle finish."

I follow her lead, making sure to mimic her tone of voice. I'm in charge of this meeting. I also think he's an ass. I didn't use him for intel. I didn't know who he was, and now he knows way too much about me. And he's mean. I thought we shared something more profound than a hookup. I was apparently wrong. I'm struggling not to let anyone know how hurt I am right now.

I get indigent and sarcastic. "Maybe let me know your name, Joshua. That way I can call on you if you have any more questions. Or if I think there's anything you can possibly help with, I'll let you know. Just raise your hand." Will snickers just a little.

"It's Josh."

"Not Joshua? Interesting. Seems there's lots of pretending going around." I push him. "Great, okay then, then please sit-down *Josh*," I say sternly. The rest of the table's eyes are wide, and I don't know what they're worried about, I can hold my own. I'll apologize if the Whittiers are offended, but I'm fighting for this job right now, and I don't lose.

Everyone shifts in their seats and two of the employees take the moment to run out for more coffee. I refocus and arrange my presentation in front of me.

I've been so disconnected from any authentic over the last year or so. I've been traveling in a haze of glitz and glamour. I'm so tired of pushing luxury brands to people who just buy things because it's what's new or next, no regard to need or quality. This place is genuine and pure. I want to be connected to something real, not create an air of authenticity around a product. I want to be associated with a true thing, not something I have to convince people to believe in. These people are real, and I'd like to honestly help them.

I want this piece of business, and no glorified farmhand will get the best of me.

I was raised on a farm in Kansas. A real working farm, with animals, wheat, and corn. I know about living and dying by the harvest and weather, hoping your family will have a good crop. I stood up to every farm boy in the county. I know all about soil and clean air, asshole. Sit the fuck down.

I don't tell anyone about the farm. I try to maintain a very polished and chic exterior for my clients. I deal in high-end luxury, and I'd lose most of my clientele if they knew I was just Brittany Noelle Doyle from Ellsworth County, Kansas. Noelle Parker gets shit done. Elle Parker is a force of nature sophisticate that gets results. I may have fooled you with my no make-up sloppy hair and submission last night, but buckle up, vineyard boy, this is my show right now.

Then he leans over the table, placing his large and commanding hands on it. Despite my new distaste for this man who's made me feel used and cheap in a matter of moments, my stomach flutters. Those are the hands that were inside me just hours ago. He's staring directly into my eyes, and I can feel myself want him.

"My name is Joshua Lucien LaChappelle Whittier," he says. "You know nothing about me, Cosmo. And you can call me Josh."

My heart drops to my stomach, and I instantly want to puke. Joshua picks up a bottle of wine with his name on it, turns the label towards me, and pushes it across the table. Visions of LaChappelle/Whittier family tree choke me. It's the son who doesn't want the winery.

Then he walks over and kisses his mother on the cheek. He places his hand on his father's shoulder before sitting. Oh, god. No. No. No. Oh no. I fucked their son. A lot. I screwed him a lot. I dirty fucked their son. I slutty fucked their son. I know what their son tastes like. Oh, god. Composure. Shit. And he's treating me like shit. I have to get past my hurt and the absurdity of this situation. I'm so pissed. Did he know who I was?

Joshua says, "Go right ahead and tell me how you know this place better than me."

Everyone laughs and the rage red flips to embarrassment

pink. It's all over my cheeks along with the egg on my face. And I hate Joshua Whittier.

I soften my tone but maintain it. I must continue, or this is all a farce of who I am. I do know Joshua Whittier, no stone unturned. Research is my weapon and religion. I smile like it's a nutty madcap mix-up instead of the most embarrassing moment of my life. He looks nothing like his over-done persona that's splashed all-over multiple bimbos' Instagram accounts. I seriously didn't recognize him last night. His hair color is so much lighter in person. *And* he's supposed to be in Santa Barbara, where he lives.

Take back your moment. You're terrific in the room, Noelle. Do it. Throw it back at him even though you're sore in every cell of your body because of things you let him do to it. And your heart aches a bit that it all meant nothing to him. He's turned so quickly on me. I'm not quite sure why I'm the enemy when it's his parents that are selling. Take it back. I throw my shoulders back and stare right at him. I'll show him Hellcat.

"Oh, but I do, Josh. I do know you. You graduated from near the top of your class at Stanford, but not with a business degree. You were pre-law for some reason. You took the LSAT and probably could have gone to law school, but I'm going to guess the siren song of money called to you. You left Sonoma eleven years ago to join your venture capital firm, Magnus, in Santa Barbara. At thirty-four, you're one of the most successful at your firm founded by Cross and Baum, but you're not a partner. You do a lot of tech offerings and own a large steel and glass home on the ocean and multiple flashy cars. You have an assistant named John and no student loans, you paid them off your fourth year at the firm. You also paid John's student loans off as a bonus last year. You speed too much and have racked up seven speeding tickets in the last year. You paid handsomely to keep your license. You eat way too much cereal and yogurt. You enjoy dating vapid amazon brunette women but only if they have more than fifteen thousand Instagram followers. And I'm sorry, but I wasn't aware you wanted anything to do with the wine business." Will claps and I nod at him but stare at Josh.

His expression changes to blank. Then he crosses his legs as his mouth opens slightly. That's right, asshole, I know exactly who you are. And the women who fawn over you and the men who scramble to be in your sphere. He's the darling of Santa Barbara's social columns and social media. He gets major movies, apps, and software companies financed. He has yet to make a misstep in business. Well, maybe just one. He underestimated me. I've never been impressed by money or status. "From my research, you don't want to be a part of this vineyard. You have no say in the sale or any piece of this business at all. I return to my original question, what are you doing here?"

He sits straight up. "Sale?! Mom. What the hell is she talking about? What's going on? Was the idea of a sale hers or did that come from Asher as well?" His father leans over and puts his hand on Josh's arm.

"Later. We'll talk about it later. And watch your language."

"What the hell happened to your arm, Mom?" He references Sarah's new cast.

"It's just a slight break. It will be off in like a week. I tripped while weeding at the amphitheater. Sit. Let her finish. Elle, I'm so sorry for the interruption. I'm terribly embarrassed. I'm so sorry for my son's behavior. Please go right ahead."

"Thank you. Now let's get to the plan."

Josh snarls under his breath. His mother places her hand on his shoulder, and he backs down.

I go through my ideas for exposure and media stunts.

Everyone seems to be laughing and enjoying themselves. Then I go in for the kill.

"I don't think you need to be any different than you already are. The buzz phrases in my business are building a brand, launching a new deck, or creating taste-making moments. Any firm would usually strive to get your name on the lips of 'influencers.' But LaChappelle/Whittier doesn't need any of those things. New labels or a new name will all just be a waste of money. Rebranding, repackaging, and relaunching is a tremendous waste in this situation. This vineyard, this family, and this wine already have everything it needs to succeed. It's an enormous testament to the quality of people who choose to stay here for decades and to most of the family that treats the land and their people with the utmost respect." I take a breath, and everyone is hanging on my words, including Joshua. I launch into my strategies and the particulars.

As I go into my closing, Josh's eyes have softened and I can see a glimmer of the man from last night. "My only job is to let people know you're here. I don't have to trick or con or need to come up with gimmicks. I plan to simply expose as many people as I can to the perfection tucked away just beyond 8th Street East."

And that's how it's fucking done. You take off your underwear and wait on the bed for me, bitch. I glance at Josh. Oh shit. Holy fuck, he has my underwear. I see the black peeking out of his shirt pocket like a dirty pocket square. He must have had it in his jeans pocket and moved it there while I was talking. I AM DYING.

Will starts to clap a bit, and the others join in. "That was wonderful. Thank you."

I sit down. "Please stop clapping. I meant everything I said. If anyone has any questions, I'd be happy to make time for you. I know you're on a busy schedule today, and I don't want to take up more of your day." I stand and shake every-one's hand. People are talking to me, but my entire attention is drawn to the sandy blonde broad-shouldered figure cutting through the room and out the door.

I walk into the narrow hallway with Sarah and Will. "Where are you staying?" Sarah inquires.

"I was at El Dorado the last couple of nights. But Asher has offered to let me stay with him until I figure out our next steps…" From behind me, I hear a scoff.

His booming voice trails down the hall to me. "Asher Bernard."

CHAPTER TWENTY-FIVE

JOSH

THAT FUCKING WEASEL IS THE REASON I CAME UP HERE TO THIS meeting. I heard he had positioned a woman to work for my parents. A friend told me. But I do not trust Asher, and they shouldn't either. He's even screwed my parents over in the past. They're too softhearted for business, and they have certainly been taken in by this harpy. As I was. Fuck. Why did she have to be this woman? The woman I need to get away from my parents. And what is her relationship with Asher? I only wish I wasn't fucking hard just looking at her. I remember every second of last night. I've been thinking about it all morning.

It was different. Elle couldn't have targeted me, I rescued her. And no one would have anticipated that I'd be at Steiner's. Only my parents knew I'd be in town. But still. I'm so pissed. Pissed that I still want her. Pissed she's selling my parents' winery out from under them. And pissed that Archer is anywhere near them or her. I'm furious at the idea that Asher's even shaken her hand. Shit, did I just get jealous? NO. It's just anger at her and what she's doing.

I'm in my head, until she answers me, pulling me back to

the present. "Yes. Asher. Why?"

She turns her delicate face to me. I wish her skin didn't blush the way it does. I saw the red indicating she hates me, and I saw the pink blush on her lush cheeks when I embarrassed her. I couldn't stop myself. I'm so angry that she lied to me. She's not a simple, no makeup girl. She's a fucking shark. Her soft pouty lips are drawn in a straight line now, looking at me, trying to intimidate me, but all I can think of is my cock between them. Hellcat. Fuck. It was a fucking spot-on pitch. She owned the room and me. And that doesn't happen. What is it about this woman that makes me think and do things that are not in my norm? She's a wizard who put some kind of jinx on me.

I push the thought away. Asher is bad. She doesn't know shit about this world or me. I don't back down and certainly not from someone I'd like to throw over my shoulder and fuck raw in the vineyards. Her attitude and stature as she pops her hip are making my stomach flip a bit, but not scaring me.

She's inconsequential in this business and in my life, but she's still insanely hot. She's all I thought about since I left her side. I wanted to get back to her. I was contemplating staking out the El Dorado after this staff meeting. She felt different and significant even while we were anonymously fucking.

But this morning's Elle is a lot different. There were shades of her holy bitchiness last night, but I thought it was sass. Her blown-out hair and blush nude lips are the opposite of the girl I was so captivated with last night. She's too polished. And too corporate. She doesn't belong here.

Her cheeks flush, telegraphing her thoughts to me while I make her wait for my answer. I do not need this woman in my head, and my parents certainly don't need anyone connected with Asher Bernard anywhere near us.

She turns away from me to talk to Randy, the tasting room manager. I get to look at her ass in that body con dress. Only highlight from this morning.

Asher's such a slimy weasel. He's smarmy, charming, and dressed for the part. Lots of people have fallen for his act. It took a while for everyone to exchange notes and see what was happening, so he did well for about a decade.

Asher's main scam was to offer consulting services to wineries. He promised boosted reputation, sales, and visibility. He'd wine and dine people all the time. Turns out it was usually his friends on the winery's dime. Then he'd pour at events for the vineyard all over the country. Then after a couple of months of no results, he'd create an excuse as to why it didn't work. Then demand his payout fee on his contract. Every wine shop, restaurant, and winery he's been associated with ended up light a half pallet of wine and a significant chunk of cash as he moved on to his next mark. Then he'd turn around and sell product privately to collectors, the wineries never seeing a dime. He profited off his incompetence.

A friend at some Healdsburg dinner last week told me Asher was poking around my parents like a vulture. And then the guy overheard my parents get super excited about the girl he was with and working with her. They can't be together. Is she working with him?

Asher's reputation proceeds him now. He's been kicking around the area for twenty years, and nobody really knows where he came from. I think I was fifteen when he first came to town. He's about a decade older than I am. My grandfather was in charge back then. He steered clear of him. Lucien, my grandfather, was a ruthless man and had strong gut instincts when it came to business. A trait that skipped a generation, my mother is too soft-hearted.

Once my parent's took over the winery, Asher reared his

ugly head again. My parents are the sort of people who see the good in everyone. They trusted Asher years earlier and got burned. He's apparently made amends to them over time, but fuck that guy. I didn't get my parents' forgiving genes.

Asher's reputation is built on a house of cards. His current scam has him building up other people's cellars with his so-called knowledge. He claims to have gone to UC Davis, but no one knows him. Asher's the guy who always purchases two bottles of an exclusive reserve vintage at cost, but mysteriously only one ever gets to his clients. Asher attends the opening of an envelope. He's also always ready to be an "expert" for any occasion or article. If it's free, he's there to pimp himself out. And if they'll pay him, he'll travel anywhere.

Most of his current reputation was built outside the bubble of California wine country. He flies to wine competitions in places like Traverse City, Michigan, and Niagara, and he's touted as the "esteemed California wine country judge." Even though he has a shit palate. They pay him and reimburse all his expenses. If she came to my parents through him, she's tainted too. Probably a complete grifter.

I step down the hallway away from everyone else. I call out to her. I want to see if she'll come to me.

I answer. "Figures."

She moves towards me. That's right, come to me. Damn, her hips when she walks. She says in a pointed pinched tone. "What does?"

"He's too cosmopolitan for the area as well. He'd never throwback whiskey in a t-shirt and jeans. But then again, looks can be deceiving."

She fires right back. "Deceiving, huh? Like promising that something would last all day but seems to have faded at dawn?"

Fucking bitchy comment. She and I both know she still feels my cock. "Asher's a self-made asshole."

"Same could be said of others." She chuffs at me.

Mom approaches us, and we shut up. There's a tense moment, and then she breaks it again, trying to bust my balls. Mom continues to the front doors.

"I'm from New York, he seems quite homespun to me." Elle says this hoping it will make me feel like a hick. It doesn't.

"Whatever you say, Cosmo. Been nice, umm."

Go away, little girl. I see those heels you're tottering on, raising you up, giving you false courage. My job is to size people up, and I got you, girlie. Lust may have clouded my vision last night, but I'm all awake now.

She smiles at me. "It certainly was, but that's clearly over."

As she walks past, her intoxicating scent fills the narrow stone hallway. The lilacs and orange blossom. I shake my head to refocus on how I now distrust and hate her.

This community was founded by farmers. People who loved the idea of hard work and creation. They still feel the soil, prune the vines, and cultivate the rootstock themselves. A world and a craft that someone like Elle Parker plainly saw dollar signs in.

That bullshit she was shoveling seemed to have worked, but wait until I talk with my parents. I'm sure she doesn't believe it and will turn right around and rebrand the shit out of my parent's winery for no reason other than money. They don't need her or anyone. The winery is in the black, we don't need more, they don't need more. And sell to whom? Why? What would they do? Retire? They're like sixty and vibrant. Fuck this and fuck that girl. Oh, that's right, I already did.

She finishes her glad-handing. I position myself at the door. She won't leave here without knowing in no uncertain terms that she's not welcome. I don't care how fucking charmed her mouth is. The entire reason I'm up here is to stop Asher's plans and now whatever this sale bullshit is. My parents suck at business, so I hauled my ass up here. And thank god I did. There's no reason for her or a sale.

She walks down the hallway and out the door. We're alone in the parking lot, and I'm blocking her path. Her scent is overpowering.

She says haughtily, "Please move."

"Listen. You're going to do exactly what I tell you. Just like last night."

"You think so? Last night, I was a girl who needed to get laid. Today, I'm a woman with a job to do, and no one fucks with my business no matter how good they are at fucking."

She's good. But she will listen to me, or I will break her. I'll buy the firm and get her ass fired. "You'll drop this entire plan. Walk away from my parents, take your gorgeous ass to the airport, and fly home to New York. Report to your superiors that you lost this piece of business. Tell them the client says we're not for sale and we don't need a new slick marketing agency."

There's electricity to what's passing between us. It's making me twitch below. I tuck Elle's panties deeper into my pocket as she watches. Then she glares at me with those green globe eyes, and I can see vibrant gold flecks dance within them. There's a moment where I see the girl from last night. And then like a veil her eyes cloud over and she straightens her posture. As if she was pushing me and whatever we feel away.

"You're not my client. And I don't have superiors, asshole. I am the superior. My name is on the door, is yours? I mean, in Santa Barbara." She knows it's not. And now I can't stand her and can't stop myself from wanting her.

"See ya, Cosmo." She gets right in my face, no one else is

around. I can see her slight mask of freckles hidden under light powder. The ones I saw naked last night. She grins insidiously, and I'm not sure if she wants me to kiss her or slap her. But I feel the same.

"Don't fucking call me that. Josh."

"It's Joshua to you."

Her voice lilts with a sarcastic tone, "Whatever, Suit. I'd say see you later, but since you've abandoned the winery for most of your adult life, I won't worry about you getting in my way."

I hold her wrist lightly, and she gasps. And there's that damn spark between us. She turns towards me, fire in her eyes and lust flushing on her chest.

I look at her earnestly, trying to bury my fury at being lied to and seduced. I feel betrayed. And I need her to define what the fuck she's doing near Asher.

I ask, "Which one's the real you? This outfit is gorgeous on you, but it doesn't compare to the girl I met last night. This one is too cosmopolitan."

She doesn't hesitate to ask the same, "Which one is the real you? Josh, rumpled linen bourbon drinker or Joshua, expensive suit Instagram model fucker? Open-air or steel and glass?" She knows full well, my house is made of steel and glass. She researched my damn house.

She goes for the jugular of guilt, but I made sure she doubted herself too. Direct hit but I don't let her know. This woman needs to go. And she pulls out of my face, leaving me standing there with a slight erection and my nostrils coated in her heavenly and infuriating scent.

She's wrong about one thing. I have no intention of getting out of her way. Not if the winery and my parents are under her spell. No one takes advantage of me or my family. Fuck this arrogant girl. She goes down, and I'm the one to keep her on a short leash.

CHAPTER TWENTY-SIX

ELLE

WILL AND SARAH PUT THEIR FOOT DOWN AND TOLD JOSH THAT I was hired, and that he didn't need to worry. I'm glad they stood up for me. I'm glad he's gone but I hate that I think about him all the damn time.

I'm about ten days into this gig, and the commute from Asher's to Sonoma is killing me. He lives about forty minutes from here, and in California traffic time, that translates to about an hour and a half each way. I slept at the hotel, MacArthur Place, a couple of nights just to get a break from the road.

Also, Asher's overly flowery house decor is a bit much to take. I have been sleeping in the guest room, and he's not pleased about it. Most days, I leave before he gets up and come home super late. I could just get another hotel room, but I don't know how long I'm going to stay. I met a girl named Poppy who owns a little cafe in town. Her parents have a winery just up on Highway 12, and it has a guest house that will be available in a couple of weeks. Not sure I can hold out.

So far things have been uneventful, and it's a lot of set up.

There's been no word from Josh, which I tell myself is a good thing. I hate him, but it doesn't stop me from masturbating to him all the fucking time. I mean, the thought of that night replays in my head constantly. I imagine that he finds me at that meeting and everyone leaves us alone in the room. I imagine he takes me in the Cooperage in every way imaginable.

I must separate that night from the reality of their jackass son. It still burns my heart a bit at how dismissive he was with me. His eyes that were so full of hope and surprise that night turned so cold and angry the next day.

I steer way clear of Asher. That's another reason why I need to get out of his house. It's strange and awkward. After I went to New York to pack up a bunch of clothes for this extended residency, I never really unpacked at his house. I have a few items in the bathroom and a couple things of jewelry in a drawer. That's it. I don't want him to think I want to play house with him. I had a conversation with him about we're better as friends and associates. That I'm so busy with this project that a relationship is not something I'd like to pursue right now. He keeps leaving me little notes on my pillow. I have not been subtle, but the dude is not listening.

He doesn't understand why I don't want to be with him. He brings home giant bouquets of tacky-ass spider mums for me all the time and still calls me angel. I need out.

I'M PRESENTING the updated but very similar logo to Will and Sarah. Evan wanted to clean it up a bit. It's not going on labels, but in printed pieces and any new merchandise they might need to order. The old one will remain as long as they need it. We're not rebranding, just modernizing the logo on the remaining pieces. They're selling, so no need to update.

"I like the use of color and the picture of Emma Farm on this piece. So beautiful. It's fun to see it through someone else's eyes."

"That's a direct marketing piece for high-end wine shops who might want one of you or Alena to come and do an event at their place. Evan needs an excellent set of pictures for the rest of our strategy. He has an extensive shot list, and I've lined up a photographer you will love." I pull up her portfolio on my laptop for them to approve.

"Wow. These are gorgeous. Alena said that *the Chronicle* called her for an interview on winemakers that dabble in heritage vines." Sarah seems impressed.

"Yes. And she'll be getting more like that. I'm glad you like the photographer. I'll start nailing down dates. And we need the entire staff's cooperation for what Evan has in mind with the photos and the personalized spots."

They agree to everything, which makes my job delightful. Our meeting is over, and there are scones. I love Sarah's scones. Will closes the folder in front of him and smiles.

He says, "Well, it's noon, you should probably start your schlep home. With traffic, you should get there by around eight, eight-thirty."

I smirk back at him. "That's helpful, Will. Real helpful. I do get some of my best work done in that car." I'd leased a Mercedes convertible. Why not have a gorgeous red car for a minute? I don't drive in New York.

"Stay here. At least for a little while." Sarah offers up.

Will begins to clarify what she just asked me. "We have a ton of room. You can have the left side of the house. We'll take the right. Put a big tape line down the middle ala Brady Bunch style."

I look at him quizzically. "You know that's a super old reference. And I don't get it."

Will explains, "Well, I am super old. And the brothers

were fighting over sides of the room and divided it with a tape line. And now you have to binge Brady Bunch. I command it as your employer. I'm going to put it in as a rider to the contract."

I roll my eyes at him. "You couldn't just say we'll divide the house?"

"Look, Josh isn't here. You can take his room or the smaller one. Both have bathrooms and little sitting areas off the bedrooms. We can put a desk in there if you don't want to work in the Cooperage."

"Hold up! Are you asking me to move in with you, Will? It's all so sudden. What ever will people think of me?" I bat my eyelashes at him, and Sarah laughs.

He gets down on one knee. "Noelle, Elle, Parker, virtual stranger, I know this is all moving so fast, but will you share our home with us please?"

"I'd be honored. And I need to get the hell out of Asher's."

Sarah agrees with me. "Yes, you do. He's fine in doses, but I can't imagine him longer than a dinner."

Will says, "Glad that's settled. Phew." He hugs me. "Elle, you seem a bit of a lost soul. Sarah and I can't help but take in a stray. For god's sake, how many freaking cats are around here?"

I answer, "And the dogs."

Will quickly answers, "And Mrs. Dotson."

I giggle at Will and then keep smiling. Wow, even though the lost soul statement cuts a bit deep, doesn't mean it's not true. I'm never without a plan or a blueprint to how it should all shake out. And here I am, moving in with strangers three thousand miles away from everyone I know and my own home.

CHAPTER TWENTY-SEVEN

JOSHUA

"WHAT THE HELL'S WRONG?" I'M ON THE PHONE, AND THIS idiot who has a fat chunk of freaking cash doesn't want to give it to me. "You wanted in on tech that's going to matter. This is it. This is the opportunity for you to make more money than you thought fucking possible. Don't ask your planner. He won't know. And if it all goes to hell, I'll fucking pay you back personally."

"Joshua, you know I trust you. We've done some good deals, but tech is so volatile. It's just not me."

I ask, "Are you in town?"

"We're in New York for the week."

He's lying, and I'm going to catch him. I'm relentless, and I don't lose. "I'll be there tomorrow. We can sit down."

"Way to call my bluff." I smile knowing full well he has small kids and doesn't like to be gone on weekends. He occasionally travels to Seattle or LA for the day. But currently, this cocksucker is calling me from the golf course. Don't fuck with me.

I bark out an order to him, "Be at the fucking Finch and Fork at 7 p.m."

"Joshua, you are going to end me."

"At least you'll get a good cocktail out of it if nothing else, right?"

"See you later."

I own him. I need to secure fifteen million, and then this piece is totally financed, and I can hand it off to legal. This the third tech deal I've worked for this gaming company, and it's going to be a nice little paycheck for me. My dad keeps texting. I really don't have time to clean up his mess with that girl. She freaking haunts my dreams. I need to leave her as jerk-off material in my mind. I can't know anything she's doing up there that will piss me off. And I certainly don't want to know anything more about her and Asher.

I scream to my assistant. "John! Finch and Fork for two at 7 p.m."

He sings his answer to me. "It shall be done, my master." He's uber-efficient, doesn't ever chitchat, and is loyal as hell, so I put up with his theatrics. Best assistant ever.

I stand and stretch. Time to look at my phone. It's been buzzing all morning.

DAD: I need a favor, boy.

DAD: Seriously, you're that important you can't text back?

DAD: What if we were trapped under something heavy?

DAD: I see you don't care that there could be a wild animal terrorizing your mother and me from inside our home. Your home, Josh. There's a wild boar in your ancestral home. Do you care?

I laugh at my dad and respond.

JOSH: Then that girl you hired to sell your winery would gain the strength of ten Grinches and lift the thing off you. Then she can fight off the wild boar with her sharp Manolo Blahniks and a butter knife. She's resourceful, right?

DAD: LOL. Can you come up here this weekend? A favor for your mother and only for your mother.

JOSH: I'm going to hate this, aren't I?

DAD: Most assuredly, yes. But your Mom is so pretty, isn't she? And sweet and kind. And birthed your dumb ass.

JOSH: I have a thing tonight but can be there by tomorrow afternoon. But leaving Sunday. Plan what you need with my limited availability. This is for MOM only. Is that girl there?

DAD: Your mother? Of course. She lives here, silly.

THE LAST THING I want to do is jump on a plane and go up to Sonoma today. I secured all the tech deal money last night. I celebrated with lots of gin and the company of a mediocre woman, who did the job but didn't excel at it. Sadly, I can still taste that damn devil woman, even when eating out other women. Everything about her, except for her bitchy side, still plays through my brain a couple of times a day.

It's been almost a month, and I can't shake her. I saw a picture of her on Instagram in New York posted on her firm's website. I may have gone to look for it, but I'm happy she's safely in New York.

I know she'll fade in time. I still don't know what the favor is, but after my engagement debacle of last year, I promised my parents I wouldn't completely shut them out anymore. I hitched a ride with my boss on his private plane up to Napa. I keep a beat-up Jeep at his hanger.

The drive from Napa to Sonoma takes you through the Carneros Valley, and it's this strip of land that's so beautiful. It's a small but mighty wine area. You get to pass by the regal-looking Chateau of Domaine Carneros Sparkling house and the hidden and amazing architectural Artesa Vineyards & Winery. If I had time, I'd stop in to see the Truchards and their charming and delicious vineyard. I haven't seen them in years. But I don't have time. I never have time.

We're well past bud break, and the leaves are green and lush. The smell of the air has me a bit nostalgic for the good things about the area.

I pull into Emma Farm. It was named for my great-great-great-great-grandmother who founded the joint. We usually refer to her as the 4G. Her husband always referred to it as Emma Farm, and we all still do. She was the original LaChappelle and a descendant of a storied wine family from the Rhone region of France. She married a DuPont but refused to take his last name. Eventually, he took hers when they came to America. She was focused on getting to California; it took them four months to get here. She was determined to make her way in the world, and her father wouldn't let her be a vintner. She was a ballbuster if there ever was one.

I exit the car, and there's a choice red Mercedes parked at the Farmhouse with the trunk open. Did my dad finally buy himself a decent car? He's usually a Prius fellow.

I round past the trunk and am confronted with an ass I was banking on being in Manhattan. It's displayed for me in white denim. These may be the most perfect jeans ever made. Her fuchsia print blouse is sliding up her back, and her mint green thong string is peeking out to say hello. I really want to snap it. I stand there staring at it as she clearly searches for something on the floor of the car.

It's taking every ounce of self-control not to smack her ripe peach bottom and see where the afternoon takes us. Maybe I can fuck her out of my system. How can the world's most perfect ass be attached to this harpy? I can't stand this fake woman's act. And then there's the Asher factor, which means I don't trust her. He's not to be trusted so how can I trust her? And then her flawless flowery scent wafts up, and my hatred wanes for a split second.

I watch for a good couple of minutes until I think my

dick might never come down. I adjust my hard-on to hide it, and I speak to startle her. "As much as I love this view, what the fuck are you doing here?" She falls flat into the car and then screams.

"You scared me."

I say to her. "Good."

She scrambles to right herself and then stands up, pulling down her blouse.

"Why are you here?"

"Really, Josh? Were you at the same meeting I was at? I work here. You look good."

I crook an eyebrow. Is she hitting on me? She's staring at me up and down. Seems a bit forward considering we hate each other now.

"This will work well. It's good. You don't have to change. Go throw your stuff down and meet me up on that hill by the tasting room," she says.

"Lucien's hill?"

"Didn't know it had a name. But, sure."

I say very forcefully. "No."

"What do you mean, no?"

"I mean, no. I'm not meeting you anywhere, Elle."

She shoots back at me. "This is the reason you're here." She stamps her foot, and it's kind of adorable.

I'm confused. "Can we clarify a few things?"

She shifts her weight and sighs. Her left hip popping out just slightly as if to entice me. Won't work, woman. I don't like you right now.

"What do you need, clarified?" She shakes her head at me.

I cross my arms and ask, "Where are my parents? What the fuck are you still doing here? And why am I here? Please tell me you didn't summon me."

"I'm doing my job. Your parents wanted me to be boots on the ground for them through the sale. I'm running my business remotely and taking care of my west coast clients. And yes, you're here for me. Yes. I summoned you for the photo shoot today. Go join your parents on Lucien's hill."

So much is wrong with everything she just said. I had no idea she'd be staying in California for longer than a sporadic day or two. I turn without saying anything and head into the Farmhouse, so I don't strangle this woman. No one summons me.

CHAPTER TWENTY-EIGHT

ELLE

THAT CERTAINLY DIDN'T GO WELL. I WANTED TO BE COOL AND confident the next time I saw Josh. How fortunate that as he walked up my ass was sticking out my car. Dammit. So stupid. I want to be in charge and intimidating, and my ass is in the air for him to see. I still can't find my stupid phone that fell under the seat. Could not be more vulnerable. He better get down there for pictures in the clothes he had on. A simple pressed white button-down with the sleeves rolled up and jeans. It was perfect. His forearms looking tan and his eyes sparkling off the white of the shirt.

Dammit, I wish my pussy and my head could get on the same page. Intellectually, I hate everything he is and has done to his family. The way he treated me after the night we had. Research shows he's a leaver. His history tells the story of the man beyond our night together. He's walked away from the winery, his family, a fiancée, his gang of Sonoma friends, business ventures, meetings that don't go his way, clients, and even famous friendships. But my freaking body wants him so badly, or more to the point, wants what he can do to my body.

I scurry down to the tasting room where I have a glam squad set up to make the staff and the Whittiers look the best versions of themselves. I walk around the tasting room and courtyard, moving things around to make everything perfect. I pop down to the block of Pinot Noir that they're currently shooting, and it looks like it's going well.

Will and Sarah look beautiful and in love. That's their story, love. It's powerful to observe and fantastic to be around. I wrap it around me like a blanket. I like watching them interact. It's a masterclass in relationships.

I hike back up to the courtyard to make sure the next shot is all set. The photographer's assistant approaches me. "Um. They won't do it."

"What are you talking about? I'll get them. Just make sure the bottles are set inside, please. Thanks."

Randy, the tasting room manager, is standing off to the side with some of the senior staff, and they're not looking very friendly. He keeps looking at his phone, laughing, then looking pointedly at me. I thought we were good, but clearly, something's changed.

"Hi, Randy," I say. "Your turn. We're going to start with the four of you pouring in the tasting room, and then Randy, I'd like you to do the cave set up as well. This is all for the website and new boutique brochures."

Randy crosses his arms and says, "No."

I take on my kind-but-authoritative tone. "I'm sorry, what?" Now, I'm baffled. The photographer is on her way up here, and this setup was his idea. I don't have time for whatever this is.

I do not know why the staff is scattering. I spent a fortune to get this particular photographer, and we only have her for a limited amount of time today. We're losing the light, and now there's an insurrection.

I try to get everyone back. "Hold up. Before you go, can

we chat? Have I done something wrong?" Randy turns and heads into the tasting room. I follow him and the others back inside. "Randy? Talk to me. Don't walk away like you're having a temper tantrum."

He says over his shoulder in a bitchy voice, "You don't belong here. This all feels wrong." He's texting and ignoring me.

Now I'm getting pissed. I measure my voice so that I don't come off as furious, which I fucking am. "You were all on board with my plan. This is just a photo shoot. This is what Will and Sarah want."

He gets another text and looks down, then says in a cruel tone, "Don't speak for Sarah and Will." This seems a little too Cyrano de Bergerac, like someone is feeding Randy lines to say.

I try to salvage the moment. "I feel as if we've gotten off on the wrong foot."

"You don't have a good foot, lady. Just overpriced shoes." He texts and I hear a ding close by. Out of the corner of my eye in the tank room, there's a flash of a white dress shirt reading his phone. Then all my anger funnels with pinpoint precision on the childish fucking jackass. I'll no longer give him the satisfaction of watching me be rattled. Try harder, asshole, to make me look the fool.

My photographer says, "Hey, Noelle, we're all done out there, but I need the son. And then I'm not sure we have enough time to get the rest of this. I thought you and the assistants were setting up the next shots. We're losing the light, and you said no lighting package."

I don't hesitate with my answer. "The son didn't make it in time. He's kind of a flake. Irresponsible, arrogant, and to be honest, kind of a failure. Also, it's probably for the best he's not in the pictures, he had a disfiguring accident in his youth and never learned humility. Poor guy." I hear a colossal growl from the other room as I make fun of him.

Randy defends Josh. "He's not a failure, and he's beautiful."

I can give as good as I get Randy. I say with a dripping tone, "I know you two are close. It's hard to see reality sometimes, but I think he uses you. He's not in a good place. You're dismissed for the day... Sandy, is it?"

His face is beet red as his employees open their mouths in disbelief, but no one else steps to me.

I turn to my photographer to save face. "We go without the son. And as for here, I don't think we need it. If we do, I'll see if you're available and we can just hire someone to pretend they're staff. The pictures will be better that way."

I hear a scoff behind me. That's right, Randy, you out. Model in.

I turn to the photographer. "Thank you so much for everything. You can wrap up for the day, and we can circle back later. There are two cases for you of different varietals to shoot in the studio. Keep them after your shoot. I'll pay you out for today's full shot list."

"Noelle, you're the best. You know I adore working with you."

"We were the lucky ones to find a window in your schedule. We should get drinks next time you're in the city."

"Yes. I'll be back in a couple of weeks to shoot Gavin in Sacramento. We'll make time." She leans in and gives me the biggest hug. And that's how you do business with a velvet glove instead of a wrecking ball. Asshole.

CHAPTER TWENTY-NINE

JOSHUA

I SLINK OUT OF THE TANK ROOM AND FIND MY PARENTS IN THE vines. I don't feel bad about screwing with her. And I'm not done driving her away. If my parents won't get rid of her, I'll make her quit. She's a bad influence on them. They don't need to be slicked up. My mother's never worn that much makeup in her life. I'm not sure how Asher and this woman convinced them to sell. I'm missing several pieces. Nothing makes sense. I need to figure it all out, and I don't think I can do that from the outside.

Standing with my parents, I explain why I wasn't in the pictures. "I don't know what happened? She sent the photographer away. I guess this is a wasted trip for me."

My mom looks to my dad and then throws her arms around me. "It's not wasted if I get to cook for you. Bolognese?"

I kiss my mom and put my arm around her as Elle approaches.

My dad speaks first, "Hey, Elle. If you didn't need Josh, we needed a heads up. He didn't have to come all the way up here."

I grin at her as my chess game begins to take shape. I took her pawn when Randy did my bidding. And then she took one right back. But I got you, girlie. Check.

She puts on a smirk and looks directly at my dad. "Oh, there you are. I couldn't find Joshua anywhere. He disappeared after he arrived, and the photographer had to leave. She had to go and we've lost the good light. But the good news is that she promised to come out here tomorrow at dawn. We can still make this work. It's nice to see you again, Joshua. Thank you so much for being here for your parents. It means a lot to them and me. I'll see you guys later, okay?" Then she winks at me.

My dad smiles at her, "That's works perfectly. Josh can totally do that. We'll text you later, Elle."

She nods, grins widely, and takes off.

Checkmate goes to the harpy.

Now I have to get up at 5 a.m. to stand in front of barrels for marketing pictures. At least it will be a lovely evening with my parents, and maybe they can tell me what the hell is going on with the winery. I need to start drinking now. I grab my mom's hand, and we walk up to the Farmhouse while my father goes to lock up the cave and tasting room. I see her car pull out of the farm and breathe a little easier.

AFTER A SHOWER and a few emails and calls, I smell dinner downstairs. We have one of the nicest meals we've had in ages. I've been a shit to them in the past, but we're trying to rebuild a bit. I'll get up and take her stupid pictures. We didn't get to the subject of the sale. We were laughing too hard at my dad's impression of the photographer and Mrs. Dotson. We'll get to it. I owe them more time before they confide in me what's really happening here.

I wonder what time Elle will have to get up to get here on time. I enjoy that it will be long before me. Fuck me, now I'm thinking about her curled up in bed. That goddamn Hellcat purring after I gave her everything and she gave me all she had.

I want to take a run before the shoot. I love running up here, and it's been an eternity since I did it. Most days lately I'm on a treadmill. I want to see the trails again with the mist rolling off the vineyards. I want to smell the greenery and be a small part of it again. I do need to get back tomorrow though to make sure no one backs out of the tech deal. I need all the money wired before I can put it to bed. But then I've hit more than quota for the quarter. I have some minor stuff brewing but nothing major going on in Santa Barbara.

I pass out with a belly full of pasta and Malbec. I haven't been to bed before midnight in ages. It feels decadent. I drift off not thinking about Elle Parker.

———

SHE DOESN'T EVEN FUCKING show up. It's all art directed by some pissant assistant. I do my due diligence and pose in the dawn. I did not get to run this morning, too much Malbec last night. Now, I'm in a shitty mood. Good thing she's not around.

CHAPTER THIRTY

ELLE

I CREEP DOWNSTAIRS, MID-MORNING. HE'S LEANING ON THE counter scrolling through his phone in workout gear. I didn't get up for the shoot on purpose. I thought my presence would just piss him off, and I needed a good set of pictures. I had a late-night meeting with an old colleague that works at Everlane. It went exceptionally well. We might get to pitch to them soon. I'm in a t-shirt and LC/W yoga pants. I sneak behind him to a grab coffee cup. His head goes up as he sniffs the air.

"Is that you?" It's like he smelled me or something.

I say quietly, "Morning."

He turns to Sarah without looking at me. "Mom, why is she here?"

"She lives here, dear." Sarah sips her tea.

I turn to him with a giant grin on my face. "Yeah, I live here, dear." Then I smack his ass and walk away. He reacts to me but doesn't turn. Sarah thinks I'm being cheeky. She has no idea what happened between us. She only witnessed the tension at the meeting and knows of his hostility about hiring me. I've given them no reason to think I have an opinion about Josh one way or another. But it appears I like to give him hell.

Still only addressing his mother, "Why?"

"She needed a place, and we have room. Your father offered. You know how he is."

"Jesus. Fucking stray cat syndrome. How long?"

I shrug as I put a splash of cream in my coffee. I stand right in front of Josh and answer for myself. "Like two weeks or so."

He looks down at me, and damn if he isn't gorgeous. Annoying, infuriating, and arrogant, but really hot.

He demands an answer. "No, woman. How long are you *staying*?"

Will answers from the bottom of the stairs. "As long as it takes, son." Now inside the kitchen, he flashes a smile and kisses me on my head. "Good morning, Elle."

I look to Josh with a shit-eating grin.

He doesn't miss a beat in his emotional counterattack. "Dad. What would you say if I stick around for a while?" Then he raises his eyebrows to me.

What the fuck is he up to? He's trying to undermine me. Go right ahead and try.

Sarah responds, "Are you serious? Don't toy with your mother."

"Mom. What do you think if I spend more time up here? Now with you about to sell, it could be closure for me."

"That would be fantastic, son." Will hugs him, and I see Josh waggles his eyebrows at me again. Game on. Will turns to me. "That's okay with you, isn't it?"

Yes! Ha-ha. They asked my opinion. I answer in a voice dripping with sweetness, "Oh my gosh. It's his home. Of course, it's okay. I'm thrilled to get to know him better." I could not be more sarcastic.

"Josh, I know you don't trust Elle completely, but I'm

going to need you to lay down your sword." Take that, Suit. Will's got my back. I don't know why because ultimately he'll always choose his son but for some reason, I feel like I'll get a fair shake.

Josh says, "Dad. All that's behind us, right, Cosmo?"

Oh, he needles me. I want to bury him. "Of course, Joshua." I use the name he gave me that night.

Will turns to me and asks, "Elle, how did Everlane go?"

"Really great, I think. I'm headed to the city this afternoon for a casual meet-and-greet with some of the department heads."

I push down bread in the toaster as Will and Sarah head outside. It pops, and he says nothing. I shove the bread in my mouth. And as I do, I turn around to discover Josh staring at my ass.

I put my hands on my hips. "If you'll excuse me, I have a meeting to change for, jackass."

He speaks in a casual tone, "Are we supposed to be openly hostile to each other now? I mean, you're the untrustworthy usurper here."

I shake my head at him. "You don't know whether I'm trustworthy or not. I don't know what to do with you. I don't know you. And I'm not sure I can be totally civil, but I can try."

He grins at me. "You shouldn't change." He nods at my yoga pants.

"I should meet Everlane in yoga pants?" I blow him off.

He smiles a wicked smile, and I want to eat him up. "Those are perfect yoga pants. Especially on you. If you feel the need to do some stretching or quick poses, just let me know. I can help or watch. Whatever." He's trying to set me off.

I tease back, "My ass is that good?"

He talks through a spoonful of cereal in his mouth. "Epic. It's your attitude I can do without."

"Again, are you just here to shit on everything?"

"I'm here to watch you."

"Really? All of me or just my ass?"

He puts his cereal down and says, "I will need to hear a lot more about this sale from my parents. There are a lot of things I need to be clear on. But they did say they're going to sell unless I want the place. I do not. I don't want it for future generations or a legacy, so selling is the option. But I need to make sure you don't fuck this up for them. I'm a god at business. The deal is my religion. So, watch yourself."

I come back into his face. I go up on my tiptoes and try to look intimidating. I hate being short. "You have no idea what I'm capable of. Back down your concern."

I go to leave, and he puts his leg up, resting it on the kitchen island. I'm caged there. I look back at him as he says, "The facts I do know are unfavorable at best. The most disturbing is that you came from Asher. That's enough to put anyone on alert."

I don't get the Asher thing. "I don't come from Asher. I work for myself. Asher just introduced us. He's fine."

"Then you're a shitty judge of character."

"You don't scare me."

He lowers his leg. "Case in point. Shitty judge."

CHAPTER THIRTY-ONE

JOSH

IT'S BEEN ALMOST TWO WEEKS THAT I HAVE BEEN IN TOWN. I'VE sabotaged all the little things I could. I even removed the printer ink when she was in a hurry. She resorted to bending over in those pants every morning. She also stole my favorite blanket from my bed. I'm better at this than her. She hid my phone the other day in a pile of kale in the fridge. I hate kale. She did set up a fake conference call with my assistant. John put it in my calendar, and I hung on the line waiting. Then she got dialed in about an hour and ten minutes and just laughed at me.

I retaliated with a fake dinner last week. She sat at Café LaHaye, believing she was meeting with some group of people thinking of buying the winery. She sat there alone, stood up, for like an hour. John pretended to be a potential buyer, after I told him about the fake conference call, and called her at to set it all up.

It's been back and forth with this annoying person and I'm no closer to understanding the sale or why they need her. She has produced amazing results though. Their online sales are up, their distribution is up, and my parents have been profiled in the Sunday New York Times. I still masturbate to her incessantly. But I've kept enough distance that I haven't made a move. But there have been moments, mostly over breakfast, where we connect and actually talk.

Asher hasn't come around or up in conversation and watching her relationship with my parents has made me trust her more. But the moment I get wind of Asher anywhere near this, I'm going to freak the hell out on her.

I'm finishing up dinner at Della Santina, a fantastic Italian restaurant with craveable gnocchi. The table has some potential money at it, they're new to town, and I met them through my best friend's mom, Theresa Langerford. Langerford Cellars was my second home growing up. My best friend is currently out of town, or I would have made him tag along with this dinner. Instead, I'm joined by his younger brother Jims, who've I known my entire life. I was three when he was born, and I remember going to the hospital to meet him. He's the annoying little brother no one wants, but I love him anyway.

Dinner is going exceedingly well until she walks in. And as always, I feel that spark between us. The one we deny exists so we can go on with our lives.

I turn away, hoping she doesn't spot me.

Elle walks to the back of the small restaurant and picks up a giant to-go bag. She hugs and kisses Rob, the owner. She's been here like six weeks, and everyone knows her. When she turns, we lock eyes. I like making her skin instantly blush. Last day or two we've avoided each other. But she invades my mind all the damn time.

I shake my head, hoping she gets the drift that this is business and not to fuck with me. I turn away and pretend to listen to this couple talk about their house in Majorca. But then she's standing there next to me. Her intoxicating scent rising above the tomato and garlic and making me hot and hard. Those damn yoga pants again.

She says brightly, "Hi, Josh. I didn't know you were here." Jims crosses his legs and looks intrigued, then reaches his hand across the table.

"Hello. I'm Jims Langerford, and you are?"

"Elle Parker, working with the Whittiers on marketing. I met your mom, Theresa, last week."

"You're the blonde, aren't you?"

"Whatever that means, I guess so." Jims' brother must have told him what I think of Elle and the 'accidentally fucking her' story.

Jims' eyebrows flash as he says, "This *is* a pleasure." He knows that she got the best of me a time or two so far.

She grins and responds in kind. "Mine as well."

I interrupt before Jims starts asking annoying questions or invites her to join us. "Elle was just leaving. Wouldn't want your mountain of food to get cold."

"It's for your parents."

"See you later, Elle. Thanks for stopping by." Get the message, you dense woman, go away.

"See you soon then, Jims. And you two enjoy your dinner."

I look up at her. "Time to go, Elle. Let the adults talk." This gets a big laugh.

She leans down to my ear, turning my head away from the table, and uses her greatest weapon against me. She whispers my name as a moan as sexually as she possibly can. It's the fucking sound. Then licks just behind my ear and stands up. Devil woman.

"Sorry, I just needed to tell him a quick personal thing. Goodnight, everyone."

My dick is so hard it's going to punch through this fucking dinner table. I can't put a thought together. That fucking moan. Her voice, that shrew. My face is now a bit flushed as I keep rearranging my legs and pants. I see her through the front window. She inserts her middle finger all the way into her mouth, sucks the length of it for a moment, and then flips me off.

The couple takes my distraction to make their exits. I'm pissed. This was about a four-million-dollar piece of business that I could have used. I mean, I don't need it, but I have missed the art of the deal and she just fucked up my business. She just raised the stakes and she doesn't even know it. And now all the energy I was putting into separating these people from their cash will go into my next plan. Hopefully this will be the one where she decides to abandon this idea of finding a buyer for my parents' winery. Time to ramp up our game.

CHAPTER THIRTY-TWO

ELLE

I'M SITTING IN MY MERCEDES IN THE WINERY PARKING LOT, staring at my phone in disbelief. I'm cold all over. I'm numb. Evan just ripped me a new asshole about losing clients. Like, all the clients. Google and Apple are beyond pissed. And my carefully orchestrated prospects of Twitter, Pacific Union, Everlane and The Gap are gone. Vanished. They want nothing to do with unprofessionalism like this. I don't know what happened. I invested so much of our money and time in caressing those people. They were all but signed and now gone. Our slate is empty, and I've been on a fucking farm instead of tending to my business.

We're screwed if I can't figure this out. It will all crumble and I don't understand how this happened. I have to calm down and figure out what the fuck to do. I have executives in the air coming to town for this now-canceled dinner. Their hotels were canceled according to their extremely angry assistants. Evan is scrambling to find somewhere to put them up for the night.

I don't know how or why it was all undone. Could it be a competitor or that hacker Melissa woman? She wouldn't do this. There was an email that no one in my company sent. We can't figure out who or where it came from. The address simply says ParkerCo72@gmail.com and the body of the message was clipped and cold. There was no explanation as to why everything was canceled, and these people weren't welcome to do business with us again. It simply stated that everything was canceled and would not be rescheduled.

I call The French Laundry, the not just five-star restaurant, but three Michelin starred one that carries more clout than almost any restaurant in America. I call their event's person, my contact, looking for answers. This was an exclusive client dining experience I've been finessing and working on for a year, and it's evaporated. I already spent a fortune to make this night perfect.

"Hello, Jennifer. It's Noelle Parker and…"

I FLY into the Farmhouse screaming before the door can close behind me. I'm yelling in a voice I've never heard before, pure rage. I come in hot. The dogs cower in the corner.

"JOSH! FUCKING JOSH! ARE YOU IN HERE? JOSHUA FUCKING WHITTIER. GET YOUR ASS DOWN HERE *NOW!*"

He emerges from the back sunporch with Will as Sarah bolts down the stairs. I stride across the room, covering the distance between us in seconds. I get right in his face. I'm grateful I have sky-high heels on to see his smug face better. Mine is scarlet with heat, and fury is radiating off me.

He speaks patronizingly, "Did you just fucking summon me?"

I breathe through my gritted teeth and lower my volume. "Yes! Why did you cancel my French Laundry dinner?"

"Oh, that." He turns away from me.

Will opens his mouth, and I hold my hand to stop him from speaking. No, no Will, I'll bury this asshole all on my own.

"Look, you muthafucking cocksucker."

He turns back towards me, placing his hands on hips. His legs are in a wide and commanding stance. I'm not intimidated, I'm in the red zone and I drop my purse to the ground and mirror his stance.

I continue to yell, "I don't give a shit if you call me stupid names, convince Randy and the rest of the staff that I'm the devil, avoid photo shoots, waste my time, and do everything in your power to undermine my confidence and job. I don't give a flying fuck about the stupid ass games we've been playing back and forth. I've taken a lot more from men in this business and in my lifetime. You're a fucking amateur at it."

I take another deep breath and unleash. For a second, I worry about Will and Sarah and look to them. Sarah nods as if to tell me to keep going. Will puts his hands in his pockets as he locks eyes with me. He seems concerned but not angry at me for screaming at his son. The longer I don't speak, the tenser he becomes. I see the strain in his neck.

I breathe in and out. Then I attack slow and low. I don't care if they learn of our history, I don't care if I lose this piece of business right now. This is my whole life he fucked with.

"All those games are nothing. But this stunt of yours is unfathomable. A bit of a disproportionate response for simply giving you an inconvenient hard-on." He shifts his weight, and I lay into him further. "But now that your arrogant, selfish, useless ass fucked with my livelihood, my career, my reputation, my employees, and my fucking company, I feel an intense need to tear your balls from your body and feed them to the fucking dogs! You muthafucking asshole prick."

His arms are still crossed, and his blue eyes cold and unfeeling staring at me. All my blood is pounding in my ears. My veins pumping pure fire and rage. I want to fucking kill him.

He speaks in a condescending tone. "I lost a possible four-million-dollar investor because of your little hard-on stunt." Sarah smirks.

"Four million your company can afford to lose. And if you couldn't close the deal, that's not my fault. I was only in the room for five minutes. Tell me why you did this?"

He raises his voice and it's stern as if he's trying to scold me. "I canceled your little dinner because we're not going to have anything to do with your boyfriend. End of discussion." I'm going to eviscerate this dickhole.

Will speaks before I can, "Son, what are you talking about?"

"Dad, stay out of it. I canceled her LaChappelle/Whittier wine expert dinner that's on your calendar. I sent an email to all attendees telling them the dinner was not only canceled but won't be rescheduled. That they are not welcome to do business with us. I called the restaurant, car service and Fairmont Hotel and canceled all reservations this morning. This winery will have nothing to do with Asher Bernard and his fake…"

I push my intense nausea down. A yell erupts from the bottom of my soul, and I shove him. He stumbles backward. He looks shocked that I pushed him. "IT WASN'T A WINERY DINNER!"

I'm shaking all over, but I continue yelling. "Asshole. Oh. My. God. I can't believe you did this to me. I can't believe you hate me so much that you would ruin me. Ruin my business. You hate me so much that it's not enough to fuck up this job but my entire life and the lives of my seventy-four employees and contractors. I knew you were an asshole, but I had no idea you were this cruel and calculating. Where are your ethics? Who the hell are you?"

"Stop being melodramatic." He turns, and I shove him again.

"This was a client dinner for *MY* business. This is my reputation and my company's reputation you screwed over. My life is not a game for a bored venture capitalist slumming it at Mommy and Daddy's. It was a Parker & Company event. My largest clients and four enormous prospects that I have romanced and massaged for two fucking years. It took me six months to get everyone to agree on a date. It took thousands of dollars in deposits, hotels, and plane tickets. I lose all that money." I'm pacing, and I realize something else, "Fuck me. I paid Chef Keller a large deposit for an exclusive buyout. And you canceled on him last minute. I will get nothing back. No one will ever take me seriously again. The clients are gone. So bad. This is so bad. Fuck you so very much, Josh."

His face is sallow. He moves his hands into his pockets and stares at me. I continue my tirade, so I don't fall in a weeping mess, rage fueling me forward.

I say in the coldest voice possible so that I don't start crying, "It took my whole fucking career to plan that dinner. This has nothing to do with you. But I guess you couldn't help but make it about you. I thought you'd have more respect for someone who built their own business. Are you a misogynist or unscrupulous? You just fucked me up the ass for at least the next five years, if we survive this. You fucked my employees, their families, my partner, and screwed over my business and me pretty fucking good. If I can't fix this, we'll be dead in the water within a year."

"Your dinner?" he croaks out without displaying emotion.

Now I need his ego crushed. I go in for the kill. His guilt and suffering will be my only solace. Suffer, asshole. Bow down to my fucking revenge rage. I glance at Sarah, who is ashen, and Will, who nods to me. They know what's coming next. They look a bit horrified to see their son in this light, but this isn't even the worst of it from their perspective. I look again to Will to see if he wants to be the one to tell him the rest of the truth. Or if they want me to keep that to myself.

"Go ahead, Elle. Tell him. We got you." Josh's head jerks to his father, and he turns and walks to the other side of the room.

His mother takes a deep breath in and then exhales loudly. "It's okay, dear, tell him."

Josh looks thoroughly lost and turns back to me. My voice becomes steely as I say, "And you know what, you self-centered prick? What about the words "wine expert" made you think it was Asher? I paid a handsome sum of money to secure two people who have been authorities and leaders in the wine industry for thirty-seven years. I was going to feature their innovative, exciting female winemaker who has over twenty years of expertise."

"Who?" he commands.

Sarah speaks from the bottom of the stairs, and our heads snap to her, "Us. You myopic, foolish little boy. I'm not sure how you got so much of your grandfather in you and so little of your father and me."

She runs up the stairs, cutting him down with a soft sentence and a look faster than any tirade of mine ever could. With my adrenaline overtaking me, I have to leave before he sees me sob. I can't take the pressure anymore. I'm going to explode into a torrent of tears.

Josh nods at me like he's going to speak. I run from the building.

"Let her go, son. Leave her alone." I hear Will command as the door to the Farmhouse slams behind me.

I barely make it to the hill that leads to the amphitheater. I'm out of sight and standing there stunned. I hear his commanding footfalls as he calls for me. I stay hidden, falling sobbing to the ground.

CHAPTER THIRTY-THREE

JOSH

I DON'T KNOW WHAT TO DO. I CAN'T FIND ELLE. I'M NOT SURE what I'd say if I did. I'm an arrogant, cocky piece of shit. I have so many apologies to make. I fucked up. Fuck. My guilt bubbles up, and I punch the door to the tasting room, cracking both my hand and the thick wooden barn door. The pain momentarily puts a stop to my crushing guilt. Back in my parents' kitchen, I thrust my bloody hand under the faucet.

My father's been waiting for me and is leaning up against the fridge. He wears a look I saw my whole childhood. I can see the level of his disappointment, and it's too much to fucking take.

"Damn, boy. You fucked up. Seems you brought a canon to a knife fight."

"I know, Dad."

He asks, "Is your hand okay?" His genuine concern shreds my heart.

"Fine."

My mom crosses the room, her face wet from tears. I'm reduced to a raw piece of nothing seeing her face. She pulls out an icepack and wraps it in a towel. She places the icepack on top of my already swollen knuckles. She's taking care of me after I disappointed her so desperately. She puts her hand on my cheek, and I squeeze my eyes shut. She grabs her tea and leaves the Farmhouse. I assume she's heading to find Elle. And then a wave of nausea overtakes me, and I puke in the sink. I spit, wipe my mouth, and face my dad.

"I'm sorry."

"You better be. I'm going to take this in pieces, the personal first. The thought that your parents are wine experts never crossed your mind. Do you think your mom and I are up here pretending? That what we do is inconsequential? That we're as flighty as you were taught by your grandfather? He's been dead a good long time, and the winery still thrives."

I lift my hand in front of me and settle back against the kitchen island. My father stands directly in front of me. He's the most forthright man I know. As much as I want to run from his disappointing look, I owe him this. I will take this like the man I hope I can become.

"You're the one, despite how your grandfather, Lucien fucking LaChappelle, tried, who has little to no knowledge of this place. You aren't the expert here. We have almost four decades of rising and falling with the harvest and keeping this farm and these employees in the black. Four fucking decades, son. That was Lucien talking today, out of your mouth. That was your ruthless, cruel, and imprudent grandfather guiding your actions, right down to the violence you clearly exhibited. And despite your incredible insensitivity towards Elle—that's why your mother's crying."

"Dad."

"I must have done a shitty job teaching you respect, honor, and compassion if you'd do something this brash and selfish. It's our business to ruin or thrive. Not yours. You're not part of this sale. Even if it were Asher at that dinner, you have no authority to act on our behalf. Is this what you're like in the world?"

I am. I take, conquer, and have no remorse. I never think about the businesses I might be ruining by providing capital for a rival company. I'm thunderstruck by this revelation. I do think it's a game, but I never thought I'd gone that far over the edge. It's all relative. Everyone I know outside of this world is like that.

"Answer me, boy. Dammit. You fucking wrecked your mother. Talk to me."

And my answer roars at my father. "I am that. I am cruel and cold in the real world. Fuck. How did I end up like Lucien? I left so I wouldn't become him."

My dad crosses to me and takes me in his arms, not an easy task as I have three inches on him.

"You're not him. I'm not going to let you be. Show us you're not Lucien. You fix this with both of those women. I know Elle's not important to you, but she's important to us. I know you don't care about her at all. But at the very base of this, be a human being. You had no right to do what you did. But you better figure out a way to save her business without compromising her integrity. Put away the wrecking ball you just used to destroy her life."

I step back from him. We stand there for a while.

I finally break our silence. "Can't. That wrecking ball is the only thing that might just save her company."

My mind is reeling with the favors I'll need to call in and for all the money I'm going to spend. I turn to leave and go find my mom. But my dad needs to know something despite my best efforts. Nausea rises again. Despite my irritation and anger at her most of the time. I hurt her badly and honestly that wasn't my intention. I wasn't thinking. I was trying to win the game. At this point, I'm not even sure why I was trying to stop the sale instead of talking to my parents about it.

I clouded her usually vibrant green eyes with tears, hate, and betrayal. It's killing me. How could I do that to her? I will fix this shit. I am shit. I came home to save my parents and the winery, and I just got fucking lost. They didn't need saving. I have no place here, but if I ever want to fit back into my family, I'm going to need to make amends for more than just this. Afterward, I'll figure out what to do about Elle and myself. I know I don't hate her, but I'm pretty sure she despises me now.

"Dad. You're wrong. I do care about her." I tried to deny the connection I feel. But it's always simmering just below the surface. I will address it head-on, but first I need to solve my mess.

"Another thing you're wrong about, son, Asher's not her boyfriend. Never really was. They dated a couple of times. He's nothing to her. He just brought her to the dinner. Divine intervention sat her next to us at that table."

CHAPTER THIRTY-FOUR

ELLE

I CHECKED INTO THE RITZ CARLTON SAN FRANCISCO four days ago without seeing him. I've been on the phone and down to Silicon Valley trying to salvage my existing business. The business was shaky to begin with, and then to fly their executives in from across the country with nowhere for them to stay and getting that terrible brush off email, I've had to assure them over and over that it was a mix-up. I think I put a lid on them, leaving me for being inconsequential, unprofessional, and rude. I told them what happened in a manner of speaking. I talk of crossed wires. Their mistrust in Parker & Co. might last for a minute or so, but we can repair that.

The prospective clients didn't give a shit about excuses. They shuffled me off the phone and out of their buildings. They don't know me or the way that I work or how terrific my company is. They just see that I blew them off. They see Apple getting nervous and we look a bit like a sinking ship who can't manage a simple dinner. I won't get another shot at them. I'm headed back into prospector mode. It's all I have.

I have to make up the lost projected revenue somehow.

LaChappelle/Whittier goes to the back burner. I head to New York the day after tomorrow. Sarah and Will understood but were disappointed I'm leaving. I am too. I'll manage them from New York. I never really needed to stay here. I just liked it. It started to feel familiar and comfortable. I've spent three months in constant contact with them, and we've grown close.

Oh, but there's no way I'll ever get to eat at French Laundry. They didn't give a shit why I wasn't there, just that I wasted their time and effort. They demanded all the money for the buyout. Our corporate account couldn't handle the added last-minute cancellation fee. I pulled money from my personal accounts to cover it. I should send Josh the fucking bill.

I deleted the email Josh sent to me without reading it. He has no idea where I am. I never have to see him again. Despite whatever I felt for him or thought he might be, he's proven that he's the last thing I want. Even when we were fighting the last three weeks, it felt like teasing or flirting a bit. But now I know the truth. Not only did he prove that our evening meant nothing to him, but now I know how inconsequential I am to him. I'm a joke in his eyes. It's the only justification for how he could do that to me.

After I talked to Sarah, I realized what he did to me was business, but what he did to them was personal. He has lots of repair work to do there. She was devastated to see herself through his eyes. I hope the stress doesn't trigger tremors or anything worse. We're having lunch today to discuss an account manager so I can go back to running my company. In such a short time, these people have become so important to me. When I talk, they listen. I hope I can be there for her today the same way she's there for me.

I'm wearing a bright pink fluttery springy dress from Nanette Lepore, and I leave my hair down and have matching pink lipstick as well. I love lipstick names. This one is called *Boom Boom Bloom* from MAC. It's like raspberry, and it reminds me to smile. Whenever I get depressed, a new lipstick always helps. I bought seven of them in the last couple of days. When I was sixteen, it was Maybelline and Wet n Wild from Walgreens, now it's YSL, MAC or Tom Ford.

I bought the dress and makeup yesterday. I may have to eat ramen and dye my own hair for the rest of my life because of all of this, but I'm going to look damned good doing it. But Maybelline, here I come again. There's a knock at the door, and I rush to see Sarah, my heart full. I open the door—and lose my breath. His large and dominant hand blocks my attempt to close it.

"Please just listen for a moment, Elle, it's important."

He's wearing the hell out of a navy suit and subtle blue plaid tie that picks up his damn eye color. His hair is coiffed again, not like it has been around the winery. He ruined me, and I don't know how to get past that. He has so little regard for who I am. It hurts professionally, but it's a bit devastating personally. His face used to send me to fantasy, but today I want to kill him.

"I'm not proud of my actions. Elle. I'm incredibly sorry for what I did. I'm not proud of the man I showed you. You should know that other than my parents, I don't think I've really ever said 'sorry' to another living person."

I sigh and cross my arms. "Continue."

"I never should have inserted myself into matters I had no right to be in. I got swept up in a trivial retaliation. I think you're a remarkable shark. Your business acumen is right on, and I'm a fucking asshole. It was a game. I never meant for this to happen, especially knowing you got hurt. You have to know that I did not think for one second that this was Parker and Company business. That said, I shouldn't have been anywhere near my father's calendar or your event. I unwittingly revealed the beast that I am to my parents and destroyed your business all with one stupid, ignorant, petty move."

"Did you apologize to your parents?" I snap at him.

"We've had a lot of conversations about my behavior and who I want to be in this life. Seems I've gotten a bit lost."

My lips upturn despite my hatred. Josh smiles back. I scold him a bit. "They didn't deserve that."

"That relationship is between my parents and me. I appreciate your concern and devotion to them. Something I didn't realize had developed so deeply between you all. Please bring your focus back to how I've treated you. If someone had done that to me, I'd burn their world down and salt the earth."

"Oh, don't worry. I have shit in the works. Just you wait. I will ruin something of yours. Once I figure out just exactly how your business works. And what you actually like." His lips curl up at my joke. I'm still angry, but the idea of me ruining anything for him is absurd. And he seems to be here with an olive branch. And he doesn't think I'm foolish. He never did.

"I take business very seriously. I should've had more respect for you. You should also know that I'm an equal opportunity asshole. I would have done the same thing to a man as I did to you. The answer to your question was unscrupulous, not misogynist. Not that I'm proud of that, but I wanted you to know it wasn't about your gender. I'll be out of your hair, I promise. I'm heading south. No more games. No more stupid sabotage. Clearly, my parents are in the best hands." He hands me a thick folder, and I look at him puzzled. "They're waiting for your call. And if these people don't take your call after tonight, please let me know."

He hands me his card, and on the back is a handwritten phone number. His touch still electrifies me despite what he's done and what's he shown me. The air once again crackles all around us. This man right here in front of me is the one I knew he could be. This Josh is the one who made sure I had a bottle of water and Advil before he left that night. The one who tucked me in at the El Dorado hotel. The one who shared stories of his childhood friends and listened to me talk about my mother. Although he is still the man who leaves, I don't feel used anymore, but it's best if he goes.

He points to the handwritten phone number. "That's my private cell. My parents have it now as well."

"What's in here?"

He nods his chin at me and smirks. "Leads. Tesla, Trader Joe's, Seagram's, and Conde Nast." My jaw goes slack. "Research, key names, and numbers."

"Why? How?"

"Because I owe you. I'm pretty good at business too. You'll have to close the deals, but I have no doubt in you after watching you take me to task. There are powerful people who don't dare speak to me the way you did, Hellcat." My body eases as he uses his little name for me from that night. Maybe I'm not crazy. He does feel about that night the way I do. I'm so confused now.

I can't let him off the hook that easily. I say, "Maybe more people should speak to you like that."

He laughs and says, "I don't think so, and I'd prefer you don't do it again."

I curl my lips and crook my eyebrow. "I can't promise that."

"I had a hunch that would be an empty request."

I smile at him, and it seems like the first real exchange we've had since we played Gin Rummy. But right now, there are no sexual motives, no vying for dominance or pretending to like each other for his parents' benefit. Just a genuine conversation and that damn charged connection.

He then tells me, "You have dinner at The Progress restaurant tonight. Elleole and Stuart, owners and chefs, will be there. Alena's already there as they build out the menu with our wines. My parents will pick you up in a couple of hours. The bill, tip, and transportation of your guests have all been taken care of. Evan should be here by five."

I interrupt him, "Hold Up! You flew Evan here?"

"I did. I figured you could use some moral and emotional support after I fucked you over. And if he is pissed, you need to be in the room together to work it out." I smile at him, and he continues speaking, "All of the prospects and clients' accommodations and return travel are taken care of. If there's a hitch, call my office, and it will patch you to my assistant, John, who did the logistics. He's at your disposal, day and night. As am I."

I'm overwhelmed. A tear builds. As it falls down my cheek, he catches it with his thumb and holds my cheek. "I don't want to be the man I showed you and my parents. Certainly not in your eyes."

"I'm glad I knew a better one already existed. I think it's why I got so angry and hurt." He drops his hand from my face.

"Was it the sensitive raw dogging or the ass worshiping that tipped you off that I could be this guy?"

I laugh, and now I'm squeezing my thighs together. "It was the expert hair washing and the way you tucked me in."

He rolls his eyes to the sky, and his grin turns up. "I hate that I hurt you. Apology accepted?"

"We'll see if all of this makes it up to me. I might come up with a few more things for you to do." I lift my eyebrows at him.

"Hmm. For you or to you? If you didn't have research to delve into, I'd say that might be an invitation I'd push for, but I should go. Good luck tonight, Elle. Goodbye. Take care of yourself."

I may have just flirted with him. Shit. "Thank you for all of this."

His tone turns sharp. "No. Please, don't say thank you. It's my mistake to rectify. I colossally fucked up."

I nod at him. He did. And then there's a moment where he looks completely vulnerable. We pause and stare into each other's eyes and for a split second it's as if we're a 'we'. I blurt out, "When will you be back?"

He answers with a small smile, "I don't know. But call me if you need anything. Or if my parents need anything. Or if you need to talk strategy. Call for any stupid reason you can think of. I'll be there."

He seems to have shifted again. This is the Josh I thought he was. He seems less angry. Maybe I can be less bitter as well.

"I will."

"I hope so." His eyes sparkle as he smiles at me.

I grin, and as he turns down the hallway. A bellman passes him with several large boxes and bags. He turns and winks back at me. My stomach flips.

The boxes are placed on my couch. I open the card first, and it's a handwritten letter. His handwriting is strong, but there's a feminine tilt to it.

Elle,

Slay them tonight.

Choose either one of these dresses, but you should wear the hunter green Halston Heritage halter dress. The Dolce Gabbana metallic mini, is nice too but the Halston... And with your eyes and hair. Trust me, the Halston. MUA will be here in an hour to get you ready. And either dress will look killer on you and highlight my oft-mentioned favorite body part. I didn't think you'd want to wear the LC/W yoga pants, but they'd get the job done as well. And one more gift, a little edge.

- *Tesla likes legs, and yours are worth showing off. He's a pig but harmless.*
- *Trader Joe's can't hold their wine, get to them early. But the wife is funny after three or four. And they want to connect with people personally. Open up a little to them.*
- *Conde Nast is only looking to highlight Town and Country and the bridal mags differently. They don't want to discuss any other magazines. Don't bring anything else up. And she's someone who will also enjoy your legs and that ass of yours. She's also insanely smart, you'll be more than fine to hold your own with her. Don't flatter her. Be your blunt self.*
- *Seagram's is a hard bitch to crack; you'll get along famously. She loves her shoes, the enclosed Louboutins are only available in Paris. She will notice. Tell her they were a gift that someone purchased at Le Printemps de l'Homme 64 Boulevard Haussmann shop.*

I wish I could be there to watch you rip them apart and empty their wallets. The thrill of the hunt, I guess. Eat 'em up. Go forth and conquer.

Until Later Hellcat,

Josh

He cares about all the moving pieces of this solution. Josh might have pulled off a miracle. The clients he chose fit our company perfectly. He also knew I needed research. His

letter is oddly romantic and incredibly respectful of my business savvy. And he gave me exclusive, to-die-for shoes that I
might want to buried in. They're heels that are so high that I
might actually look formidable and be able to carry off that
Halston. Did he fly in shoes from Paris? I might not hate him
as much anymore. Also, how much money does he have?

CHAPTER THIRTY-FIVE

JOSH

I DRAG MYSELF INTO MY OFFICE. EVERYTHING LOOKS THE SAME, but I can't help but feel something has shifted in me. John hands me a cup of coffee as I enter the building instead of leaving it on my desk. Our offices are down and around the corner from the reception area. The coffee smells delicious and very different than the burnt sludge Mrs. Dotson usually makes. I shouldn't miss the sludge. John tugs me back to reality. I've been back for two days, and there's a shit ton to be done.

"Why are you out here instead of at your desk?" I cock my head to John and narrow my eyes.

"Because he's in there," John says matter-of-factly.

"You're fucking kidding me." I sigh.

"No. I don't fuck or kid with you. I'm going to work out here. Mr. Mr. is in quite a snitty mood. He's been here for an hour and a half. Godspeed. Let me know if you need me to take the cannoli."

"Stop it." I chastise John. Sal is a difficult thing to explain, but he's still business.

"Sorry."

"Regardless of who you think he is, he's still a legitimate client and should be treated with respect even though he's a giant pain in my ass."

John grins and touches my arm. "I'm going to run errands. Is that okay?"

"As long as you pick up my dry cleaning, I know I don't usually ask you to do that shit, but I keep forgetting and it's been there like a fucking month."

"That's what happens when you hide out in the rolling hills of the wine country playing games with girls." I shake my head at him and head towards my office and Sally Pipes. Sally Pipes, or Salvatore Pietro as he's known in the legit business world, sits in my office with his back to me chomping on an unlit cigar looking every bit the part of a cleaned-up gangster. He was raised as one of those who never earned the initial fortune but was taught how to protect and hide it. He grew it and has now legitimized a large portion of his once underground family empire. With my help.

We had a chance meeting in Los Angeles at a bar about a decade ago. We were both getting into new businesses. At the time, I was unaware of what his was. He told me he'd inherited the family business and although it was successful, he wanted to change things. He didn't want to do what had always been done. I respected and identified with it. He's a couple of years older than me. That night I talked to him about venture capital ideas, not knowing where the money would be coming from. It's been in the last year that he's told me more details about making the business clean. I had ignored all the signs of what his business really entailed. I don't know all the specifics of what he does or what his parents, grandfathers, and godfathers did to earn the money.

All I know is the bulk of Raptor Industries money was

made during Prohibition, and that's a similar narrative to LaChappelle, so I had a soft spot for him.

His family ran the downtown tunnels and the Mayor's office in those days. A series of underground tunnels were the speakeasies of LA. The only specifics I know about his current dealings are that Salvatore has vowed to pass on a clean legacy to the next generation.

He staked me in my current company. In exchange, I've gotten him into some pretty incredible investments. He was the first whale that got me noticed in the venture capital world. I was fresh out of college and running away from Sonoma.

He's become a confidant as well. He knows all about my rift with the winery. He knows bits and pieces about my grandfather and his demands on me. And his edicts of honor and glory. And because I had a similar narrative to his, I'm his soft spot. Both of us wanting a different outcome for our lives than what was expected.

His portfolio boasts Twitter. He's one of the original investors in a lot of California tech. I paid him back for his initial investment in me after three years. He let me escape what my grandfather tried to make of my life. He helped me achieve the one I have.

We've made a lot of money together. I've never felt threatened by him, but I have an inkling of the wrath that can ensue if his wishes aren't followed. I keep him at a distance, though. I like him. But I've never said no to him either. I don't think many people ever have. And if they have, there's not a second time.

"Sal. This is a surprise considering we had a meeting on the books for next week."

"Joshie." He stands and we embrace. I sit behind my desk, and I watch this massive man sitting across from me. He crosses his right ankle over his left knee and sits back in his chair. He's always confident that he'll get what he needs.

"Why are you here, Sal?"

"Cutting to the chase now, aren't we? No chitchat? How's the folks?"

"Fine. What do you need, Sal? The deal I'm presenting to you next week isn't close to being ready."

"The folks are good?"

"What are you playing at?" I lean forward. I'm not intimidated by this man, but I am wary. He drops his leg and puts his meaty paws on my desk and leans forward.

"How do I know you've got my best interests at heart when you've been so far away from your office? That was an awful long vacation for you to take."

"My time with my family is none of your concern."

A giant grin breaks across his stubbled and chiseled chin. "Ha. Busting your balls, Joshie. You know I'm all about familia. Good on you to be with them."

I sit back and laugh at this man. He's insane. "Again, you fucking idiot, what can I do for you?"

"I got issues, Josh. People coming at me. I'm not going to go into all of it."

"Please, with all respect, don't ever go into all of it. I love living in the margins with you. No narrative. How much do you need to invest? How soon?"

"This. This here is why you're my guy." He stands up and I expect him to be slapping my back. He smiles. And slides a piece of paper across the desk. It simply says *$6m*. "As soon as fucking possible. It's sitting in the escrow account that you have access to, and I'm getting a bit jumpy about it."

That's a pretty big number for this guy. It's usually one or two at a time, but six is a big ask for him.

"Sal, I can do it. I'm used to dealing in much higher

numbers, but to be delicate, I didn't think you could invest that much at a time without drawing unwanted attention."

"No fucking choice. I'm protecting the future, and it can all get unfucking raveled if I don't move this now."

"This is legit cash, correct?"

"Of course, you asshole." He looks offended.

"Sorry."

He nods at me and shrugs with open hands as if it's a way of saying it's all okay. Then he turns to leave. At the door, he turns back to me. "Josh, I don't expect you to understand all of what I'm asking but know I'll never fuck you with this money shit. I got honor and so do you. But I need you here in your office at my disposal."

"I'm here, Sal. And I have an idea for the cash. But next time you can call."

His lip curls up to the left as he winks at me. "I'm a face-to-face guy. It's the only way to do business." And then he's gone. He looked frazzled to me, and he never looks like that. He's always impeccably dressed and appears well-rested. The slight wrinkles around his eyes and on his shirt have me a touch concerned.

CHAPTER THIRTY-SIX

JOSH

AFTER THREE WEEKS, THINGS ARE BACK TO SEMI-NORMAL around Santa Barbara. Except now I look forward to a daily phone call. The call usually comes at the end of the night. I sit and look out over the ocean, and she looks at the stars in Sonoma. I've stopped staying out late, so I don't miss it. Three weeks ago, she called to thank me and update me that she nailed three of the four pitches. I made her give me the play-by-play. I love a deal. She really is a fucking shark. I will not mess with her again.

The entire thing cost me forty-three grand. It took a teacher's salary to undo my own dumbass mistake. But the lack of guilt and renewed relationship with my parents was worth every penny.

After she called that day, I had her number. I texted her the next day with something to mock my dad about. Then she texted back. Then I called the next day under the pretense of asking her a question about the marketing dinner she's putting together for my parents. But she has yet to send me a picture of her in the Halston.

We're becoming something else. Not friends exactly and

indeed not lovers, but we're no longer enemies. I don't understand it, but she's proven that she cares more about them than I have in quite a while. And Asher really is a non-factor. I put my feet up on a chaise lounge and pull a cork. I'm on the deck just off my kitchen. The whole back of the house is glass to the bluffs and then down to the beach. My deck wraps around to the back where I have an infinity pool. The hot tub is just off to the left and off the bedroom deck. My bedroom can open out to the ocean breeze. I laid out specifics of how clean and masculine I wanted everything, and John made sure that happened. I do not pay him enough; he seriously is the best assistant. There was only one thing I insisted on decor-wise. Well, two. One, no throw pillows. No extra fucking clutter that makes people want to cozy up. The most comfortable thing in my house is my bed. And there's a picture I had printed that most people overlook as just something cool, but to me it's a piece of who I am. I thought it would keep me from tipping over the edge to becoming another douche with too much money. I have more money than I ever thought possible.

The first couple of years when I started making a shit ton of money, I didn't spend it. I lived in a small apartment, drove my piece of shit Honda and barely did anything but work. I had people I admired invest for me. I bought modestly into some groundbreaking tech and it all snow-balled from there. Now there's more than I could spend in several lifetimes.

JOSH: *How did dinner go? Did Adrian go with you?*

Adrian Schroeder is Dad's best friend and a fellow vine-yard owner. I grew up with his kids. Their winery isn't far from ours. And his son Baxter is one of my close friends from childhood.

ELLE: He did! They're hysterical together. My stomach hurts from laughing. The prospective buyers had a really good time too. And met his daughter Tommi. Love her. They left, but I'm still there with the remains of the prospectives. Call you in like 30.

JOSH: If Tommi's still there, tell her hello from me. She can be a riot, but she's a bit extra sometimes too. I'll be here when you call.

ELLE: Good. I like to keep you waiting.

I like that we're getting to know each other. And I do like that this powerhouse of a woman wants to make sure to get back to me immediately. I still think about her naked way too often. Despite that, we're becoming friends. I still imagine the night I drilled her senseless. She totally submitted to me without ever losing her power. No one would suspect that. And now I'm hard. Insanely hard. Always for her.

I'm still wearing my workout shorts, and now they're just a tent. I pull them down and tip my head back, stroking my cock easily as the ocean breeze blows. I imagine her raspberry pink lips wrapped around my tip. My Sonos is blaring, but all I hear is her sexy growl of a moan in my head. I stroke it faster. Now I need to release to even have a conversation with her. Back and forth. I imagine her rocking on top of me, and oh fuck. That was like record time. From her text to cum was like five minutes. I remove my shorts, wipe down my stomach then jump in the pool naked. A perk of no neighbors. I own the lot next door as well. It started out that I was going to build a garage for cars I dreamed of collecting, but I like that it was wild and untouched. I also like that it hides my house. The beach below isn't that accessible to random people so I can have all the privacy I want. I also never really got around to collecting cars. I just have a couple. It's really all I need.

I swim some laps, hoping to shake the image of her. I have to shake this woman off. She's heading back to her life in New York in six weeks. I gave her west coast contacts on purpose, to keep her out here. Then she told me she hands the business off to account managers after the initial meetings. My phone rings and I answer it in the pool. I know exactly who was at the dinner, and it's why I'm anxious to talk to her.

"How does something like Asher happen?"

"No, hello? Stop it. He was good to me. Kind of. He still thinks he's a boyfriend or a potential." She says with a lilt to her voice that I don't want to be there when she's discussing Asher.

"I might puke but continue. And no. Asher can't be anything to you."

"I've told him numerous times we aren't dating. But he acts as if we are. But we never really were. I just stopped seeing him. I stopped everything."

"Everything?"

"Yes. I have had a dating life before you."

Dating? Is that what we're doing? Huh? "Hellcat, you had no problem telling me to fuck off multiple times, surely you can tell this weenie to take a hike. How did it happen?"

"You know how we met. At first, he wanted to whisk me off to Lake Tahoe."

I'm laughing and can't stop. "Whisking is for Paris, not Tahoe."

"Romantic nonetheless!"

"Did you go?" I hear her suck in wine through her teeth, and I want to know what it is. "What are you drinking?"

"The new Zin."

"Is it good?" I wish I had some.

"Fucking amazing. But I've already had like a shit-ton a Schroeder Petite Sirah so what do I know. It could be shit."

She giggles and my dick stiffens. And now I want to taste that Zin on her tongue.

"Schroeder makes a hell of a Petite. They have those good benchland and hillside slopes to pull it off."

She giggles again. "They also have all those sunshine vectors and the sharp pointy blue rocks in the soil."

I ask, "What the hell are you talking about?"

She shoots right back. "What the hell are you talking about?"

I laugh long and hard. "Sometimes I forget you don't know shit about wine."

"Oh. I know shit. I know this shit I'm currently drinking is yummy. That's a technical term."

She's cute when she's buzzed. I don't know how drunk she was the night we met, but this might be the most adorable she's ever sounded. My dick is thickening again, she's like human Viagra. I'm always hard for her. There's that four-hour warning for Viagra, but there's no warning on Elle Parker. I spend my day semi-hard all the time. Like I'm always DTF if she happens to pop by the office in Santa Barbara.

I grab my glass of Cab and move to the hot tub. The heat should shrivel that fucker up.

"What are you doing?" She's slurring a bit.

"Hanging out. Literally."

"Meanings what?"

"I just worked out and then took a swim."

"Josh. You don't have any clothes on, do you?"

"Not a goddamned thing but a smile." Fuck me. I would give anything if she'd talk me through jerking off right now. I say slyly seeing if it could lead anywhere, "What are you wearing?"

"Snake print DVF wrap dress. It has cute ruffles and it's flowy and I like it. It keeps gaping and showing my favorite bra though. Wait. Hold up! Hell no. I see where you're going with that, big boy. We're not doing that. I can barely tolerate you."

I picture the dress and hint of bra. I want it to be a black bra.

"One question and then we can drop this subject."

She pauses and then relents. "Okay. One."

"What color bra?"

"Black." Jackpot. I push her to see how far I can get. How far I can stretch her. I want to be stretching her cunt around my dick right now. It fit so perfectly like she's made for it. "Why not?"

She sighs, and I don't know if I'm getting the shoot down or about to get lucky. Then her tone turns earnest. "We're friends now. You know that can never happen again. I'm not in a place where…" Her voice drifts off.

"What? Tell me. Tell me anything, Elle. I'm listening."

"I'm afraid to tell you." Fuck. Fuck. Fuck. Why is she afraid of me? That is not a good thing. Is she afraid to open up to me or just afraid of me?

"Elle. I never want you to be afraid of me in any capacity. You've never shied away from telling me exactly what you think, don't hide now. Don't make me into something else. Do you hear me?"

"I do. I know you've apologized, and we're in a different place now. But I can't forget how deeply it hurt that you didn't trust me. Or that you turned on me so quickly that you didn't believe in me. Or that you dismissed me. That you left. The night we met and after my client dinner. You left. You left your parents. And you left your fiancée. I think that's who you might be. You might be the guy who leaves. I'm happy to be on the phone with you every night, but as for opening a different part of me to you, I can't do that."

That's what she thinks. Despite my best efforts to be a

cold asshole, now all I want to do is prove I'm not. I want to believe in her. I want to build trust. Leaving has been a lot of my past, but perhaps I can be the guy who doesn't go. Shit. I'm usually a 'turn it and burn it' guy in relationships, but lately, there's an appeal to building something.

I want to see where this goes. Shit, that switch flipped. I want Elle in my life. I also desperately want to fuck her again. If I'm honest with myself, I'm not worthy of her. But I am going to show her she is dead fucking wrong about me leaving.

"Perhaps I'm the guy who comes back?"

"Perhaps."

I ask, "Are you there next week?"

"No. Homesick Candles is opening a brick and mortar in Austin. We've worked on the launch for a year. I'll be there for a day, then off to New York for an Xfinity meeting at NBC for a seasonal tie in things. Then to my abandoned office. I suck at being in New York after all my California time. The pace is relentless. Can you hang on while I pee and get more wine?"

"Sure. I'll be here."

"Promise you won't leave?"

"I promise." She giggles again.

Shit. I need to see Elle face to face without asking. Without forcing it. I have so much ground to make up from the last decade of denying who I was or could be. This woman cracked me wide the fuck open. I don't know how to stop having all the feels lately.

I want to make up for alienating my parents and most everyone I love for the last ten years. I have one solid tie to Sonoma, but it might be time to repair the arrogant damage I've done. What has this woman done to me? I sleep with her one night, and my entire world flips. I want face-to-face time with Elle. She won't Facetime with me, so until I can convince her to video chat, I'm going to have to figure out a way to see her.

I'm going up to Sonoma for my mom's birthday next week. I don't want to tell her I'm disappointed that she won't be there. I can't ask her to stay because I don't know what the fuck I'm doing. I just can't leave her alone, and I certainly can't leave my cock alone when I think of her. But I'm still the asshole who didn't trust her at the bottom of all of this. And apparently, the guy who leaves.

If I think practically, she lives across the country and her life is far away from mine. Then a different part of me—an emotional part me—dreams of her soft glowing skin, those dancing green eyes, and that ass. It will haunt me when she leaves. Maybe we can figure it out. Perhaps we can land on the other side of my ego and her doubt, together.

I'm about to find out. I respond to Elle like a friend but know that we're far beyond friends. Now I need to convince her of it. She's mine. Buckle up, Elle. You're not going to know what hit you, Hellcat.

CHAPTER THIRTY-SEVEN

ELLE

"Back," I announce, and he just picks up the conversation where we left off before my bathroom break.

"I'm sure the pace is so nuts. You're kind of a Northern California girl now. And I'm sure your desk is covered with all kinds of crap people thought you should see. You seem like you belong here now." Hmmm, he wants to keep me here in California. That is too hot of a subject. I back off by flipping the conversation away from New York and back towards explaining Asher.

"To answer your other question. Asher had seminars in Tahoe and invited me to tag along. I didn't go but joined him in Healdsburg the next week and never left. He extended a generous invitation to me to stay at the Hotel Healdsburg, and the fancy wine dinner was with your parents."

"I know him. This doesn't sound like him. He's a hustler. Not a giver."

"He's not a hustler."

"I will bet all my fucking money you paid for your plane ticket and the hotel room."

I pause, sucking on my lips and raising my eyebrows.

Then bite the inside of my lip. He's so Josh lately. 'Joshua' the dick hasn't been around in a couple of weeks. I don't know why, but I find these nightly conversations to be grounding. My head's spinning and swimming with him. But the pit of doubt that sits at the bottom of my stomach stays firmly in place. I'm curled on the cozy chair on the porch and looking up at the stars. I'm sipping, and suddenly, I wish he were here.

I say resolutely, "Yes, I paid. Do I hear water?"

"Yes, non sequitur. I live on the ocean."

I clarify. "No, like bubbles."

"Hot tub."

"Really? Is your house like a hotel? It looks like one."

"Have we been googling? Or was it Realtor.com?"

"Realtor."

I giggle, waiting for his response, and he sucks air in quickly. "I redid the master bath, the kitchen, and put in this hot tub. Now can we please get back to the Asher thing?"

I admit it all. "Is the hot tub like your infinity pool?"

"You did do some research. Yes, similar style."

"Mmm. Sounds nice."

"You should come over sometime. Like right now." He says this as a growl, and I feel it in my nipples. They rise to the sound of his voice. Friend. I need to bring him back to the friend zone.

"Yes. I bought the hotel room and a plane ticket. And the car rental."

He's laughing at me. Then he says, "You know if he took you skiing, you would have ended up paying for…"

"Lessons, lodging, and ski rentals?"

"You're an idiot, Elle."

I laugh loudly. I can't stop giggling like I'm twelve. "Yes. Yes, I am. I paid for it all. Someday you'll need to explain your hatred of him in detail. But here's a gift." I'm too drunk to keep secrets.

"I like presents." I can imagine the smile breaking across his face, and now I wish I was there in his hot tub. No. I need to stop that thought.

"He's terrible in bed. I mean *terrible*. I was beginning to think it was me. It was so bad. And kissing. Ugh. He's got a blobby tongue and no clue what to do with it."

"Trust me. It's not you. You are not bad at sex. Is that why you came looking for me?"

Ahhh. This is the first time we've ever really discussed that night. But I need to stop talking about sex with Josh. "No. I went looking for the old letch. You found me." I swear I can hear him smirk.

"Yes, I did." He growls and it's sexy as hell.

Then I'm honest with him. "Yes. I went looking for you."

"I didn't know it, but I might have been looking for you too." No, he did NOT just say that to me. That's too cute and vulnerable. I have to lighten this all up.

"What's the worst sex you've ever witnessed?" I ask.

"Bad porn. Overacted."

I laugh easily.

"Asher's the worst you've ever witnessed?" He pushes on this line of questioning.

"No, he's the worst I've been involved with. The worst I ever witnessed, that honor belongs to the ex-fiancé, fucking my assistant in the ass on our shared desk."

"OUCH! Damn. He's a fucking fool. There's no way her ass is better than yours."

"I need to stop talking. And you need to stop talking about my ass while you're naked in a hot tub. Change the subject, *friend*." Visions of him from the shower drift across my imagination. The water pouring down his abs and falling onto that giant root vine of a dick he has. Wow, I need to get laid. He breaks the silence.

"Yes, ma'am, I'll stop talking about your ass. But you are the one who brought it up. Tahoe can be good, but it's not where I like to ski."

"Where would you invite a virtual stranger, you thought was a 'potential somebody' to go skiing?"

"First off, we'd fly private if I really like her."

I'm intrigued. "Private really? Yours?"

"No. I'd rent. Plane maintenance is too much."

"Samesies. Such a hassle. As is docking the yacht, do not get me started."

He laughs loud and long. "Second, we'd stay in the Fairmont Lake Louise."

"But I love a Ritz-Carlton." I snicker. I can't stop with the innuendo tonight.

"I know you do. But this one is smack in the middle of the mountain, it's like a castle. And third, this mystery woman would have an all-mountain pass, all new equipment, champagne on tap, and refresher lessons on me."

"Champagne on you? Interesting idea."

"Stop playing with fire, woman."

I need to stop.

He asks, "And where would you invite a gentleman to snuggle up and be an adorable ski bunny?"

He called me adorable. My skin is tingling. "Skiing wouldn't come to mind. Bali. And I'd pay for everything."

"Bali?"

"I'd always wanted to see it. I did a report on it when I was little, and it was the farthest place from my home and my life I could imagine. When my parents died, I went there by myself."

"Oh, Elle." His voice drops and I hear the concern, but not

pity. That's important, I don't want pity. "I'm so sorry. I didn't know."

"I know you didn't. Car accident. I was in college. I dropped out for a bit and flew across the world to run away. I drank, snorted, and smoked everything they had to try and forget the pain. Eventually, when that didn't work anymore, I began exploring a lot of 'potentials' in Bali. Each one held a promise."

"Like a boyfriend?"

"No. A promise that for at least twenty minutes I wouldn't have to think about the bottomless pain. I wouldn't have to remember that I was alone in the world."

"Elle." He says with a level of concern I need to ignore. I continue telling the story that only my therapist knows.

"I relentlessly pursued pleasure in twenty-minute intervals. I wanted just twenty minutes to not be sad or alone. And eventually, like with the drugs and alcohol, even those twenty minutes didn't help anymore. My tolerance for sadness was too high. That's when I came home. Back to school and counseling."

There's no response. I wipe the tears from my eyes, glad Josh isn't here to see it, but a little sad he's not here to catch my tears again. "Wine's done its job tonight and turned me into a sappy mess. I'm going to go to bed. Goodnight."

I hang up quickly, slightly embarrassed. I head upstairs with a full glass in hand. I don't even know why I just shared that. I've never done anything like that before.

In business and relationships, you want to screw me in any way possible, that's fine. Just don't ask anything personal. I don't share. Fuck. I've never even told Evan about Bali, and he's the closest thing I have to a best friend. I have lots of people that I hang out with, but even they don't know my path.

My phone rings as I turn down the hall to my room. I pick up, and he starts talking.

"I'm confused, Elle. You want to take someone back to the place you tried to bury your pain?"

I roll my eyes at how persistent he is. "Please hold while I get my jammies on."

"Did you just say jammies, like you're a six-year-old?"

"Yes. Jammies."

His voice gets that raspy wanton tone to it. "I can't help but recognize you're probably naked right now. And by coincidence, so am I. Just saying. It would be so much easier to hear you rather than imagine that moan again tonight."

"Oh my. We've covered this." I hear a big roar of laughter as I put my phone on the bed. I remove my wrap dress and climb into my favorite LC/W yoga pants. I take a picture of my ass with no shirt on and text him. Just to mess with him. It is a good ass.

"Did you just text me? Oh shit. That is *not* fair. You want a picture of mine?"

"No, I have a good memory." I grin at the thought of his gorgeous dick and ass.

He jokes, "Can I use this?"

"NO!"

"Too late."

"Don't, Josh. Take your hand off your dick right now. I'll send you something better." I can't stop flirting with him tonight. I have no power to stop.

He growls at me. "There's nothing better than those yoga pants."

I send a picture of the Halston. The dream outfit of my lifetime. I didn't send him one before now because it felt too personal. Like I was showing off for a boyfriend. He knew how to make me feel stunning and confident. He thought about how my body would look in certain clothes. Color, cut, shoes all of it, he envisioned it all for me.

Then he chortles. "Never mind, you were correct. I don't need the yoga pants ever again. Holy shit, beautiful."

"Me or the dress?"

"You. You are breathtaking. So utterly splendid. Heart-stopping stunning. So confident and strong. All of you striking."

"Please stop. Thank you for it. It's the most amazing thing I'll probably ever wear. I do love it so."

He keeps up his reverent tone of voice, "Won't stop complimenting you. That's one of my new favorite past times. That dress was made for you. It's perfect. You look so elegant and just kick-ass cool."

"I kept the Dolce Gabbana even if it looks like crap in comparison."

"It's hard to imagine you looking like crap in anything."

I laugh again to try and break up his compliments. "Josh, listen up."

"You have my full attention. Trust me."

"Bali. I want to make the most beautiful place I've ever been whole again. I don't want to be sad thinking about those stunning beaches and amazing people who took care of me at my lowest moments and all of that delicious food. I'd take the person that finally made me feel not so alone in the world. He gets to go, no one else. But I'm paying for everything."

"I hope you find him. Just out of curiosity. Why was your pleasure limited to twenty-minute intervals?"

"Sex. It's average."

"Amateurs. That's a lack of discipline right there. I'm just saying from personal experience."

"Oh, that's *right*. You could go pro, you know."

"You're just remembering we had mind fucking blowing

sex for hours on end? I can still describe what you taste like. It's like it's on the tip of my tongue. You do remember that part? The tip of my tongue and your face riding it?"

I roll my eyes at his crassness, but it's turning me on. I like it. It just comes out of my mouth. "It's hard to forget when you replay things so often in your mind."

I shouldn't have said that. But I'm wet thinking about that night and currently wine-soaked. I should be angry when he says things like that. Instead of getting mad, I'm going to have to get off the phone with him, so I can get off to thinking about him.

I make an excuse to get off the phone. "I have to go. I'm saying all the things."

He's quick to respond. "I like those things."

"They are drunk things." I need to get a grip on myself before I begin to believe and hope that he's actually something.

He sighs. "Sweet dreams."

"Night, Suit."

Then he says the words that put me to sleep most nights lately. "Until tomorrow, Cosmo."

I barely hang up before my hand is between my legs, flicking and swirling as I slide two fingers inside slick from memories of his tongue. I moan his moan as I begin to build my orgasm. I think about him throwing me against the shower wall and fucking me so hard I couldn't speak. I think about the dirty words that came out of his mouth and how deep down I want him to tell me what to do. I can't explain it, but my body isn't listening to my mind when it comes to him. My nipples are hard as I stretch, gasp, and then I shudder. I come hard but not as hard as he can make me. I wonder if he's doing the same. Shit. I think I miss him.

CHAPTER THIRTY-EIGHT

JOSH

I DRIVE THE JEEP UP MIDDAY ON FRIDAY. I'D TAKEN IT BACK TO Santa Barbara, and it belongs back up there. I like the long drive. It clears my head, and I can feel the switch from work to home happen as the familiar roads twist and turn into Sonoma.

We missed our calls for the last couple of days. I've been immersed in closing this insane deal for this persistent and insistent Sally Pipes. He's the one I'd like to ditch. I'm not sure how to get out of this sensitive situation. I'll talk to him when I get back about backing off his business a bit. We had dinner the other night, and it was a good time, but we didn't really talk business.

This week has been nights at the office asleep on my couch and my personal phone off. I warned Elle that I'd be unreachable for most of this week. She called it lockdown mode and totally understood. I left her a good luck text from the work phone about the stuff in Austin, but there's been no answer.

When I couldn't sleep last night, I looked up the event online on her Instagram. It looks like it was insanely cool.

She convinced the company to create a six-foot candle that smells like Austin to burn out in front of the store. Not sure how she convinced the city to let her do it, but she did. She told me that she was working on a limited-edition cross-promotion between Homesick and Sonoma County Visitors Bureau creating candles based on varietals. She's really good at her job.

I cyber-stalk her from time to time, but she doesn't seem to post much. People post more about her on the winery profiles than her own company. And fucking Asher displays any time he's with her. He keeps bringing buyers to the table so she keeps meeting with him. And he's done some events for her. Of course, he posts all the fucking time like he's a twenty-year-old. How can someone so unscrupulous in his work and word get away with a happy-go-lucky Instagram account? I loathe him. He posted a really hot picture of Elle about a week ago, and it fucking twists my insides to know he touches her. He blew his shot with her. Thank god. I scoured social media, but no one else has posted about her in two days. She's all I can think of as I skid up the familiar, gravel winery driveway.

I'm slipping into town to grab a beer or two, celebrate my mom, and then I need to get right back to Santa Barbara and the firm. It's for the best she's not here. I've been fucking dominating at work lately. It would be too much of a distraction. No one can touch me at that office, and they'll crumble without me. I'm the only one who makes that much money in one fucking day. Pussies. All hail the conqueror.

I'm making it right on time for Mom's birthday party that she didn't want. Dad always insists we celebrate everything. I haven't been to her birthday party in years. But it's usually a lot of the earthy-crunchy yoga pottery set that attends. Should be a patchouli sandalwood smell fest but it will be nice to see the folks.

I enter the house through the kitchen door, and the smell is indeed overwhelming, and I might puke. Not sure what it is about this kitchen that gives me a weak stomach. My father is giving his annual toast which always includes a new poem about Mom. It's the sappiest thing in the world. I move quietly into the house so as to not disturb anyone. And then there's a whiff, just a hint of lilacs and orange blossoms and my dick wakes up. It's like it's got Spidey senses when I smell her. She must have left a scarf here or something. Fuck, I must maintain. And then I see a flip of a blonde shoulder-length hair in the small crowd in front of me in the living room. My dick outright pushes forward like it wants to say hello to her first. I want to smack that ass so fucking badly. I'm so excited she's here.

I walk up behind her, staring at her tight black capri pants and hot pink cold shoulder silk shirt. I want to eat her shoulders. I take a picture of her ass and text it to her. I see her instantly open the text that I sent from behind her. And she doesn't react but texts back.

ELLE: Stalker

I grin widely at this cheeky girl. I stand directly behind her, and she backs up into me. That's right, give me that ass, sweet girl. I can see her chest begin to flush as I look down over her head. At six-foot-three, I tower above her by almost a foot. The view is spectacular as I discover her nipples seem happy to see me. She reaches back and squeezes my hand as we continue watching my father fete my mother for her birthday. She doesn't pull away, so I don't let go. I don't know what any of this means. Our DL hand-holding seems forbidden and that makes it hotter. Maybe it means nothing, or maybe I finally get to see my handprint on her luscious ass and perhaps we can find another bed to break. I wish she'd stop listening to her head and listen to her body that's clearly responding to me. I also don't know if she found out I was coming and canceled her trip.

She sneaks a look at me over her shoulder with a tiny little smirk. Fuck me. I'm done. I'm done pretending I don't want her. That I can't have her. I will have her. I want to throw her down here in front of everyone, fuck her raw to show everyone in here and prove to her that's she's mine. I don't ever feel like this. Hell, I was engaged and didn't feel this connected or drawn to my fiancée. Noelle Parker, you are my undoing.

CHAPTER THIRTY-NINE

ELLE

I FELT HIM BEFORE HIS TEXT. I KNEW IT WAS HIM BEHIND ME. He has a presence and a heat. It's like we exist on the same wavelength. When his cedar scent overtook over my senses, my nipples instantly pebbled in my silk shirt. He's so tall and commanding behind me, and I want to melt backward. Instead, I sip my wine and let go of his left hand. He shifts, and his right hand finds its way to my hip. He pulls me to him. I struggle to keep my knees from buckling at our close contact. My chest blushes red with lust, and my panties instantly flood. I look over my left shoulder again and part my lips. He bends down to give me his ear. It's been five weeks since we've been in the same room and four days since we've spoken. I whisper something true.

"I missed you."

I hear his breath catch. His hand curls tighter around my hips as he pulls me closer. "I missed you too, beautiful."

I'm instantly aglow, and my stomach flips. I didn't want to ask Will if he was coming, possibly ruining a surprise for Sarah. All I know is Will asked me to postpone my New York trip until next week, and I did. Because of schedules, we haven't talked in days, and I felt the impact of that every night. I didn't realize he made me feel safe.

It's been so long since I had someone to share my day with and I forgot how nice it is to not feel alone. I've made it my mission to not let anyone get too close because I never want to go through the pain of losing them. That pain is too intense. Everyone knows me to a point. And then the damn Whittiers happened.

First Sarah and Will accepted me into their hearts and home before I realized what was happening. And then there's this one. This fucking Whittier who might be more than I initially thought. Well, initially I thought he was an Adonis with a golden cock. I only wish I could trust him. I don't know if I can rely on him, and since I'm an expert at relying on only myself, it's a hard habit to break. I couldn't bear to be left.

We all clap as Will finishes his speech. Josh's hand leaves my hip and the warmth that was filling me recedes with it. I turn to him, and his eyes are adoring, and his mouth is upturned on the left. He embraces me in a giant protective hug. I melt into him. He kisses the top of my head and picks me up off the ground. I kiss his neck with my arms around him.

"What are you doing here?" I squeak out.

"You know it's *my* mom's birthday. What are *you* doing here?"

"I went to Austin and came right back. New York week after next."

He takes me in his arms again. I wrap around him in a hug that seems more familiar than we should be in front of these people. No one knows we've been talking every day. Most of them think we still hate each other. But I don't even care how they perceive it.

Will approaches and says, "I'm thrilled you're here, son.

And that the two of you aren't scratching each other's eyes out." He winks at me and I think he knows. Josh isn't all that subtle, and it's not like I wasn't just in his arms.

Will hugs Josh heartily then puts his hand on my shoulder. "Are you mad I didn't tell you he was coming?" Will winces.

I pretend to be annoyed. "In the future, I'd like a little heads up so I can put on my armor in anticipation." Josh's laugh booms through the room, and his mother's head turns at the sound. She's at the far end of the house surrounded by her friends.

"Josh!" She rushes over into his arms. "You haven't been to a birthday party in a while. Come say hello to Theresa, Tina, and Goldie." And she whisks him into the party leaving me alone with Will.

Will moves the cake knife away from me. "Don't cut him."

"I won't. We're in a good place. I'm not ready to flip a table today. Can't promise Josh won't piss me off tomorrow but tonight, you're safe from a scene."

"Good. Because you're scary when you're pissed."

I wink at Will. "Only when I'm pissed at him."

"Interesting. Very interesting." Will jokes with me and raises his eyebrow.

"What is?" says Samantha, one of the newest tasting room hosts. She butts into our conversation. She's funny, and I like her a lot.

"I was just assuring Will that I wasn't going to cause a scene because his son is here."

Will says, "Hey there, Samantha. That's Josh right over there with his mother."

"It's Sam."

"Sam. Of course. Have a good time."

Will nods and walks away. She leans into me, staring at Josh. We're both looking at him. "Well, oh my damn. That's delicious. I mean, why not cause a scene. That much of a mountain of a man deserves to be climbed."

Suddenly I want to rip this woman's face off. My mountain. Don't you fucking climb him. Oh shit. I'm jealous. I say nothing, but I'm white-knuckling my wine glass, and she laughs at me.

"No worries. I prefer someone more rugged. Maybe a little more meat. He's a bit extra. Too pretty. Nice to look at though. I prefer a good beard and flannel."

"You like your men a bit more mountain man than a mountain of a man?"

"Exactly. And you?"

I try to bluff. "I'm not sure."

"Oh shit. I don't know you very well, but you can't even fool a stranger. You're hot for that man. Also, your chest and cheeks are flushed fire engine red when you look at him. Undies wet too?"

Fucking Irish skin.

I HAD the best time with Sam. She may be the first real friend I've made since college. I didn't try to impress her, and I didn't lie to her or skirt the truth. She's kind of awesome. But my entire night was a series of check-ins with this man and an unspoken agreement that there'd be a moment for just us later. We would get each other drinks and touch elbows and backs. His hand sears my flesh with each innocent touch.

Everyone finally leaves around one. I'm doing some dishes with Will drying. Josh is changing out of his suit and putting his mom to bed. She probably won't be able to do much of anything tomorrow. Usually, if Sarah has a long hard day, the next one is just rest. I've loaded her with Netflix and Amazon suggestions, so she stays in bed tomorrow to get back her strength. The new meds are kicking her ass. But the disease seems to be stalled, according to her doctors. There's no cure so it's simply a reprieve for now.

Will heads upstairs after bidding me goodnight. Within seconds of Will turning upstairs, Josh is at my back. His hands are on my bare shoulders and his fingers caressing circles. He leans to my neck, and his lips graze it. Too much. My skin prickles, and my head is light. He's too much.

I exhale as I say, "Porch?"

"Farmhouse porch? Is that where you take my calls?"

"Most nights, listening to the land and looking at the stars. There are no stars in Manhattan. It's a magical place, but no stars." I don't turn around. If I do, I'll be in his arms. That can only lead to chaos and I'm not a fan of chaos.

"Come with me. Bring your bottle."

He grabs his wine, and I grab mine. We go outside, and he takes me down through the parking lot towards the tasting room. He guides me through the darkness with a hand on my back that's a little lower towards my ass, but somehow I don't mind him copping a feel tonight.

We climb up on the side before the road slopes down and around to the entrance of the tasting room. They mostly keep extra merchandise and boxes up in the stuffy attic space. But he pulls a ladder from a secret area and lays it against the old stone building. He hands me his bottle and climbs up one-handed while not spilling a drop from his very full glass. Probably not his first time climbing with wine.

I hand him my glass and the bottles then climb up. There's a flat space in the middle of the roof where he's placed our things. He holds out his steady hand to pull me up. My skin warms under his touch. There's a flutter in my belly. I'm not going to judge, just tumble a little deeper into him and this moment.

We lay down next to each other. The stars are going to swallow me whole. There's so many of them from this vantage. The temperature is warm up on the roof, but I'm shaking a bit. Without saying a word, I reach out for his hand and he doesn't resist. We lay there in our truce watching and occasionally lifting our heads to sip our wine. This is the least lonely I've felt in a very long time.

CHAPTER FORTY

JOSH

THANK FUCK'S SAKE FOR THE DARK, SINCE CERTAIN PARTS OF me are a little too excited by her touch. When she took my hand, it was the most restrained I've ever been. She fucking said she missed me. That means I'm gaining ground. I missed this tiny dynamo of a woman who makes me laugh and feel all kinds of scary shit.

"Can you tell me things?" she says in a lilting tone that melts me.

I brush my fingers through her hair. "What sort of things, Hellcat?" She sighs.

"Lucien things. And something about Santa Barbara life before I met you."

"Tall order, Cosmo. Why?"

"I want to trust you and I don't know how you feel about your history. Only research."

I kiss the top of her head. "And that will help you trust me?"

"It's a start."

"I was engaged."

"I know."

"Research."

"Yup. Did you love her?"

"No."

She was supposed to complete my perfect life picture. After my first multimillion-dollar deal, I leased a Porsche. The car completed a childhood dream I thought I wanted back in my dusty Farmhouse bedroom. My Santa Barbara house is steel and glass. It defined my successful transformation from Josh to Joshua. At parties, I always drink whiskey or beer, never letting on that I know anything about wine. I successfully became someone else.

I didn't have a tragic upbringing, but I was stripped of choices. I was being forced into a life laid out for me by my grandfather. When I rejected it, I thought it made me a better person. I rebelled against the world I was locked into by becoming insanely successful at something else.

The wine business comes with such strings, especially this one. My parents never had a choice. When my parents got married my grandfather legally changed the name of the winery to LaChappelle Whittier so he wouldn't be forgotten. He tried to get my parents to legally change my name to LaChappelle. My mother being an only child, the last of the true LaChappelles wasn't good enough for Lucien. That misogynist needed to know a LaChappelle man would run things. My grandfather was a hard man and never truly believed in my mother or that she could run his empire as he often called it.

My father is an affable guy who had promise as a business journalist or a scientist. And then he loved her, and his fate was sealed. He had to become a vintner. No choice, just Lucien's law. They protected me from him the best they could. But in the end, I severed all ties to get out from under his large shadow.

I glance over in the darkness at hill where dear grandpa

used to stand with a giant stick and overlook his kingdom. As a kid, my grandfather would take me on tractor rides through the vines. Not a fun ride with a loving grandpa in the grapes, it was mandatory and part of my life curriculum. Before I could go to school, I'd have to identify not only the varietal but the clone and the age of each block. And he wasn't too kind when I forgot one. At one point, I knew the exact age of every vine on property. I almost failed geography in fifth grade because I couldn't memorize world capitals. But I could find the Zin clone 68 blindfolded in our vineyard. Late nights and early mornings I was bombarded with information that I was told was vital for survival.

He told me I could go and study anything I wanted at college. He'd happily pay for it but with the understanding that I was to return to the vineyard to take over for my 'foolish lighthearted father' and his 'inconsequential flight-of-fancy daughter.' This was his command. His words and feelings towards them may have played a part in how easy it was for me to cut ties with them for a while.

I shift my body and tell her a bit. "The man spent my youth telling me the only way this place would survive is if I came back from college to rescue it from my parents. I've never told my parents the terrible way he spoke of them. But I'm sure they knew. He used to say to me I had no choice but a duty."

"That's terrible."

"It was Lucien and we all accepted it."

"My parents were treated like stewards of this land, and they never knew it. My mom used to paint. I didn't realize this until I was seven and found a bunch of her canvases in storage. She wasn't allowed to paint anymore because she needed to tend to the merchandise or the deal with label design and getting it approved through the liquor board. He made her learn graphic design, but she found sneaky ways to create. Like the pottery that she now sells in our tasting room."

"I love that she found a way to express herself despite him." I lay back down and think about him again. She caresses the back of my hand.

The bastard died when I was a junior in college. Lucien's last Christmas, when I was home from school, he sat me down and showed me his will. The winery would be mine. It was cruel to my parents and a legacy I wanted nothing to do with. The damage was done, and we had a relationship that was no more than shambles. After he died, I gave it back to my parents. I was old enough to realize no one could tell me what to do and that my parents weren't everything I'd been force-fed.

I'm excellent with math, and I can talk anyone into anything. I had no interest in a world where my grandfather marginalized not only my parents but had taken away my entire future before I even figured out what I wanted it to be. My parents can mine joy from everything, especially each other. So they thrived here. I'm a different breed.

"You don't have to tell me anymore if you don't want to." She whispers to me and I revel in her trust. I'll let her know a bit more.

"Lucien lived for revenge, duty, and Martial law. I wanted to be the master of my universe, not thrust into someone else's. He was the most black-and-white man who ever lived. There were no second chances and no second impressions.

Lucien sent his best friend and CFO to jail for embezzlement, and he probably cooked the books himself. He ruined the man's life and the lives of his family because he believed his friend cheated him and was disloyal. Completely cut him off without another word. That was the kind of man Lucien LaChappelle was."

He took possession of me from the very beginning. My

mother got to pick Joshua, and of course I have my father's last name, but the rest of it was mandated by my grandfather. It's literally his name bookended by mine. Bastard. I set out to be Joshua Whittier instead of anything Lucien LaChappelle."

My heart tears a bit when I think of the winery becoming someone else's home. I know I gave it up a long time ago but it's still hard to think about. A feeling I didn't even know I could muster. It's buried pretty deep down under glitz, money, and ambition. Then there was Elle. The woman unearthed a whole slew of feelings I didn't think I was capable of having. She did it without trying, just by being Elle. Seeing this all through her eyes reminded me that I don't have to reject all of my childhood. That Lucien was only a piece of it. I have a universe of people and support. I do love the smell of the soil and the bitter taste of a grape right off the vine. Elle busted that door open when I thought it was sealed off. We stay still in all that I've revealed. After a while she shifts to her side and looks at me.

"Josh, why aren't you hitting on me?"

"Do you want me to hit on you? Because I don't do that."

"Yes, you do. You hit on me at Steiner's." She chuckles that deep throaty sexy fucking laugh. And my resolve weakens.

"No, I didn't. I conquered you that night."

She laughs again, "I wasn't putting up much of a fight. I'd call it more of a checkmark on a to-do list than conquering."

I can't help but laugh. "That was then, but last week you said no. You've repeatedly told me to stop, so I am. You said that was off the table because you don't trust me. So let's just look at the stars."

Fuck me. This wooing shit is hard. I want to flip her over and eat her pussy until she wakes up all of Sonoma with her screaming, but I'll bide my time. I'm pretty sure I could get her, I'm just not sure I can get her heart yet. I don't lose, and I need to be careful not to fuck this up. I want all of her, not just the parts I've already had. As sexy as she is, for once it's about more than just sex. I'm feeling things that don't relate to my penis while I hold her hand, and I like it. I want more of this.

I WAKE up a couple of days later still in Sonoma. I was supposed to leave the next morning. I can't find the motivation until she goes to New York. The night of my mom's birthday, I kept reaching for her hand, or she kept reaching for mine. I'd like to blame it on Syrah, but she was different. Something has shifted and cracked wide open. She's changing me too. I got up early and went out for a run, so I didn't have to see her at breakfast.

Nothing happened last night, only wine and more stargazing, but for some reason that awkward morning-after feeling was taking hold. I need to connect with nature.

Last night she snuggled into my chest. I've never been so chaste in all my life. I just put my arm around her, and we both pretended my cock wasn't at attention and my balls weren't blue.

No one has asked when I'm leaving, and honestly I don't have a fucking clue. Instead of phone calls, we sit on the porch each night and reveal a little more of our dark and twisty shit. She knows more stories of my grandfather and his domination over my childhood than my father now. No kissing but I don't think I can be patient much longer. I swear I heard her masturbating last night and the idea of that set me off. Our rooms are next to each other, and it's killing me to know she's so close. My parents' bedroom is on the other side of the house.

Today I need to focus on some of my own business, and

then my dad asked if I'd look over the reports that came in from the vineyard manager. I just dove right into vineyard life. I was in the fields today too, my childhood chore skills coming back like long-awakened muscle memory.

He also said he made progress on restoring the outbuildings on the property. Dad's always envisioned restoring the crumbling buildings scattered throughout our property for historical tours. Mom and I believe they should become vacation rentals for an immersive experience. Either way, it's time to deal with the some of the salvageable ones. Maybe Elle has an idea.

After I shower, I head to the Cooperage excited by this thought. Usually, Sundays would be quiet, but today there's a bustling office full of employees getting the end of the quarter crap together. My emails can wait. I scoop up my mom and call out for Elle.

"Elle! Get out here, now. Where are you?"

"WHAT!" She bolts up from her chair in the conference room where she usually works, acting like something is terribly wrong. She's dressed in faded, ripped jeans and a heathered gray V-neck clingy t-shirt. The shirt perfectly frames the spot where her emotions show. She stops my heart for just a split second. So, fucking beautiful.

She runs out of her office with her hand on her heart. She says, "Why are you so loud? Jesus, I'm right here."

"Come with me."

She shakes her head. "No. I have work to do. You seem to be annoying right now."

"I'm super annoying, but you still have to come with me." I motion to her to hustle up by waving my arms at her to usher out of the building.

"Why?"

"Because I said so. And when have I ever commanded you

to do something, and it went badly?" I wink at her, and her cheeks flush.

Elle says, "That's ominous. I don't like it. Where? I need to know where I'm going. I need a plan."

She looks adorable as her vivid green eyes glare at me, and the gold flecks dance in the streaming sunlight beaming from the windows.

I say, "It's fine. I'm not kidnapping you. Too many witnesses. Mom's coming too."

"Is she done with her luncheon."

"Yes. I promise she's coming too."

"If Sarah's there, then you can't very well leave me in a ditch. But I do not like not knowing where I'm going."

"Trust me, I get that. Come on." The entire office laughs at me teasing her as she flips them off. Hellcat.

WE SET off for a tour of the property along raggedy roads that haven't been groomed in years, but I know the paths well. I shouldn't be looking, but the bumpy ride is managing to make her perky breasts bounce most delightfully. Her bra doing nothing in the way of keeping them in place. We almost go off the road. They're so hypnotic. And now, I need to look away because I apparently have awoken my favorite appendage. There are multiple twitches down below at the thought of seeing them bounce without Mom in the back seat.

Focus. I need to focus on the task at hand. Damn her tits. We pull up to the caretaker cottage, and the path to it is a little overgrown. It was a guard shack of sorts during Prohibition. We refer to it as Lookout.

"Are we hiking? I'm not so much an outdoorsy woodsy girl."

"Shut up and follow me."

My mom is smoking us, she's way out in front. She's always been fit, but she seems off her game lately. Glad to see she seems to be back to normal. The cottage looks great. It's been stripped of vines and brush. The foundation looks like it's been reinforced and the inside has been overhauled. There's tarping and a temporary roof.

"Mom. When did you guys do this?"

"Your father started this project a while back. We just never got around to finishing it." The building looks fantastic.

As Elle makes her way through the trees out to the edge, she sees it, she looks fucking fabulous in a simple t-shirt. Her eyes get all soft and sweet. Almost as if she's falling in love. My mom is circling the building, and Elle joins her as I stare out at the view of our vineyard and the valley. Lookout's pretty big though, approximately eight hundred square feet, for a cottage.

"What is this, Sarah? Like a hobbit house? It looks a little bit like a fairy cottage with the gingerbread exterior."

CHAPTER FORTY-ONE

ELLE

SARAH SPEAKS, "THERE ARE SEVEN ABANDONED BUILDINGS ON property all similar in states of disrepair. Same limestone and river rocks that build the Farmhouse, the Cooperage office building, and barn that's the tasting room. Some of them were homes, and some were secret warehouses to house wine barrels. There's one super long one on the end of the property over there. Will and the crew did a lot of work on this one and the one we call, Longhouse. But then well, you know, time got away from us." They must have gotten the diagnosis in the middle of the construction.

"And the story is that Emma LaChappelle also believed seven was a charmed number so she wouldn't allow any other tiny buildings. There were originally only seven varietals, and now we only have dividends of seven for tradition's sake. I'll bet if we look at them on a map, if connected, they might have a pattern or something. She was a bit mystic."

"Like a pentagram or something?"

Josh laughs and says, "Yeah, the 4G, Emma, was a brilliant genius whack job."

Sarah points towards the big hill before the little lake. "That one was where they'd bottle in secret."

"Why secret?"

"This one was called the caretaker's home in the twenties and thirties, but that was code. They used it as a lookout point during Prohibition. They called him the caretaker, but his whole job was to sound that bell if he saw a raid approach. It's called *the Chappelle Bell*. Part of the cover for police was that we were religious zealots."

She gestures to a rusted-out bell that sits between two very sturdy trees still tethered. The clapper is long gone, but the bell remains. The trees grew around it. I touch it then sit on a rock for the rest of story time.

Sarah speaks, "All the buildings and the cave were retro-fitted with false walls to hide the extra wine we were producing. We had a license to produce sacramental wine for Catholic churches in the area but produced ten times the amount needed. It's how my great-grandfather was not only able to survive but expand the winery. That's when he bought the coastal land out near Bodega. It also enabled my father to be able to jointly purchase a monstrous track of land in Lodi. That's how we can keep up with commercial production. Lodi produces a ton of Cab and Zin each year. We don't mix it with the Estate vines but produce the…"

I interrupt, "The Chapel label, I know. But you own the property with Schroeder, right? They produce the Bellamy's Ghost label."

Josh chimes in, "Exactly. And the LaChappelle and the Whittier labels can remain certified organic and estate. As can Schroeder's. It's second labels, like Chapel, where the real money is. Alena maintains the proprietary white and red blends each year, but we have little to do with it after that. My dad and Adrian Schroeder expanded the Lodi vineyard to accommodate Trader Joe's demand."

A Trader Joe's light bulb goes off. That's how he knew them.

"You are aware that I know all this. But what I've never asked is, why not just sell the juice?"

Josh explains, "We do some. It's a lot of juice. But by owning the name, blend, and production facilities, it makes more money for us. And we maintain quality control. We may be in a position to produce some cheaper wine, but the quality is still excellent. It's how we can keep creating world-class rare vintage wines because the ten-dollar dinner party wines provide the capital for the collector and higher-end wines."

Sarah lights up as Josh becomes animated, telling me about the business and their family legend. She's proud that he's not been totally swallowed up by Santa Barbara. His face softens, and his eyes gleam in the sunlight.

Josh finishes her story. "The LaChappelle legend is that we were the only vineyard to never have a drop spilled, confiscated, or destroyed during Prohibition."

I ask, "I knew lots of wineries produced sacramental wine, but did they all bootleg?"

Josh raises his eyebrows before he continues, and it's insanely hot. He says, "Yes, but not as well as we did. Langerford got close, but just before the repeal, they got raided and lost a ton of barrels."

"You're descended from bootleggers? That's cool as hell. Can I use that?"

Sarah laughs. "I don't see why not."

I ask, "What are you going to do with these buildings?"

"We were going to restore them, put them on the historical register, and then either conduct tours or let people vacation in them."

"You don't need more tours. I love the idea of little cottages tucked away for vacation," I say.

Josh is standing a couple feet from me, and the sun is in his sandy hair, making it all the more enticing. He's still an untrustworthy asshole, but when he turns towards me with one corner of his mouth in a semi-smile, the distrustful knot in my stomach loosens. He's different. We're different. It's like we're laying the groundwork for something else. Here's the part that makes me the most nervous about him being up here this last week. I've discovered I don't like to be too far away from him. I wait for him to fall asleep each night. If I leave my door open, I can hear him snuffle and lightly snore. It's adorable and comforting.

His shirt is unbuttoned one too many. I feel as though it's not usual for him, but I get a view of his pecs. They're granite-hard, like the rest of him. Tasting room Sam is crazy. This is how a man should look.

I start to envision the cut vee that leads me to his sandy glistening hair that surrounds his magnificent dick. I flick my eyes in that direction, and he catches me. We both realize that we're kind of staring at each other when Sarah interrupts us again. And I look away quickly as his smile gets dirty and he licks his lips.

"I would have loved to restore them, but there's no reason now that we're selling," Sarah says.

The sun ducks behind a cloud, and Josh's smile disappears. I've seen that negative veil settle over him before. In some ways, I represent the sale. He doesn't want the business, but he doesn't want anyone else to have it. I'm not sure why he wants nothing to do with all of this when clearly, he loves it. It's a part of him. Get that all too well. Someday we should talk about his farm and mine.

Even though I sold my parents' farm, there's a part of me in that soil, no matter what happens to it. I heard part of it is a housing development. Kids now play in grass that will always have a piece of my family and me in it. We belong to the dirt, and that dirt belongs to us. I know why I couldn't stay there, but I'd like to see why he chooses not to stay here. The more he shows me of himself and of the property, the more I see that it's possible that 'Santa Barbara Joshua' is a façade.

He becomes abrupt and says, "Doesn't matter. Let's go. Just thought you'd want to use the story for marketing. I have a shit ton to do, let's go."

Sarah reaches her hand to help me off the ground as Josh stomps back to the Jeep. I want to change Sarah's mind about renovating. It seems to mean something to Josh as well.

"Sarah?"

"Yes, dear."

"You have the means and the vision, why not do some of the buildings like a parting gift? You don't give up on anything, why this?"

"It's a lot of work. And I'm tired a little too often lately. I'd rather spend my energy with Josh, Will, and my friends."

I remind her, "It could be beautiful. I'll help."

She touches my cheek. "I'll think about it. We do have the permits, materials, and supplies. We'd need labor."

She yells after Josh. "Honey, can you send your father up to get me in about an hour? I want to hike around a bit."

I panic. "Are you sure, Sarah?"

"Absolutely. Today is a good day, Elle, thank you for asking. And I want Will and I to talk about the buildings."

I breathe a sigh of relief that she feels strong today. She hugs me tightly and says, "Thanks for reminding me that we haven't sold just yet. And that I'm not done for, yet."

Will is going to be pissed at us that we left her up here all alone, but she's too headstrong. Josh seems oblivious to the health concerns of a woman with Parkinson's left up on a mountain by herself but whatever.

His chiseled chin taunts me. I want to grab it and suck on

it right now, but I also want to push him out of the car and make him walk back. It's not my fault they're selling. I text and let Will know where his wife is, and he tells me he'll head right up there. Then I buckle in and stare at that damn chin with a fucking sexy dimple.

"What?"

"Stop being an asshole. It's your parents' decision."

"I can't help but think you had something to do with it."

"How? What are you talking about? They had buyers and paperwork in motion long before I started putting you guys in magazines and all over social media."

"About that. I'm done being your poster boy for the wine country."

"No, you are not, Suit." He's breathing intensely and driving erratically. My head and chest are bouncing every-where. I hold down my boobs as we take a particularly harrowing turn. "Can you slow down please?"

"No."

I plead. "You're making me nervous." He speeds up, and I hold on the bars of the car while we turn on a switchback. "PLEASE."

He glances over to me and shakes his head. Then the car slows down a bit. I breathe a little bit more regularly. Then I smack the shit out of his arm.

"Hey!" He jerks his arm away. "You want me to be more careful driving, then don't hit the driver while I'm doing it."

"You scared the shit out of me on purpose."

He smirks at me and says, "Maybe I like the terror in your eyes."

I roll my eyes and say, "I need a favor."

"Don't you always?"

"You have a photo shoot this afternoon at El Dorado."

"Hmmm. Do I?"

"Oh. No. I'm not joining you there. I'm not sure my

whore ass can ever be seen there again even after all this time."

"We did wreck the room." I laugh at the memory.

My tone softens, and I say, "We were different people."

"Were we?"

I shift the subject slightly. "Did you know we cracked the headboard, chipped the sink, broke a chair leg and shredded the sheets and mattress pad? I'm not even sure how the hell we did that one."

"You paid for the repairs?"

"Of course."

"You paid to have sex with me." He needs to stop referencing that night.

"Jackass."

"It's my fatal flaw."

I know exactly who told him that. "Sarah told me that mine is being too in control. I find it endearing."

"A controlling bitch and a jackass. We're a match made in hell." I laugh at the thought.

I defer back to his schedule. "You'll be in the pool with a glass of wine and a bimbo showing people the good life."

"Now, that I can get behind. Hey!" He reacts as I hit him again. He says in a deeper tone of voice, "I know it's not your fault. But you're here actively helping them sell this place. I can't wrap my head around how I feel about that or lots of things these days."

"Someday I'm going to need for you tell me what the fuck it is that bothers you since you've been all but absent from this place for almost a decade. There's more to your grandfather's stories, aren't there?"

"That will require lots more wine and some stars. "

"I happen to know where we might be able to find some."

"When I get back."

CHAPTER FORTY-TWO

JOSH

SHE QUICKLY ASKS, "WHERE ARE YOU GOING?"

Her voice pleading with me makes me realize that more than anything, I don't want to leave her side. I don't want other men looking at her without me around. I don't want to miss out on saying goodnight to her or good morning. But if I miss this week, my career is done. I'm only going home to get this deal done. No other fucking work matters.

"I'm headed to work right after your photo shoot."

"Now? You have to start telling me things!" She's standing on the other side of the Jeep demanding to approve my schedule.

I ask earnestly, "You want to know about where I am?"

"Yes!" Her face reacts to how intimate that statement is. She instantly blushes with embarrassment. Her skin telegraphs each mood and feeling. I'm starting to know which shade is what.

"Then you'll just have to go to New York. Go today."

"Because I can so afford a last-minute ticket." She rolls her eyes at me.

I pull out my phone. "When do you want to come back?"

Her jaw drops. "Don't. You don't have to do that."

"Leave this afternoon. It's Sunday, traffic will be light to the airport. Let me skip the photo shoot, and I'll go with you to the airport. Then I'll meet you back here on Friday." If she's occupied for the week, I won't miss out on anything. "You know this is a good plan, Cosmo."

Elle's eyes are wide as I keep my phone out. She asks sweetly, "Do you have another lockdown week?" She's still talking to me across the Jeep, afraid to get closer. I can see her hands fidget. And a smile breaks across her face and I know I have her.

"Yes, Cosmo, a lockdown week. But you can tend to your messy New York desk. John's sending you a ticket. Consider it my apology for not telling you I was going sooner. Meet me back here in two hours, and we'll take a car."

She simply stares at me with a ridiculous grin, shaking her head in disbelief. I like keeping her guessing. I return the smile, and we just stare at each other like moony-faced morons. We've just made our first joint plans, and it's not lost on either of us. They may not actually be together, but they are in tandem.

Then she walks away towards the Farmhouse. She doesn't look back as she yells, "You're watching my ass, aren't you?"

"Fuck yeah, I am."

"Good."

I see her skip a bit into the Farmhouse, I assume to pack. This week is going to suck.

CHAPTER FORTY-THREE

ELLE

"I GOTTA SAY, MY LOVE, IT'S FUCKING STRANGE TO SEE YOU AT that desk. And as power-hungry as I am, I adore it."

"I missed you, Evan."

I haven't really been in my office in three and a half months. Evan is set up on my office couch. This is exactly how we used to work when I started in this business. We were paired early in my career, and he would just plop down across me, and we'd work. Sometimes in silence or talking through things as we went along. He's the other half of me business-wise and pretty much the only person I trust in the world.

I did pull in a shit ton of business to justify my extended California vacay. But my office is foreign to me. I use LC/W as a base of operations now, but I think I might want to open a branch office and get out of the winery. Sarah said they know a lawyer that might be able to help me out with the practicalities of getting a California business license. I might hang a small West Coast shingle.

"I love seeing your face. But you're in jeans. And are those Adidas?"

"Yup, limited edition."

"At least tell me they're designer jeans?"

"Lafayette 148 New York."

"Thank god you're still you. The sneakers are the strangest. Don't they make at least a wedge?"

Not sure which girl I am. But I'm not so sure I miss all the makeup and maintenance. My nails are bare right now. I don't think they've been naked in a decade. Maybe I'm both of them. Both Noelle and Elle. Time will tell.

Evan and I laugh a lot over the morning's business. Then he hauls in most of the creative team so we can hammer out a schedule. They all call it 'pitches and problems.' Evan and I secretly call it sitches and bitches. It's a moment for the staff to be heard, but it can get bogged down in annoying petty shit. My mind drifts as someone complains about the quality of copier paper and how it doesn't have an accurate Pantone read.

Before I left on Sunday, I sat down with Sarah and Will and scheduled the revitalization of the Longhouse and the Lookout. They started construction today, and it's where my head is dwelling. I got them a double crew and paid for overtime myself. I won't tell them I paid but I want it done quickly. My gift to them for taking in a stray. I pulled some strings with a decorator friend of mine in San Francisco to get the building sites inspected first thing this morning. I want to give this to them. In exchange for all the kindness and housing they've given to me.

Will got all the permits and materials to surprise Sarah nine months ago. He'd gotten far enough in the projects that they were plumbed, wired, and inspected, but they dropped them cold for the exact reason I thought, the diagnosis. But everything is there to finish at least three of the buildings. Two of them might be almost done by the end of this week.

Evan pulls me back to my reality. "Do you like the blue? Hello?!"

"Yeah. I do." I mean nothing I'm saying. I'm so distracted by the other life that I've apparently been building.

It's two hard and productive days. After some client drinks, I head back to my apartment. It's Tuesday and tomorrow I have a ton of meetings during the day. It will be dizzying. I forgot how draining meeting after meeting could be. And without running up and down the hills to the tasting room or picking up wine boxes, I remember why I used to work out so often. I've replaced spin class with hauling wine boxes and hiking the vineyard. I'm antsy. I have extra energy without the manual labor. I forgot how sitting all day long can take a toll on you.

I stop at a liquor store on my way home and discover that the wine I like is freaking expensive outside of the immediate Sonoma area. I buy LC/W Merlot and Langerford Chardonnay. I've never told anyone that it's my Chardonnay of choice, given that it's a rival winery. But I have met Theresa Langerford, Sarah's friend, and she is blunt and wonderful. And I did have that chance encounter with one of her sons, Jims at Della Santina's. I could just tell people I'm supporting the Valley as a whole.

I open my front door, and there are no stars, no one waiting, no leftovers in the fridge, just my flawlessly manicured home. My deep blue velvet tufted couch sits perfectly positioned with a shell pink woven throw just waiting for me. I have two beige chairs with blue velvet pillows that match the couch on them. Then there's a splash of bright green on the rug that gets picked up in the wallpaper in my powder room. I keep that door a tiny bit cracked so the green can harmonize. Good lord, Melissa was right. This is all way too planned. All my artwork matches the exact hue of the couch and bathroom paint.

My bedroom is shell pink and black with a touch of Tiffany box blue. My shower curtain in my bathroom and the blotter on my desk are also Tiffany blue. I sit there dumbfounded at the matchy matchyness of my home. I pull a cork and start going through my mail. I look at the coffee table. I instinctively got out two glasses. Guess I was getting used to someone being there at the end of the day.

ELLE: Everything feels foreign here. I'm not sure who to be.

JOSH: I'm sure it's a lot. You okay?

ELLE: Yes, but it's like I don't belong in California and I don't belong here anymore.

JOSH: Babe, I'm swamped. I do want to hear all of this. You know, I do. But I can't right now. Email it to me, and I'll read it before I fall asleep. I promise, my Hellcat.

I sit straight up and toss my phone on a chair nearby like it's searing hot. Did Josh just call me Babe!? And when did I become his? I have to let it go but holy shit. Can't. Did he just call me Babe and respond with a reason why he can't talk? That's not friend behavior, that's a term of endearment followed by accountability. I hear another text across the room and look anyway.

SAMANTHA: When are you coming home?

Sitting in my apartment in the city that's been a part of me for so long, I feel my entire body relax at Sam's word, *home*. This is my perfect furniture. I searched for close to a year for my prewar apartment. My ideal neighborhood. This is the perfect life I dreamed of as a little girl. And it's not home. I'm proud that I'm bold enough to face the truth. Oprah would be proud because I'm going to stand in it.

ELLE: Tomorrow.

CHAPTER FORTY-FOUR

ELLE

I NEVER ANSWERED HIS TEXT, AND THERE HAVE BEEN NO PHONE calls. But after sixty-six hours in Manhattan and feeling vaguely suffocated, I changed my plane ticket. Instead of sitting in meetings, I spent the next couple of days decorating the new buildings. They were completed in record time. Evan was in charge of my company all along. We chatted before I left about a possible West Coast office. It has been an incredibly interesting five days since I've spoken to Josh.

The buildings are magnificent. They were much further along than we thought. I can't wait for Josh to see them. If he's still coming up. He said we'd meet here on Friday, but I haven't heard from him. I should call, but the 'Babe' freaked me the fuck out. I need to distance myself a bit and figure out what to do with him. Or figure out a way to push past my fear and see if he wants to move forward.

I have to run out to the Longhouse and finish loading the new mini fridge with water and some amenities should someone find their way out to this sanctuary. Sarah actually had a small function out there today with the Salute to the

Arts committee. My friend Poppy catered the luncheon for her. I want to get out there before she leaves to say hello.

It's in the middle of the woods and feels like another world. There's still work to be done on the mini-warehouse that will house all the extra ATV parts and crap that currently litters their garage up at the Farmhouse.

They also want to build out another one to store unsellable palates of wine. The tops and tails of a bottling, for quality assurance they don't sell the beginning or the end of a run of bottling. They give it away, or the employees buy it at a deep discount. But mostly it's just to have around. I went into San Francisco for the lighting fixtures and small deco pieces, calling in a few more favors from the designer who redid my offices in New York.

I arrive at Longhouse, and it looks like I've just missed Sarah and company, but Poppy's is still here.

"Poppy!" We're getting closer, but I really like her more every time I see her.

She hugs me and says, "Elle. I thought you were in New York?"

"Came back early. How did it go out here?"

She's bubbly and bright. Her red hair bouncing with excitement when she speaks. "It's so good out here. You thought of everything to help a caterer make this place work really well. I'm just wrapping up now. I'll clean up and get on my way. Have you eaten?"

"Sadly, yes. But is your restaurant open tonight?"

"It is. Come by for a drink. I got some wonderful mussels and oysters in today. Not sure what I'm going to do with them yet, but they'll be delicious."

She's the best chef. She does this kind of high-end comfort food thing I can't get enough of. I eat there all the time. "Done. I can't wait. Hey, can you do me a quick favor and stick some of these water bottles I just brought into the fridge? Just to replace what they drank."

"Of course. I'll see you tonight."

"Thank you. You're my favorite person today. I need to book back to the tasting room."

I skid Josh's Jeep into the tasting room parking lot and jump out. My breath leaves my body, and there's a thrilling cold sensation overtaking me. He's wiping his brow with his t-shirt that he apparently just removed. This view should come with a warning label. Josh is back. And then I become panic-stricken that I'm in nasty shorts, a dirty LC/W t-shirt, and a crazy high ponytail. I try to fix it before he sees me, but I can't stop staring at his rippled back.

Randy, the tasting room manager, looks thrilled with this Josh show as well. He's in his running shorts. Did he work out? How long has he been here? I've been in heavy prep mode for the upcoming Winery event and putting the finishing touches on the outbuildings. I approach them and Randy's talking.

"Tell me you'll be here tomorrow night?"

"Yes. I'll be here." Josh answers.

"Because she…"

Randy points to me. Josh's head whips around, and an enormous fucking smile overtakes his face. I'm instantly light-headed as his eyes rake over every inch of me. I feel them. Randy hates me. Josh does not.

Randy continues babbling while Josh stares at me, walking towards him. "She sent your parents down to the city to glad-hand at some event. We need family here for our party. Not usurpers."

I hear all of this as I walk back past them and into the tasting room. I keep walking, so I don't mount this man. Fuck. A booming voice that rumbles in my nether regions and instantly soaks my thong calls after me as if he's simply having a conversation. But he's mocking me.

"DON'T WORRY, ELLE WILL BE THERE TO HANDLE ANY AND ALL CONCERNS AND QUESTIONS THAT OUR WINE CLUB MEMBERS MIGHT HAVE. AND SHE'LL BE WEARING A THEMED OUTFIT TOO. TROP-ICAL THEME, IS IT? LET'S GET LEI'D."

Without turning around, I put my middle finger up in the air. Of course, I'll be at the event. I planned the damn thing. But I'm not quite dressing in theme.

I hear Josh again. "YOU CAN'T DO THAT TO THE BOSS."

I scream back without looking. "YOU'RE NOT MY BOSS!"

CHAPTER FORTY-FIVE

JOSH

I'm grabbing a linen shirt from my car to chase her down when a massive amount of noise takes over the property. Everyone begins to gather. I have been in town exactly five hours. Apparently, that's too long. There's a helicopter landing on the road that leads up to the Farmhouse. I know exactly who it is and what's going to happen. I'm about to get a lashing. I've left the office, god forbid. Then I ignored the wrong email and a phone call this morning.

"Everyone, it's fine. Go back to work. He's here to talk to me. It's just a client."

Elle has reappeared, and I need to get her away from this guy. There's no need for them to know each other. She begins to step to me, and I commandingly say, "Elle, go back inside *now*, please."

I have no clue what the hell he's doing here. I wrapped up a ton of business for him in the past month. He should be more than fine.

He's a massive man at six-foot-five with coal dark hair cropped to his head, dark chocolate eyes and biceps that can and routinely do crush walnuts. I stroll towards this man in his ten-thousand-dollar, custom-made suit as the dust from my family's dirt road kicks up around him. As my worlds collide, I see Elle watching as she heads up to the Cooperage from the tasting room. I wave her off. I don't want him anywhere near her or my family despite my affection for him.

"Joshie! Joshie! Joshie!"

I rush to him with outstretched arms. "Sal! What the *hell* are you doing here? And you couldn't be a little more discreet about your arrival, asshole?"

"Mohamed, mountain. You get that shit, right? First time in ten years you don't answer a fucking email. And you ignored a call. I came to check out this new set of giant balls you've found. I think I can see them in your gym shorts."

Fuck him. At least I have on an oxford. I run my hand over my hair to slick it back a bit. It's shaggy lately, but I haven't had a chance to get it cut.

Sal looks at me very directly. "Is there someplace we could talk?"

"If you're willing to get on an ATV in that outfit, then yes."

"Hell yeah." He whips off his suit jacket and flings it at the even taller, beefier, and well-armed man standing behind him. Then he hands him his holster and gun. I didn't know if he carried one or not, but fuck me this is strange. Fortunately, I've never seen it. He waves his security off, and I shrug to the gathered crowd.

On ATVs I get out of our garage, we wind and twist through the old paths that lead to the Longhouse. My friends and I used it as a broken-down fort when we'd play Army growing up. The trails, although overgrown, are the same as in my memory, but the fort is not. Longhouse is now modern and designed with gatherings in mind.

It takes my breath away. Holy shit, this is amazing. Seventeen-foot floor-to-ceiling glass windows line the sides of the building. It highlights the landscape, and the vaulted ceiling's exposed beams have been stained a rustic reddish brown. There's an extremely long and large oak table that spans the building. I hear someone rustling from the back of the building and there's scattered dishes around the table.

"Hello!" someone squeaks from the back.

"It's Josh. Who's here?"

"Ah! Fuck. Me, Josh. You scared me. I'm just cleaning up your mom's luncheon."

"Poppy Gelbert!"

I cross the room quickly. Sal hangs back as he observes me, greeting my old friend. I haven't seen her in forever. After we hug, she unleashes her long red curls from a green and white flowered headscarf. They cascade down her back and her dark brown eyes narrow as she spies Sal in the corner. She's about the same height as Elle but without her curves. She's got a delicate doll appearance to her. But don't let her sweet and kind exterior fool you, she's a slow burn. She'll take teasing, but only to a point, then she lives up to the clique of a redhead temper. She's also the first one to show up if you need help with anything.

Her mom, Tina, is one of my Mom's closest friends. She was eighteen months old when she and her Mom showed up in Sonoma at their family winery. Her father has never come looking for them. She goes by her mother's maiden name. She discarded her father's long ago. Both of them did. She became our little sister. She's the same age as Jims Langerford and Tommi Schroeder. She's one of my gang from growing up. The chosen cousins, as Elle called them that first night.

Poppy calls across the room in her feminine lilting voice, "Who's the giant brooding in the corner? Hey, broody! You hungry? I know this one always is."

I rub my hands together and say, "Seriously, you have extra?"

Sal approaches, and I do introductions. "Poppy Gelbert, this is Salvatore Pietro. He's a client of mine from Santa Barbara. I've known Poppy since we were both in diapers running through the vines. She's a chef who owns a cafe in town."

"It's hardly a cafe. I mostly cater. There's a smattering of tables and a tiny bar."

"Come on, Pop. The food's awesome."

"That I'll give you. I cook a hell of a ziti if you're interested?"

Sal takes her hand and holds it with both of his. His usually hard features soften when he looks at her. He literally towers over her. He's only two years older than I am, but I always feel as if he looks more adult somehow.

Poppy looks flattered as he approaches her. They're quite the contrasting couple to look at. Not that Poppy would ever go for a guy like Sal. All her boyfriends have been of the insurance salesman variety and most of them with glasses and sweater vests. Where she's light and lithe, he's hulking, and with his deep Mediterranean coloring, they look like polar opposites of each other.

And then he pulls her delicate hand to his lips and kisses. "Well, I'm completely charmed. And you say there's ziti too. This day just got fucking perfect. Will you join us?"

Poppy blushes a bit. What the fuck? Don't blush at the almost ex-mobster. Don't do that, Poppy. I have enough on my plate; I don't need to keep Poppy safe from this man as well.

She says, "I need to get back to the shop, but let me grab you some stuff. I was just loading the dishwasher."

"Dishwasher. Jesus, Mom did a good job out here."

"You know full well who thought of the dishwasher. She

kind of thinks of everything." I know she means Elle. Of course, she knows Elle.

"So, you've met her?"

"She's coming by for a glass tonight. I like her a lot. We've become friends. And thank God you fixed that colossal screw up with her clients. I was about to go full Tina on your ass." I roll my eyes. Tina, Poppy's Mom is not one to be trifled with. She's the one who put all the teacher's in their place, kept the gang of us in line and always gets a refund for bad customer service. She's a fierce single Mom. She and Poppy are thick as thieves. She dishes up our lunch. She continues speaking, "Here you go. I have to run. Josh, are you here for the thing this weekend?"

I say, "Yes. You coming by?"

Poppy smiles and answers, "After I close up, for sure. I think almost all of us will be here."

"Jesus, really?" I can't imagine seeing all of my group of friends at once. I've been out of it for so long.

She pops her head back into the main room from the little alcove in the back. "You're usually the missing piece, but yeah, the stars seem to be aligned. Except Baxter, I think he's in DC this week." She turns to Sal. "It was nice to meet you."

Sal takes a big bite. "This is as good as I know a red sauce can be. And damn, tiny woman, you can cook."

Poppy kind of stumbles over her words, "Thanks, giant man. You know it's just... I don't know tomatoes and..." She's juggling chafing dishes and a platter. Sal jumps up and takes them from her.

Sal speaks, "It's delicious. And it's a delight to meet you. Can I put these in your car?"

Poppy says brightly, "Thanks."

Sal exits, and she crosses to me and squeezes me again. "There's everything you need in the back. My girl's got Sonoma lifestyle on lock. Go back and see for yourself."

"You're that friendly with Elle?"

"I adore her. She comes in a couple times a week to eat or hang out." I had no idea she was friends with anyone from my past. I wander back to the little kitchen area and start opening cabinets. There's a subzero fridge and a dishwasher.

"I mean there's even salami and cheese in the freezer should you want to put out an instant cheese plate. And there are gorgeous ceramic plates, platters, and mugs."

I pick up a mug and smile. My mother made them at the Community Center in their pottery studio. They're so cool and completely her style with her little hand drawn butterfly on the bottom. She used to draw it on my sack lunch bags "Okay, Pop. Thanks for the food. I'll see you this weekend." I kiss her on her cheek, and she leaves. I open a Syrah, putting a couple of glasses on the table.

Sal rejoins me and sits back down, swirls and sips. "That is some damn good vino."

"I already know that. What I don't know is why you're here, my friend." I sip the wine. It is fucking good.

"Joshua LaChappelle, we've been through some shit, haven't we?"

"We have. And it's Whittier."

"You know I got your back, right?" Sal shoves more food into his mouth. It must take a truckload of pasta to keep him that bulked up and muscled.

I don't know where he's going with this. "I do. But I also know we've always been straight with each other."

"It's one of the things I like best about you, Josh. Do you know you're probably my only friend who has zero ties to the families or the neighborhoods? And the only person outside of that collective that I trust."

I laugh at the realization. All my trusted friends come from winery families so I know what he means. I have people who think they're my friends in Santa Barbara, but I don't really trust them. It's odd how parallel our worlds can be.

I say to him, "You might be that for me as well, sir. Sal, you might come back for Poppy's ziti, but you didn't come here for that. So why the hell are you here?"

"Because you're here. Joshua. I emailed. I called, and then I flew up and went to your office and you were gone. I don't trust easily. This should not be news. I can't and won't work with your associates. I know you got issues here. And I looked into the sale."

"You can't purchase us. For many reasons."

"I know. I remember everything you tell me. I know the rules. No liquor, no firearms, no tobacco, no dispensaries, nothing that would draw attention. But why aren't you brokering this sale and then getting the hell out of here?"

"Because my parents wanted me to stay out of it. So I'm here to kind of…"

"To babysit the blonde." I swallow hard. Don't fuck with Elle.

"What blonde?"

"I make it a point to know everything about everything. She's a shrewd little act you're coveting. Parker & Co. is on track to crack eleven million gross this year. She's no joke. And your dick likes her."

I don't like that he knows anything about her. Also, I didn't realize she was that good. I suspected but didn't know the hard figure. "You let me worry about my cock."

Sal leans forward. "It's your balls I want to discuss. Not calling me back. She gave you those or you just borrowed hers?"

"Trust me. She's of no concern to me, so remove her from your radar."

"Don't ever play poker, Whittier. You need to drop the

idea of her. She's a shark that will swallow you whole. You need to get back to Santa Barbara where you belong."

I adjust my chair. This is a new level of relationship for us. "I was planning on backing off from the business in the lead up to the sale, just after harvest. It's only for a couple of months."

"Bullshit. It's the end of June. You're going to stay in this fucking cowtown until October?"

I scramble because I think a threat might be on the way. "I'll work from here. I won't ignore you again. I've just gotten caught up..."

"Swept up in this family business? I know the feeling." He puts down his silverware and sips his wine. He gestures to me with the glass, and I fill it a little more. "Joshua, when you get bogged down with family and women, you lose focus, and you'll get burned. You get burned, and I get fucking screwed. And I don't get screwed unless it's by that sweet little gingersnap that was here earlier."

"Don't you even joke about Poppy like that."

"I'm just saying I like her. I'm not going near her. No worries. I'm too busy for personal pursuits, and you should be too."

"It's not like that. Elle and I are nothing. She's not my type, she just irks me."

"Those are the dangerous ones. I need your focus, go fuck a nobody. You're backed up. And you need to leave Noelle alone."

Her name sounds like acid coming out of his mouth. "My dick is fine, thanks. Worry about your own."

Another lie. My cock does need to be serviced. It needs to be buried in Elle's sweet pussy or mouth soon. I want all of her. Shit. I need to fuck Elle soon. I haven't been with anyone in months.

"My cock is fine. I don't do attachments so no one gets hurt."

"Never a girlfriend?" I ask realizing I've never heard him talk about a particular woman."

"No one of consequence. Let's just say, in my business, the women get left, cheated on, or occasionally meet unfortunate days. There's never been anyone that I needed that was worth the risk to me or her. So, no. It's a good philosophy, Josh. You should get back to fucking supermodels to get your shit off."

"Thanks." I brush off his advice. I need off this topic. This man has no attachments that I can think of that he wouldn't sacrifice. So would he respect mine? I don't like him here in my space. I don't want him here putting faces and names into context for him.

"Now Joshie, where am I putting this eight I got burning a hole in my pocket?"

I force a laugh at this odd business meeting. Eight. Sal's numbers are increasing as well as his neediness. I pull out my phone, and I'm shocked we have decent Wi-Fi. She thinks of everything. I scroll and pull up this luxury boutique California hotel chain that I was starting to work on when I left Santa Barbara this morning. I slide my phone to him.

"Might take more than eight to play in this sandbox. The company might expand to Florida after this as well. Get in now, and it could be a good thing for you."

He bellows a giant dark laugh and lights the cigar. "There you are! Send me the prospectus. I'm about to get bought out of a decades-old sanitation deal and need to put the scratch somewhere. Should be enough to play. Next couple of weeks are dicey, and I don't need a single hair out of place. I don't have time to chase your fucking ass around the fucking state. We'll be so busy you won't see the light of day. Get a bunch of shit ready for me to unload large sums quickly."

He slaps me on the shoulder, and I sip my wine, well aware that he just vaguely threatened me for the first time in our relationship. We finish the bottle then ride back to his chopper. I shake his hand, and he pulls me into an embrace.

He says sternly in my ear, so I don't miss it. "You'll be back in the office just after that party."

I back up, cross my arms, and ask, "What party?"

"The Wine Club people party. The fucking tiki party happening here."

"You should keep my calendar."

"Your assistant is for shit, you know. No sexy voice on the other end when I call. Who has a male assistant?"

"Someone not looking to bang their secretary. But John does have a sexy voice if you listen." Sal laughs loudly.

"You'll be there. In your office when I call. No excuse and no second chances."

I'm not afraid of him, but I am getting pissed off. "Salvatore, I'll get a plan together and be there next week sometime."

And then his entire demeanor shifts. There's a chill coming off him. And I'm faced with something I knew would rear its ugly head someday. The money was just too good, and I should have ditched him long ago. Shit.

"The nice part of our visit is over. No fucking way. You do as I say, Josh."

He's clearly unaware of how big my balls really are. "Or what? You're going to threaten me? I work with you, not for you."

"It's a good little set up your family's got here. And that sweet little cunt you've been chasing. They seem like good people. They don't need any hassles or accidents."

"Are you fucking kidding right now? What the fuck are you doing? This isn't who we are to each other. I'm not a lackey. You don't fuck with me like this."

I am full of rage at a veiled threat at my family and Elle. I want to rip the man apart, and now I'm screwed. Fucked in the ass by this capo cocksucker.

I will figure a way out of this before it gets too fucking deep. Shit. Maybe I should get to know more about him. I need to know his business as well as he knows mine. I've had a 'don't ask, don't tell' attitude up until now.

His voice is gruff and resonates in the air, "I got shit, Josh. A ton of it raining down on me right now. You're my shit umbrella, Joshie. I gotta get out of it, and you are the one I need to fix it. I'll do whatever I can to protect my family, and you'll do whatever I need you to do to protect yours. Get your ass back home after that party. No more fucking around Josh. You fucking get me? Do *we* have an understanding? You help me fix shit for my family, and yours stays out of all of this."

There must be some legal pressure on him, so he's putting pressure on me. Nobody tells me what the fuck to do. I step to him, and we're eye to eye. I don't blink, and I don't fuck around.

"I will go back to my office in a timely manner. But listen to me, hood. Don't you ever fucking even hint a threat in my direction again. I will break ties with you so fast your head will spin. And although I don't know where the bodies are, I certainly know where you buried the profits. I have people too."

"Big man talking. No need for name-calling, Joshie."

He straightens up in my face, and I don't blink but continue speaking. "I don't owe you a muthafucking thing, thug. You want my trust and loyalty? It goes both ways. You watch your tone with me. Don't ever come back here. And don't ever, ever fucking summon me again. Take your money moroned helicopter and get the fuck off my family's property."

We stand there, nose to nose, and the hulk in the background reaches for his chest. Without breaking eye contact, Sal waves him off. The man's hand returns to his side. I hate that he brought this to LaChappelle/Whittier.

"You're the kind of guy I like, but this is beyond me, Josh. My hands are tied. I will make this right by you someday. But for now, you do what I tell you to do when I fucking tell you. And everyone wins. I'll be in your office in two days, and so help Blondie if you're not."

I back up and outstretch my hand, he takes it and pulls me into an embrace. We slap each other's backs, and I'll only exhale as soon as he takes off.

"My back is up against all the walls. I have no choice, Josh."

"Then I guess I don't either. But know that you've taken us to a different place. One we can't come back from."

"So be it."

"So be it? You're a fucking son of a bitch."

"You don't know the fucking half of it, Joshie. You're lucky I still like you."

I don't want to be likable. I want away from him. He will fucking pay for his threats.

CHAPTER FORTY-SIX

ELLE

I've double-checked all of the details, and I think we're ready for tonight. I'm standing in the kitchen with Sarah; she's giving last-minute orders into the intercom. "Well, then let's make this one hell of a party, shall we?"

"You know you're going to the city for dinner with the potential buyers, right? You and the four wineries that they're thinking of buying. You have to go now. There's a car waiting."

"I do know this. Have fun with Josh. I can't believe he came back up here."

I sip the end of my water bottle and smile at her. She's so thrilled he's in their lives again. "I think he likes being around the two of you more now."

Sarah says, "Sweet girl. I'd guess it has very little to do with us."

My stomach flips. She disappears out the back door as I head upstairs to get ready for this insane party that apparently is the favorite of the season around here.

Josh is at the top of the stairs, looking stressed but still impossibly handsome in cargo shorts and an athletic fitting tank top. Damn those are some good arms. I want to bite his biceps, but I restrain myself. His look is sour as he stares at his phone. He doesn't notice I'm down the hallway.

I startle him. "Who do I need to kill?"

He looks up and smiles. "What?"

"Who made your face look like that?"

"Research. I need information. I'm not sure how to get it."

I walk to him and put my hand on his bicep. I almost swoon but collect myself. "I'm excellent at research. Try me."

"I think this is beyond both of us. Kind of an underground shit thing."

"Cool. Like secret research? I got that on lock too. I have a hook up for you."

"What are you talking about?"

"Dark web? CIA hack? I got a guy. Well, a girl."

"No, you don't. I have friends who can help." He rolls his eyes at me. I can't wait to prove him wrong. I do know someone. She said she'd be there if I needed her. I just never knew I'd need a hacker.

"Trust me. You want her?"

"How?"

"Give me your phone." I tap out an email from him to me, and the subject says, *Melissa!* The body says:

Mel,

This is Josh and his email. He needs you to work your magic. I trust him like I trust my favorite flaw. I don't know what it's for.

Hoping your underwear is clean,

-Noelle

"How does that help?"

"She reads my email. But she reads the ones sent to me faster. She finds the ones I write boring." I shrug. She sent me an email a while back just checking in on me and wondering why I was in California. I told her what was going on, and she told me about how she usually reads my incoming mailbox rather than my outgoing.

"And you let her?"

"I can't stop her. But if you meet her, she likes guacamole. A lot."

I turn tail and close my door to get ready as his mouth stays open in surprise.

CHAPTER FORTY-SEVEN

JOSH

WITHIN TWENTY MINUTES, THIS MYSTERY MELISSA TEXTED ME a number, date, and time to contact her. She did it all without ever getting my phone number. Then there's a message for Noelle that says:

BLOCKED NUMBER: Tell Noelle to be careful with her email. Flaws are everywhere.

It's a call set for four days from now. How does Elle know a hacker? Is she a spy? What the hell does her message mean?

A FILM CREW and a photographer show up, and she has yet to come down to the tasting room and barn areas. This year it's a coconut bra themed party is all set up in and out of the tasting room. On the other side of the cave, there's a large field. The cave is essentially a tunnel that leads out there from the courtyard. Elle has set up dinner on the opposite side of the courtyard through the cave. She's set up the courtyard for the cocktail hour, and then it will turn into the dance floor while everyone is on the other side eating dinner.

I look like an idiot, but it's for the good of the winery. The staff convinced me to wear Jams and a Hawaiian shirt.

My dad loves these parties, I've always hated them. I hated theme parties at college. The irony is, I'd like to be in a suit glad-handing at a swank restaurant in the city, and he'd rather be here talking about the wine and doing the limbo with some of our favorite customers. But Elle is here, so I'm here. Tonight's the night she won't say no.

Some of the wine club members have been with us for decades. I've known them since I was little. Should be an interesting evening, especially with the bulk of my childhood crew in attendance. I move tables around and help string lights. It's an all-hands-on-deck situation except for Princess Elle who has yet to report for duty.

I hustle to the cave tasting room. It's basically a winery conference room. A long table surrounded by wine and barrels. I'm setting up a legacy vertical tasting in there for some high-end wine club members, those who order a large number of cases a year. The bottles need to breathe. When I emerge, Elle is stepping around the stone, dark wood building that houses the commercial tasting room. She's stunning in a floaty white dress with large bright flowers. Her sunshine hair is twisted up and playing off the blue flowers on the dress. Her eyes, in contrast, are sparkling like the most perfect emeralds. Her peaches-and-cream skin is radiant as the sun begins to set and gives everything that golden glow. It brings out the gold in her eyes. I can see it from here.

She's looking around but doesn't see me staring. Probably a good thing because I just had to close my mouth hanging open. The dress skims the tops of her knees, and if she bent over, I'd pay someone to kick up a breeze. She's pointing to different pieces of furniture and moving them around much to the chagrin of Randy. He had a vision for the cocktail hour seating nooks, hers is better. The entire courtyard now flows and looks like a high-end nightclub. She runs away and returns with several giant bags from World Plus Market and hands them to some employees. They begin arranging tropical throw pillows on the couches and chairs at her command. Suddenly all of this seems custom instead of rented. Then she pulls out these small colorful paper cups similar to cupcake pa that she has the staff place over each individual light on the main string that runs around the entrance to the party.

She's the queen of the tweak. Of seeing what one more little thing can make something perfect. I've seen her doing this by adding one more sentence to a paragraph to a statement or email. I've also seen her angling one bottle towards the light or raising them up a small bit in the merchandise area. I've even seen her add one more piece of jewelry, from her own neck to my mother's outfit to make it perfect. She cares so much about the small and the large. Then she crooks her finger and beckons me.

"Yes?" I land in front of her.

She bites her bottom lip, and I want that lip. She says, "Can you do me a huge favor?"

I cross my arms. That's the phrase she uses to get anyone to do anything. Another amazing feature of this captivating and infuriating woman. "What?"

"Like two things."

"One."

"But Josh, I really need your help with this." She bats her damn eyelashes at me. But it's the thought of her ruby red glossed and painted lips that grab my attention.

"It's not enough that I set this entire courtyard up to your specifications while you were applying makeup?"

"I'm the beauty, and you're the beast. Look, can you not fight with Asher tonight?"

"Damn fucking straight I'm the beast. Wait, what?"

She glares at me and says, "You heard me."

"Who invited that fuck? Of course, he's coming. He wouldn't miss free food and wine. Are you seeing him again?"

She knows I'm teasing but scolds me anyway. "You know I'm not. I don't want him. I don't want anything to do with him, really. But he's been helpful with the sale, bringing a big prospective buyer to the table and he always shows up if I invite him. Tonight, I promise to make him understand that we're purely professional."

"Don't you find it kind of creepy he wears a big gold signet ring with a dragon on it?"

She rolls her eyes and wobbles her head back and forth. "Okay. Yes. I do. The ring is super weird."

"When we were joking about him the other night, I thought…"

"I feel obligated to him because he introduced me to your parents and then let me stay at his house for a couple of nights. He didn't make it a big deal when I moved in here. I promise this is my last invite to him. Unless I need him at a dinner, and you don't have to be there."

I crooked an eyebrow at her. "Is he your date?"

"Stop it." She shoves me.

I smirk. "Does he think he's you're his date?"

She pops her hip and bites her bottom lip again. Fucking adorable. Those legs perfectly shapely and long considering her height. She's all legs and I want them wrapped around my waist right now. So hot. How can she be both? She's equal parts cute kitten and sexy Hellcat.

She answers, "Maybe?"

"Let me put it this way." I walk very close to her ear as I pass by and whisper. "Is this stunning and sexy as hell dress for him?"

She turns her head to capture my eyes, not backing down. "No. Not him."

Then she grins, walking away from me. That body, that woman, and that sass all drive me out of my mind. Tonight, she finds out she's mine. She's all I think about. Damn, I need a drink. And I don't need wine. I head to the tank rooms to grab a beer and possibly a shot of Hornitos Reposado tequila from the bottle our winemaker hides for her own personal use.

CHAPTER FORTY-EIGHT

ELLE

I DON'T KNOW WHAT HE'S PLAYING AT, BUT THAT LAST SMIDGE of distrust is gone. He nudged his way into my life and heart, and I like him in those places. That knot that usually lives at the base of my belly has untied over the past couple of weeks and been replaced by a bright shiny feeling.

Randy and I meet and greet the first group of guests. We're at Fire Marshall capacity, so we need to keep count and check people into the party. A uniquely beautiful woman with big beachy wavy blondish hair is walking towards us with Wade Howell. His rich chocolate eyes and dark shaggy hair look casual and cool as if nothing could ruffle him. He's a reporter for *the Chronicle*. I invited him to cover the event. He's also written a book I keep meaning to read.

Wade waves as he comes down the hill to the courtyard. He turns slightly to his date as she trips over what appears to be her own grass skirt, and just before she takes a tumble, Wade grabs her elbow and saves her. She holds onto his arms and pulls her grass skirt up as they both laugh.

Randy was halfway up the hill to help but turns back around to me. "That's Meg. She tends to do that. She runs the local film festival. Super funny and fun but a bit of a klutz. Don't give her real stemware. She tends to break things." I hit Randy, and Meg throws herself at him. They hug and giggle.

Wade pulls me into a hug. "Ms. Parker, the pleasure is mine this evening."

"Wade. I'm thrilled you could come." Tonight's a bit humid, and he's wearing a palm tree print button-down underneath the blazer. Always in a blazer. Like it's a super-hero uniform. He's thoroughly entertaining each and every time we cross paths.

I ask, "Is this your wife?"

Wade turns to his companion and motions to me. "Meg, darling, this blonde vision is Noelle Parker. And this is my life companion, Meghan Hannah."

"What he means is I'm his plus one. It's great to meet you, Noelle, was it?"

"You can call me Elle. Are you okay? It seems you tripped."

"Totally fine. That was purely for show and to keep Wade on his toes." Meg winks at me. She is interesting.

Wade's lips curl to the left as he says, "Around this one, I should have permanent pointe toe shoes." She hits him then laughs. I find their relationship intriguing. They seem totally enamored with each other but with zero sexual chemistry.

"Well, go on in and enjoy. I'll catch you later, Wade. Text me if you need me or have any questions. There's sangria floating around, but the good stuff is in the tasting room being poured by Samantha." Wade winks at me and squeezes my shoulder as they turn towards the courtyard. Meg walks away, hiking up her grass skirt again.

"Randy, come find me to dance. See you later, Noelle. I mean Elle!" She yells over her shoulder.

Asher strolls down the hill from the trolley drop at the end of the first batch arrivals. I set up the Trolley to bring people from a more considerable parking lot towards the front of the property. I haven't seen him in almost a month. We text occasionally. I'm aware he wants more from me. My back goes stick straight when I realize he has a tall, thin, and leggy date with him.

She's wearing a gold shimmering mini dress, more Ibiza tiki bar than the cruise ship kitsch that we've set up here. She makes the rest of us look out of place. She has to be a foot taller than I am with the opposite coloring. She has that rich skin tone I envied the Balinese women. Long dark hair that cascades down her delicate back. Her alluring eyes are inky and intriguing, whereas my round green globes are too bright, round and obvious. My chest flushes and my cheeks burn as Asher approaches. She's otherworldly and clearly a decade younger than me and two than Asher. Huh. Maybe he doesn't want more from me.

"Stunning! My darling angel, Noelle, as always, you're stunning."

Asher wraps his arms around me and picks me up slightly like I'm a little girl at a birthday party.

"Asher. Good to see you."

I kiss his cheek slightly, and I see Josh come around the corner. I don't know whether he's jealous or annoyed, but he's staring with laser focus at Asher. Then to me, then to the mysterious dark beauty with the tiniest ass I've ever seen on a human adult.

"Thank you so much for the invite, my soft feather. These parties are always epic."

Did he just call me a soft feather? Every time he just digs himself deeper.

I turn to his date. "Hi. I'm Noelle." She doesn't shake my hand but lifts one arm and half-waves instead. Josh stands to the side and is staring with his mouth open. Duh. Who wouldn't stare at her? Even Randy's staring. I'm wearing stupid strappy wedges, looking chunky and clunky. Somehow my shoes are making me even shorter, and she's in black spike Louboutins. I look like a different species. This is a gazelle, and I'm like a meerkat popping up trying to get everyone's attention.

"Serena, this is Noelle. I was swept up by this stunner last week when I met her in Santa Barbara."

I don't know what to say to his sudden love at first sight. After five months of pursuing me, I find the flip odd, but I did blow him off. And I don't want him. And now I don't know what to say to them. "Santa Barbara. Josh is from there."

"Joshua." She says his name breathy, with a 'z' instead of 'j' sound and with a flick of her lips upwards. It's fucking weird. Like she's making up an exotic accent to go with her look.

I ask her, "Do you know him? Let me grab him."

"No bother, girl. Zosh-ooua always finds me."

Girl?! Then she brushes past me like she's Natasha from Rocky and Bullwinkle. What the hell does that mean? *Zosh-ooua*. He's slipped away from the courtyard. The rest of the senior staff has formed a receiving line, and I give up my place. Mrs. Dotson's already crocked and hugging every person.

I run into the tasting room looking for Josh. Someone needs to hear how strange that scene was. "Where's Josh?" My voice bellows over the room, and Sam points towards the tank rooms. She goes back to pouring after she gives me the intel. Pushing the doors open, I find him and a bunch of the vineyard workers passing around a bottle of tequila. "Dude!" I hurry to him and take the bottle. I take a long pull myself. Much to the joy of the workers who applaud me. "I just had the strangest experience. Wait until you hear this, or did you see?"

"Oh, I saw it." He seems dark and brooding again. The opposite of what his resort wear clothes say to the world.

"I think I'm in the clear with Asher. But she's a bitch. And she towers over me so I don't think I can take her down if she riles up trouble."

"You have no idea how much of a bitch she is."

"She kind of said she knew you. Not so much as knew you but enjoys saying your name strangely." I straighten up as tall as I can and imitate her, "'*Zosh-ooua* will always find me.'" Everyone laughs at my impression except Josh. I bow and do another shot.

He nods and says, "That's Serena."

"I know. That name totally matches her whole Padma Lakshmi vibe. Exotic and stunning."

"She's not stunning." He winks at me, and the corners of my mouth go up. "She's my ex-fiancée."

"Wha?"

CHAPTER FORTY-NINE

JOSH

NOT SURE WHAT THAT MONEY-GRUBBING WHORE IS DOING here or what her angle is, but if she's mixed up with Asher, my guess is it's all calculated. I can't understand what they want from me. I have no skin in this game. The winery is going to sell. I don't get the money. It'll go to my parents. And I'm not sure why Asher cares at all. I know he lives to put us down in some way, but that girl is trouble. A gold-digging piece of problem. And how the hell did he find her? This is no serendipity. He didn't just meet her. Is she here to get me back? Does Asher think it will bother me, or does he want Noelle all to himself? How does Asher know about Elle and me? What shit is he trying to stir? Does he think that if he flaunts her in front of me that I'll lose interest in Elle and he can just have her? She's not a fucking prize to win. Nothing could be farther than the truth.

She interrupts all the questions swirling in my head. The fresh breath of air that is Elle. She asks, "Are you okay? I hadn't planned on this contingent, but I can move around some tables to make sure you're seated far away from her."

I squeeze her hand. Always planning and controlling. I wonder what she's like when she doesn't have a plan or an agenda. "I am. I'm glad you're here."

And then she stuns me by saying, "I'm glad you're here too." We both take another hit of tequila.

I ask, "What's the plan?" Now she's stunned as I give her control.

"I'm going to head back out in a minute. You need to face this. Do you want me to kick them out? I can get Randy to do it. Well, I can't, you can. Randy hates me."

She's babbling, and it's adorable. Serena would sleep with me if I snapped my fingers and all I can do is be enchanted by Elle. I watch as she takes a long pull on the bottle, and it's fucking hot as hell. Serena's black heart is nothing compared to the lightness that radiates from Elle. I am well aware I don't deserve her, but that's not going to stop me from having her.

The only goal Serena and Asher could possibly have is to upset me or get me back together with Serena. They won't get the satisfaction of either. I'm going to drape myself on Elle tonight. Let me see if she'll play my game. It's a cheap move, but it puts me in striking distance while out in the open. She can be safe and dangerous at the same time. I'm going to flip her world upside down tonight.

"Elle. I have a plan. Come find me in like ten minutes. And forgive me for what I'm going to do. But I need for you to roll with it."

She's sitting up on a counter holding court with Jose, the vineyard manager, and crew. They hand her a bottle of beer. Jumping down off the table, she finds a lip to the table and opens the beer without an opener. All the while, not a hair out of place or a spot on her dress. Incredible. She's oblivious to the multitude of openers lying around.

"Sure. Anything you need. Can you do me a favor and make sure the photographer is circulating?"

I nod and head out to find the biggest mistake of my life.

I left, built a life that on paper looked perfect. Serena completed that picture for me. We dated for years. Then after our engagement party, and my parents' stunt, she admitted she knew about the winery all along. I'd never told her. I never shared any part of Sonoma with her. And when I told her I wanted no part of the LaChappelle/Whittier Vineyards, she was gone in a week. Even though I make a shit ton of money, she wanted winery money. She wanted prestige, a fantasy lifestyle, and old school wealth. She has no idea that if you're doing winemaking right, you're knee-deep in muck, not sipping sparkling on a porch. I'm also sure that she has no idea how much money I really have. I'm grateful she was vain and shallow so I didn't end up married to her.

That was a year and a half ago. After Serena, I fucked every hot woman who crossed my path without caring about their names or the day after. Until the El Dorado. Even before I knew Elle's last name, there was a connection I couldn't define. There was a moment where we saw each other for more than what we told ourselves we were. We each believed and felt there was more. We validated each other and healed some wounded buried part of ourselves.

Asher and Serena are chatting with local luminaries as I approach. "Everyone having fun?"

"Zosh-ooua, darling." She leans towards me, and I kiss her cheek. She smells spicy, a smell I used to love, but tonight it smells heavy and out of place. Almost acrid. Funny what time and distance can do.

"Serena. Such a surprise to see you here. At my family's vineyard."

"Asher."

Her annoying habit of using as few words as possible

comes back to me in a flash. She's the opposite of Elle, who uses way too many words. Asher puts his hand out to me.

"Joshie, good to see you. I had no idea you two were acquainted."

I hate that name. Pretty sure he knows that. He's greasy and dripping with lies. Serena has no idea he's not wealthy. I have no problem letting her think that he is.

I say, "That makes it even funnier."

"What does?"

"That you're picking up my sloppy seconds." I try to take him down a bit, but he gets me back.

Asher retorts, "Takes one to know one."

He nods over my shoulder, and I know Elle's behind me. I want to fucking rip his head off for being that demeaning to her. Serena deserves it, Elle does not. At least I know he's terrible in bed.

I need Elle to save me, but I only hope she doesn't freak for what I'm about to do. I never know how she'll react to something. When she's lovely, I think she's purring, but she can turn on a dime and scratch pretty profoundly. Fucking Hellcat.

I say, "Appears that way." I turn, and the last of the yellow sun is reflecting off her shoulders and into her emerald eyes. This may be a stunt, but I am going to enjoy every second of it. She stops short of me, and I snake my arms around her waist and yank her to me. With a wicked grin on my face, I wink, and she nods with a sly smile.

I brush her lips with my thumb, and her arms find their way around my neck. I have anticipation butterflies. She has goosebumps all up and down her arm. I don't quite understand because we've kissed before. Granted, we didn't know each other's last names when we began. And we certainly didn't know each other at all, even if somehow we did.

Maybe it's because we can't wait any longer. I move into

Elle as she moves into me. My mouth slants over hers. She slowly parts her soft lips and moves her head in the opposite direction. I lick her just inside of her mouth, and she draws in a sharp breath. It's sweet and suggestive. How can she make a sweet kiss dirty? We're lingering and savoring the moment. Every nerve ending in my body is tingling. Our lips barely touching and teasing. Every part of me is awake, for what feels like the first time. Then we're kissing and it's soft and intimate. I pull back from the kiss and we gaze at each other, intoxicated by the kiss.

Then she pulls my shirt towards her and finds my lips again. This time for a deeper and longer kiss. It's everything. Just like the first night, it feels as if our mouths and our bodies were made for each other.

Her tongue tickles my teeth, and I open wider to take her inside. She responds to whatever I do to her. We're pulling at each other as if this were the last time we'll ever kiss. We're milking every freaking second from it. It's no longer a performance but a connection. It's selfish. It's for us, and we flick and lick our tongues together. She gently moans inside my mouth to make this the most flawless kiss. And then she pulls back and looks just past me.

"Asher, hi. Didn't see you there. Can I get you another glass? There's a legacy vertical tasting in the cave if you have any interest. So delicious."

She's spot on fucking perfect at this moment, and I want to keep kissing her. I really do. It might be the tequila, but the heat in her cheeks tells me that she's feeling the same. She breaks our embrace, and I lightly pat her ass as she turns to walk away. She blows me a kiss, and I pretend to catch it. Then when she's around the corner, I see her crack up. I turn away from the two of them and continue over to some of the guests I recognize.

"He kissed that short, tiny gurrrl." I can hear the pout in Serena's voice with my back to her as I walk away.

Damn fucking straight I did. And I've just decided I'm not going to stop. That was the best fucking kiss of my life.

CHAPTER FIFTY

ELLE

WHAT THE FUCK WAS THAT? I MEAN, I KNOW WHAT HE WAS doing, and it felt good to help him. But Jesus, my cheeks are on fire. I felt that kiss in my toes and in my now swollen and throbbing core. There are still tingles where he was holding me. This asshole of a man who changes personalities so fast it can make anyone's head spin just delivered the most electric, vulnerable and sensual kiss I've ever had. I need him. I mean, I think I'd like to do that again. I want his lips now. I can't believe I just knowingly kissed Josh. It was so good. We've been on a collision course with that moment for a while. I'm so happy I'm too tired to fight my feelings any longer.

I shake my head like I'm trying to erase lines on an Etch A Sketch to get the memory and feeling out of my head, belly, and pussy. I point the photographer in the right direction then the staff escorts the partygoers to the dinner. The DJ should be here any minute so we can convert the cocktail area to a dance floor. I circle around the cave to the dining area, and it's stunning. There are large glowing balls in the trees to light up the tables. They're giving off a warm glow of red, orange, yellow and a very tropical blue, that all matches my dress. The tables are skirted in fake grass, and there are fire dancers in the clearing to greet them. The servers are in place with LaChappelle/Whittier's brand-new Rosé and light sangria, both adorned with umbrellas.

One last tweak. I place two large blue orbs on either side of the bars, making sure they're more visible in the dark. I tape them to rocks to anchor them in place. I look around and then open the back door to the cave to let everyone out to the alfresco dining area. I stand back and watch as everyone enters and marvels. I grin at the *oos* and *ahhs*. It's my bread and butter, the thing that makes me tick. I don't want credit, but I do love to see a great reaction. I love making a moment. Randy approaches, and I brace myself. He hands me an LC/W tumbler glass of Rosé.with an umbrella in it.

"Girl, you make me look good."

I turn quickly to him. "You don't hate me!"

"No one hates you, and that's why I hate you. I like to be different."

I nod to Serena as she enters the space. "She hates me."

"Who the amazon Bella Hadid wannabe? I think the shoes are a knock-off."

I laugh and try to see them. "Like she painted the bottoms herself?"

"Exactly. That leather shouldn't be fraying. She's just mad you're going to fuck her man tonight." I choke on the wine and stare at him. "Girl, you're going to have to give me details on that. I've lusted after little Joshie for years."

We sip and gab as everyone's served. The servers keep refilling our tumblers. I have a warm belly that's becoming liquid courage. I watch Josh visit each table. He's laughing and hugging people. There's a rowdy table that all leap up to hug him. They're our age. I've seen Jims before, he's a

Langerford, but I don't recognize anyone else. Jims stands up and looks around, then approaches me. Randy licks his lips, but Jims doesn't notice.

"Darling, that dress. You are a vision. Tell me." He hugs me. Which is strange considering we've only met once in passing. I can tell he's had several tumblers as well.

I ask, "Jims. It's nice to see you again. But tell you what?"

Jims gestures towards Randy and me. "Who is this?"

Randy holds out his hand. "I'm Randy, we've met before."

Jims turns to Randy in all of his tan glowing the moon-light. Jims is a gorgeous man, and I see why Randy is lusting after him. But Jims looks completely bored. "Randall, I know who you are. We've slept together." I choke on my Rosé.

Randy says, "I'm aware. And?"

Jims answers a question that wasn't really asked. "My darling, that was our time, and it won't come again. Now you, intriguing blonde goddess, who made this garment?"

"Oh! It's a Verandah printed blouson-sleeve cover-up wrap dress with fringe. I always say that because it was on the tag."

"Fuck me. It's floaty, fun, and fucking fabulous. It's a cover-up? You ingenious girl."

"I loved the print so much. I wear it as a dress. Justifies the cost. Can't imagine getting it wet at what I paid for it."

Jims laughs freely. He's kind of delightful. "Smart. I must return to the barbarians at that table, but my darling, I'll see you later." He kisses me on the cheek and heads away from us. Randy turns to me. Everyone at the table has looked over at me at some point while Jims was talking to me. I feel as if it was his job to point me out to the others. These must be the crew that are Josh's chosen cousins he talked about on our first night.

"And now I hate you again. Can you charm anyone? He's the most eligible man in wine country. Well, aside from yours. But the difference is that Jims has run through every man in wine country and Josh hasn't dated here since high school." I laugh at Randy.

Josh occasionally comes over and kisses me on the cheek or holds me for a moment if he notices Asher noticing him. Is this for show or does he really want me?

"You're playing an interesting game," Randy says.

"It's his game, not mine."

"You don't see the way he looks at you, Elle. Not a game."

I gulp my wine. It's the kiss I can't get over. Hopefully, Asher and Serena won't stay to dance. She probably does that "stick figure sway" and then slowly lifts her arms in the air like they're so "heavy pout dance."

I turn to Randy. "You have this handled, right?"

"Go, make sure my dance floor is ready. I know you'll have a couple of tweaks."

I roll my eyes and hit his arm. I head back down through the cave, leaving the glowing beach balls in the tunnel to light the path to the dance floor. Entrees will be over in about ten minutes. Josh needs to make a toast while they're all still sitting, then on to dancing.

I'm nearing the other side when the entrance is filled with his beautiful hard body. My breath catches, and not because I'm startled. With his eyes staring at me, I shiver in his gaze. His hair has a bit of curl to it, and its sun-kissed from all his time outside lately. Those blue eyes that mirror the colors in my dress are telegraphing his thoughts. I bite my bottom lip, and he covers the six feet between us very quickly.

He grabs me around my waist. I grab his neck. There are no words as we quickly crash our lips into each other. His hands are splayed all over my back and ass. We're a tangle of tongues and chorus of gasps. Every part of me is on fire. I can't stop myself. I pull back, and he gives me that one-sided grin. We're both struggling to catch our breath while our faces are still nose to nose.

"You have to make a toast."

"Woman. Let it go. For one fucking second, you need to stop being in fucking control. Lean into the moment." He lurches forward and takes my lips with an intense kiss that has more than my toes tingling. I gasp and grope at him. He possesses me with this kiss. He's commanding me to lose control. I can feel my shoulders relax and tension roll off of me. I want this man right here and now. His phone buzzes.

He winks and says, "I have to go make a toast."

CHAPTER FIFTY-ONE

JOSH

She giggles, looking at me. "First, you might want to let that go down."

My dick is straight up and throbbing hard. My glorified bathing suit is hiding nothing. I could come right now if she brushed by it. So fucking turned on by this vixen. My shirt's not long enough to cover my raging hard-on. She's going to need to walk away from me. And take her lilac and orange blossom smell with her. And the feel of her silky hair and her skin. Holy hell, I need to be inside this woman. I need to be filling every inch of her.

I smirk at her. "Then you're going to need to stop touching me."

"Wait. Like this?" She puts her hands on my chest and then moves them slowly to my back, caressing with her nails.

"Yeah, like that. Unless you can give the world's fastest blow job and relieve me of this, take your sexy ass away from me. Stop torturing me."

She doesn't stop. Her hands roam underneath my shirt. She's rubbing my pecs and feeling her way down across my abs. This girl. Fuck. "I'm not that fast at it, to be honest. But I am really good at sucking cock. Remember? And I really like it." She bites her full bottom pink lip and then traces the top of the waistband of my ridiculous shorts with her matching pink chiffon nail. I need her to get away from me before I bend her over a barrel. I adjust myself.

"FUCK. Not helping. You'll pay for teasing me."

She smiles, tilting her head and staring at the large bulge in my pants. "See, I'm just as turned on as you. As wet as you can remember. I guess I just hide it better."

"Don't sit down and let it seep through your dress."

"Yes, then I'd have an awful mess with my thighs so slick."

I cover her mouth with my hand. She needs to stop talking, touching, and insinuating. "Stop this or I'm going to have to exact my revenge." I roughly pull her lips to mine and lick inside of her mouth. I'm matched stroke for stroke until neither of us can get closer. "You're dangerous. Walk away." I put my hands on my hips and bend at the waist trying to regulate my breathing.

She licks her lips and leaves. She calls back over her shoulder. "Okay. I guess I'll save you a dance then." Elle then drops her phone, bending over to let her dress flip up onto her back. I'm going to tear that thong off her later. She smiles at me.

"Fuck me. That ass. That skin. Go. Or I'm never going to let you go."

I am insanely hot for her right now, but there are four hundred people here who know me. I grab a cold cup of water from the cave tasting room and douse my head. Both heads. I think of the time I accidentally saw Mrs. Dotson, my surrogate grandmother, changing in our kitchen. No bra, just swinging in the wind. That did it. I flip back my hair and slick it down. I douse the rest of my Jams so it's not obvious. Okay. I'm ready. I look like I just went swimming so I'm going to use it as a gag in my toast.

Just as I turn from the tasting area in the cave, I get a text from my dad telling me they're back and he'll make the toast. Thank fucking god. I head out of the tunnel in the opposite direction of my temptress, who I will make pay for teasing me. Everyone is wrapping up dinner, I sit with my friends while Randy and Mrs. Dotson sing a parody song to the tune of *Margaritaville* about our members. It's all sweet and everything, but I can only think of the moment when I get to launch on her. Patience seems to be my test tonight.

I exit toward the dining area and see Asher and Serena get up and begin to sidle their way to the exit. I forgot they were here. Asher salutes me, and Serena blows me a kiss. I turn away. They pause to hear the speeches. Both of them have no idea that they bear very little weight on my life right now. I look around the vineyard from this view. I've seen all the aspects of this place before. I inhale my home deeply, and it's nostalgic but also new and exciting. I'm shocked by the thoughts and feelings I'm letting my brain process.

My mom takes the microphone. I can tell she's going to get misty. They're going to tell the members about the sale. I was supposed to do it, but it should come from them.

"You're the very backbone and spirit that my father, grandfather, grandmother, mother, great-grands, and great-great-grands envisioned sharing this world with. I can never thank you enough for filling our lives with such joy. We're so happy that you believe in the soul of this place the way that we do. It's with an extremely measured and heavy heart that we tell you that within the year we'll be transitioning out of the business. We're looking for a buyer with the same integrity and love of our vineyards that we share with you. You will all be well taken care of."

There are audible gasps and lots of rumbling. A couple of the people look at me, and I redirect them back to my weepy mom. I'm focused on my mother's lined and soft face. She seems so fragile but sure of herself. And again, I think about the artist or business tycoon she could have been. The path never opened to her because her father wouldn't allow it. The way blocked by the weight of this winery legacy. The weight I thought was too great to carry. She's finally lifting it off herself.

I can never tell them exactly why I don't want the winery because it would be too cruel to say to them that Lucien didn't believe in them. I'm not sure if they know the extent he forced me to learn the business at such a young age. I can't tell them I hated him for giving me no choice. I ended up hating the winery because of Lucien's unstoppable force of will. But then I stepped away, and my parents gave me a choice. They let me go. I need to let them go as well. If their choice is to sell, then I need to let it be. But I'll miss this place. I'm beginning to wonder about the path I didn't take. What if I had done all of this on my own terms? Was this my sliding door moment? The one where I can clearly see what the other road would have given me? It's doesn't matter. It's too late. I'm secure in that. I walk over towards where the staff is holding up the wall of the cave.

Suddenly, as my father is blathering on about the terroir and overcoming root rot, my nose is filled with lilacs and orange blossoms. Like Pavlov's dog, I begin to salivate and my dick twitches. She's near me. She moves directly in front of me. I lean into her ear, nipping it, and she arches her back a bit. Randy squeezes my shoulder and disappears. The rest of the staff moves towards Dad on the other side of the crowd. I sink deeper into the alcove we've found ourselves in, pulling her with me. I whisper so low only she can hear me, "I want your perfect peach ass to back up into me and stay there." I'm going to torture her, and this little flouncy skirt is going to help.

CHAPTER FIFTY-TWO

ELLE

I don't know why Will and Sarah are back from dinner early, but I'm delighted Josh won't have to glad-hand anymore. Everything is handled on the other side, and Randy is over there putting in his Black Eyed Peas requests. He's a freak for Fergie.

Josh's hair looks like he slicked it back with water, but now it's floppy, and his bangs are falling over one azure piercing eye. He's back on my ear and my stomach flips. I cross my arms over my chest so no one can see my diamond hard nipples.

His hands are firmly on my hips as I brush my ass against his tropical drawstring. He spread his legs to lower his center of gravity a bit. My wedges make up the height difference and our parts are in alignment.

His thumb strokes my back on the top of my ass, and it's strong and powerful. He's not asking, he's just doing it. My back arches a bit to give him better access to my ass. Then he whispers to me again.

"Stop squirming." I roll my hips back just a little, to help out. "Don't help me, Cosmo. I've got this. You do what I say

right now. You've been barking and cooing orders around
here for months now, let's see if you can follow some. Don't
move. I'm looking for something."

As he says it, he hooks his thumb into my thong's waistband then removes the thin strip of material from my ass.

"What are you doing?

"I'm sorry, did someone say you could ask questions? Do
as you're told and you get rewarded. Let that Elle sassy attitude slip out, and I stop. Got it?"

I say nothing. It's the same tone Josh took with me the
night of Steiner's. It already has me over a cliff with desire.

"Words. Tell me, you understand."

I turn my head to his at my ear, nip the lobe, and whisper.
"Got it. I understand."

He's feeling my ass, searching, and it's so good. Then I
figure out what he's doing as he says, "There it is." I gasp as
he gently tugs it upward. "Spread your legs, just wide enough
so I can find what I need."

I hesitate because there are people everywhere around us.
This is so hot. He touches me, and no one seems to notice,
but they could. His leg is between mine, nudging mine apart,
just slightly. Tucked in a dark alcove, we're only partially
hidden.

Most of the glowing orbs have been moved out of this
area. As I'm contemplating how visible we are, there's a slight
smack on my ass. One that's not cute but something else. I
jerk my body for a moment, and then he's caressing the exact
spot that stings and my juices run faster than I thought they
could. There's a heat bubbling in me that I've never experienced. I'm a ball of lust with one quick swat.

"I told you to open your legs slightly." I grin as he begins
to light me up. No one has ever spoken to me that way. He's
back at my ear. "Do you trust me?"

I lean back to ask a question. "As long as the Farmhouse doesn't have a Red Room."

I hear him laugh, and then his lips kiss and peck my neck. He keeps making me feel this switched on, I might die. I reposition my legs, and suddenly, his hand is under my skirt. I suck in a sharp breath. His hand moves up my inner thigh. And then it's on my ass and clasping my thong again, but this time it's at the bottom of my ass. He tugs slightly. His nimble fingers tuck the lace panel into my folds, and I gasp somewhat. It's on either side of my clit, and it's the most erotic feeling. He moves his fingers back to my ass and hooks into the fabric. I'm his puppet right now. If I move away from him, it will dig deeper into me, and if I step back, this perfect pressure that he's somehow found with this tiny piece of lace will go away. I suck in air and let it out slowly as he wraps the elastic around his finger. The pressure increases as does the friction.

His hot breath is at my ear again. "Rock your hips back into me and then move slightly forward again."

I roll my pelvis as I'm told. The pleasure surges through me. Josh is pushing me, or pulling me in this case, towards an orgasm. He twists his fingers around the fabric again, and now the friction is directly on my clit. My thong soaked with the wetness he's created. I involuntarily gasp. Then I suck it back in through my teeth. It's starting to get to a point where I can't take it.

As the people pass us and the volume of muttering guests increases, so does his volume. His deep voice rumbling through every part of me, "Do it again. And let it out."

I rock back, and this time it's into his hard dick. I release and stand up again, he tugs just a little harder.

"Hope you're not attached to this drenched piece of fabric because I'm going to tear this off you with my teeth later.

Only talk when I tell you." I just rock my hips back again as I moan slightly while nodding yes.

"That's not quite what I want to hear. Say my name. Let me hear you."

"Josh." It's as breathy as I can make it. The 'J' getting stuck in the gasp. I'm living so close to coming.

"You're so wet I can feel you coat yourself. I need you to coat my face. I'm going to lap up that sweet pussy. Let's see if you live up to my memory of how fucking good you taste."

"I have to...." He puts his hand over my mouth. Fuck so hot. I suck his fingers. I'll tell him anything he wants if he lets me come right now. I have to. I've never been this on the verge without release. I'm so lost in lust that I do not care who sees me or hears me. There is only us. Everyone else fades from view as I stare straight ahead at the staff cleaning the tables. I don't care. Fuck them. Josh, please just fuck me. I'm a tight ball of sexual tension. I need to release.

"No, girl. You don't get to come yet. Tell me how you think you taste, and then I'll tell you the truth."

"Good. I taste good." I manage to get out.

"You taste fucking amazing. Like oranges and spice." He pulls my strings again, and I squeak. "Tell me what this feels like."

"No. Can't."

My breath catching as I attempt not to come. I have no language. I can't speak, or I'll scream. But Josh lets go of my panties, pulling them away from my body. Then they settle back where they usually are, and I'm desperate for him to pull my reins again. He pulls his hand from my skirt. I turn around and look at him. Most of the party has moved to the dance floor, and we're surrounded by servers and bar staff. My mouth hangs open in an exaggerated O.

"No. Why? Why did you stop?" I whine, and he raises his eyebrows at me.

"I told you, you had to listen. Do as I say. You told me no. Denied a direct request. You do as I say, or I stop."

"I'm so close."

"Then you'll have to wait. Do as I say and you get to come. If you don't, then I can't help you. And don't take care of things yourself. I didn't, so you can't."

"I understand you want me in as much pain as you were in an hour ago."

He grins insidiously at me and pushes his hair out of his eyes. When he does, his shirt pops up a bit and I see his abs, and I now know, I'll do whatever he wants tonight. "Not so much pain, as I want you to know how badly I want to fuck you. I want you to join me in this frenzy of desire."

"I'm there."

"Not yet, you're not. Not even fucking close to knowing how much I want you. I'll decide when we're on an equal level of lust. Let's go dance."

He holds out his hand to me. He laces his fingers in mine, and it's the most intimate we've ever been. This isn't primal desire. It's true affection.

But even that benign touch sends shots of pleasure through me. Josh winks as he sees me try to regulate my breathing. We head through the cave together. Suddenly he pushes me into one of the barrel rooms and crashes his mouth to mine. We kiss as if our plane is going down. Gasps and moans from both of us. He gropes my ass and moves his hands to my thighs but is careful not to invade my skirt. The one place I want him. If he won't give me his dick, at least a finger or two until we can be alone. He moves down my neck and licks my cleavage as I throw back my head and reach for his waistband. Perhaps I can convince him.

He moves back a bit. "No. Not yet. Come on, we need to get out there."

"In a minute, Josh." I pull his head back to mine and cover

his lips while feeling the outline of him. He moans and responds in kind by swirling his tongue in this magnificent passionate dance in my mouth. Fuck he's hot. Then he pulls away suddenly and chastises me.

"Last time you do that without permission tonight, little Miss Bossypants." I nod. No one has ever taken control of me in this way. As much as I want to fight, my body is reacting in such an unexpected way. I want to surrender to this man. Just before we exit, he lets go. I know exactly why, but I do feel the absence of his touch.

I tell him, "I agree. Let's not invite questions."

Also, it's insanely hot. He looks at me as we enter the fray.

When we emerge, there's an old Jackson Brown song playing. Turning on his heels, he grabs my hand, twirling me into his arms. He's light on his feet. So much for not drawing attention to ourselves. Our faces are close to each other as he takes the lead and whisks me around the courtyard. Everyone is so drunk. Hopefully, no one is really watching us. Then I see his mother sitting on the sidelines. Sarah waves a little tiny wave at me, smirking a knowing look.

His blue eyes are shimmering under the party lighting. It's as if they've got glitter in them. It's hypnotic, and I am more than willing to submit to him. It's just not the time to let him know that yet. I'll be his mouse in this game, but right now I want him to think I'm still the Hellcat.

My head is swirling with moments of him tonight and over the past months. It's like a new vintage, I don't know what this wine will end up tasting like, but right now the color is ruby and ready. As for clarity, that will have to be put on the back burner.

"Mr. Whittier, if you wanted to dance with me, you could have asked."

"It's the song, Jackson Browne's *In The Shape of a Heart*. It demands dancing." He sings in my ear, and it's different than the rest of the night. Passion on the back burner for a moment. He starts to mutter the lyrics. And I can't quite make them out but I don't care. *"It was a ruby ... hmmmm mmmm...in the shape of a heart"*

"And Ms. Parker, I believe I've told you already. I'm going to do whatever I'd like to you this evening."

"That's an interesting point, Mr. Whittier. But I have yet to agree to those terms."

"Yes, you already did. I heard you. I watched as your gorgeous eyes submitted to me when my name escaped your lips. It won't be the last time tonight."

"Fine."

He suddenly spins me out and pulls me back to him with magnetic force. Then he's holding me closer, and his lips are grazing my ear. He begins singing the lyrics, and they're haunting and beautiful. And with each word, my skin prickles with passion. He stops signing. I listen intently to hear the lyrics he won't sing in my ear.

People speak of love don't know what they're thinking of
Wait around for the one who fits just like a glove

It's a break-up song, but the way he sings it, sounds to me like he feels he needs to earn love by fighting through. I guess I feel that way too. That no one can go into a relationship or love without knowing there are shallows and pitfalls. The trick is that you choose to do it anyway. I haven't made that choice in a long time or ever. The feel of his arms around me, his breath prickling my skin and the smile in his eyes are the reason I can feel myself slip. It's okay to fall. This is how I'll hear the song from now on.

CHAPTER FIFTY-THREE

JOSH

SHIT, I NEED TO GET AWAY FROM THIS WOMAN BEFORE I SCARE her. I am drunk and getting carried away. Scaring myself a bit as well. This is more than lust, and I know she feels it too. I should stop, tell her I have to go back to Santa Barbara tomorrow. But I can't seem to help myself from pushing her deeper into my arms.

I'm so fucking addicted to her I'm afraid she'll take everything. I shouldn't be here, but then this temptress moved into my Farmhouse, and I haven't been able to leave or shake the feelings that grow more intense every day.

I can't walk away. Not without one more night under the stars in the Valley of the Moon that I do love despite my best efforts to leave it behind. Just another taste of Elle. I'm learning that the glass will never be full enough.

The song is almost over, and I can hear ABBA crossfading under the end of this one. I'm still holding her close. I inhale her most perfect perfume, now mixed with the smell of her sex and me. She moves her hands in my hair, and I want to take her far away from here and do nasty things to her. I also simply want to kiss her. I don't usually do sweet, but this woman's scent does terrible things to my mind. My dick begins to struggle against my ridiculous floral shorts, and I know she can feel it. She goes up onto her tiptoes. I bend down to hear her ever so sexy sigh in my ear. Then she whispers, "I'm ready as well."

"Wet?"

"Drenched. Shocked it's not dripping into my sandals."

"Stay that way."

I remove her arms from her neck. I don't want to, but I do need to settle my dick down. Seeing my mother on the couches helps quite a bit. I kiss Elle's hand and release her. I walk over to see my mom as *Dancing Queen* begins, and my father leaves her to take over the dance floor again. He's a dancer, she's not. She looks content but a little run down.

I sit down, slipping my arm around her. "You look tired, Mom."

"I'm fine. Just been a long couple of days. The party is so great, honey. You did a wonderful job."

I feel as if she's changing the subject. "Mom, in my entire life you've never been tired. You're the Energizer Bunny." She takes my hand and looks as if she's going to tell me something. She kisses my cheek and I squeeze her hand.

"Age comes for us all, my dear."

"That's it? Age?"

"For now, my darling. That's it for now."

"Okay." I'm going to keep an eye on her, but I'll believe her because I've seen my dad slow down a bit as well. He's developed quite the old man bags under his eyes in the past year. I guess I just don't want to see them age because I was an ass who pissed away years being angry at the wind and staying away from them for no reason.

"It really is one of our better parties." I sip wine from my mom's glass.

"It was Elle and Randy."

Mom corrects me, "You mean it was Randy and then Elle."

I laugh at my mom knowing full well that whatever we do, Elle will rearrange it and convince us it was our idea. Taking my mom's hand again and settling back into the couch, we watch the crowd dance.

The Serena engagement debacle was the defining moment of my terrible and lost behavior. Well, there was that flare up when I canceled Elle's dinner and disregarded them as experts. It's like a sharp stab to my heart to think of that. That was deplorable of me, and I realize that was the cold Lucien, grandfather part of my DNA.

I was so concentrated on not becoming him I left here and became him anyway. Only business, money, and power mattered. It carried into my personal life without me realizing it. I thought I had to distance myself from this world to have my own.

I'm starting to see that I was wrong. I leave tomorrow because Sal will be waiting, but for the first time in a long time, I don't want to go. For now, I'll hold my mom's hand and watch my dad be a dork surrounded by the love that they built out of this place. Even though my grandfather had a grand and stringent plan for the farm, it was my parents that made it home. They planted organic gardens and tended to the buildings. They grew the relationships with these people and the land. They started the wine club, much to my grandfather's chagrin.

"Mom."

"Yes, Sweetie J." She grins, knowing I hate that fucking name. I want to tell her how good it feels to be here. But she looks tired. It will keep. I kiss her on the cheek and get up to go find some old friends.

"Nothing. It can wait."

CHAPTER FIFTY-FOUR

ELLE

I EMERGE FROM THE BATHROOM, AND WILL IS IN THE CENTER of a large circle of people breakdancing. I stand there watching him for way too long. It's hard to look away. Josh grazes up against me from behind, and my skin instantly pebbles. I had to go to the bathroom to mop up just a bit. He makes me burn for him. I hate and love every second. I'm so damn conflicted.

"You're still going to fuck me if my dad ends up doing the worm, right?"

"We'll see."

"Yes, we will." He pats my ass a little aggressively, and my chest flushes. So do all four of my cheeks. I grab a Zin for myself and Cab for Sarah from one of the makeshift bars. Then I cross the courtyard to sit with her.

"Thank you very much, Elle."

"How did it go tonight at dinner?"

"It wasn't really our scene. This is. Josh should have gone, and we should have stayed here."

I knew that, but I was selfish and wanted Josh here with me. "I'm so sorry. I'll make a note of that for the future."

She places her hand on my thigh. "No. No. I just hope you're not angry that we came home early."

"Not at all. Did you know Asher was here?" I want a little intel on Serena.

Sarah looks surprised, "Really? I wondered why he wasn't at the dinner with us. He arranged it, right?"

"Yes. But Asher came here with Serena instead."

"I'm not familiar. Who's that?"

I'm a bit knocked over. Sarah never met her son's ex-fiancée? What the hell was that boy thinking? I know bits and pieces of this story, but maybe Sarah can round out the picture for me. I'd give anything to introduce anyone to my parents, and he cut them out voluntarily. I don't know if it's my place to tell her who she is.

"Perhaps Josh should answer that question."

"Is she the ex?" I look shocked. And she can tell by my reaction, and she turns to me and continues speaking. "We knew about the engagement, not from Josh, and he never told her about us. He forgot the wine industry is small. Some of our Santa Barbara colleagues asked if we were coming down to the engagement party that was scheduled at their winery."

"Snap! That is cold. He held the party at another winery?!"

"He told us he never told anyone in Santa Barbara about his connection to wine. It was a couple of years ago. Josh was very angry about life. He's never explained fully to us why we were cut out."

"How painful." I wish he'd tell his parents that it was mostly Lucien that drove him away.

"Yes, it was. But I imagine my sweetheart of a father had something to do with it. I trust Josh will tell us someday when he's ready. Know this, Josh will never do anything if he's pushed. Always been that way."

She smiles as her husband does the Stanky leg to the B52's *Love Shack*. She explains further. "My father was not a kind or compassionate man. My mother was, but she died very early in my life. We always hoped there was more of us in Josh than Lucien. We never tolerated outbursts or his habit of pretending we didn't exist. We always tried to remind him of humility, compassion, and caring."

"You did a good job. He's not really Lucien." She takes my hand and kisses it.

Sarah grins widely and says, "In a brilliant parenting move, Will sent four cases of Joshua Lucien Merlot to Josh's engagement party without telling him. They were just served to him with the bottles on display."

I laugh heartily and glance over at Josh. He catches my eye and winks. "Sneaky."

"It did exactly what Will wanted. Apparently, it was the first that most of his friends heard about the winery. And it turns out the fiancée already knew and had targeted him. I'm not sure if she knew he had money of his own or not, but she dumped him when he told her he wanted no part of the winery. More importantly, we heard from him for the first time in eight months the very next day. He flew up the next weekend, and we talked it through. He just forgets who he is sometimes. But he's been intermittently in our lives since then. More so in the last six months or so." She leans towards me and winks.

"I don't know if I could handle that. Him leaving."

"I don't have another choice. I'll always love my baby boy no matter what. Every once in a while, Joshua—that's what we call his Lucien side—rears his ugly head. Will reminds him the only thing we want is Josh every once in a while. That's why Will's so happy and carefree these days. We've had Josh for almost three months now, since that awful day with the Lucien moment of canceling your dinner. I don't care why he's still around, but we're grateful. I know he'll go back to his life soon, but it's so nice to have him part of our world again."

My stomach knots up at the thought of him leaving here. Maybe I'm already in too deep, perhaps he'll stay. Sarah's glass jerks for a moment, spilling a bit of wine. I quickly grab her stemware.

"Are you okay? Was it too much tonight?" She nods. I say, "You have to tell me when to back off. I won't put you in harm for the sake of a stupid dinner." She looks exhausted.

She takes my hand and smiles at me. "You think I don't know that by now? The tremors come and go, but they're getting a bit worse. Apparently, I have to start using plastic wine glasses or maybe sippy cups." I smile but don't laugh. She continues speaking, "The thing I hate the most is the loss of control of the one thing I've depended on the longest. It's like we're no longer a team. There's a disconnect between my head and my body. And I know the symptoms will come and go. I'll have to deal with a whole new set of things, but for now, I'm pissed off at my body."

A woman with this open a heart doesn't deserve this. No one does, really.

She continues, "But I did get approved for an experimental drug treatment down at UCSF hospital. They've done some of the clinical trials in Europe, but now they've selected eight of us for a control group here. I never thought a local would get picked, but I guess I got lucky." I hand her glass back to her.

"Congrats. I'm so happy. Will and Josh must be thrilled."

She smiles, sheepishly. That may explain why Josh is in such a good mood. He never discusses his mother's illness. I won't ever bring it up. It's his business to talk or not. I thought he'd chat about it at least one time when we were under the stars or on the phone, but it's his path to walk. I do know that I'll listen when he wants to talk. This is not something I would have said three months ago.

I look around the courtyard, and he's trapped by a couple of super drunk couples. The women are in flowing sherbet-colored caftans and perfectly placed hibiscus flowers in their hair and alternatingly pawing at him. Sarah sees me notice.

"They've known him since birth. But that doesn't stop an old drunk cougar from reaching out."

I laugh. "Go to bed. I'll tell Will where you went. I have this. I'll make sure it all gets cleaned up, and we'll be ready to open at noon tomorrow morning."

"I'm not sure where or why you came into our lives, but I'm so grateful to have a beautiful soul like you on our side."

I tear up and hug her again. It's like she senses how I can use a little more maternal love in my life. "I feel the same."

I help her off the couch. She makes her way over to Will, who is still ripping up the floor with the robot. I watch their unspoken exchange of how she's going to bed but wants him to stay and enjoy. I wish for that. I want a wordless relationship. To be so understood and cherished that every nuance is appreciated.

I sit back on the couch and look around the party. I finish my wine and then reach for the rest of Sarah's mostly unfinished glass. I can now focus on the task at hand, then go about taking a hand at Josh's task. It seems we're on a predestined track tonight, and I'm wet again merely thinking about it.

My skin and core are still buzzing at a low but constant frequency. I stand up to go check on the caterers and see if they need anything. I'll tip them out and let them get on their way. I'm covering for Randy who's now barely wearing his clothes and leading everyone in a dance to *Fergalicious*. I'm still on the right side of buzzed but rapidly descending into drunk and bad decisions.

Samantha should have my 'end of the night' favors set up in the tasting room, but I need to make sure the ribbons are easy to untie for the overserved guests. Also, the trolley and car service need to be double-checked. I need to make sure all pieces are moving the way they're supposed to.

The tiki bars are almost all dismantled. I grab the last of the light-up beach balls to bring back through the cave to the courtyard. I'm joined by the catering staff. We're kicking them down the tunnel through the cave and they're bouncing like brightly colored pinballs. My phone buzzes.

JOSH: Where are you? No one gave you permission to disappear.

I like that he's looking for me.

ELLE: Had to pay the caterers and supervise clean up. Randy's worse for wear.

JOSH: Not my concern. Don't we have staff?

ELLE: I am the staff.

JOSH: No, you're not. Surely, we pay people to do more of this grunt work. Where the hell is Mrs. Dotson?

ELLE: In the corner of the courtyard, making out with the City Council guy.

JOSH: Get it, Edna! Tell me you're still wet.

ELLE: Slightly. Less as I think of Mrs. Dotson but more as I think of you.

JOSH: Sending actual staff to you. Let them do their jobs. There are people hired to do the job you insist on inserting yourself into. Stop fucking doing other people's jobs. Now come to me right now and let me fix this wet pussy situation. Or you can head to the barrel room and narrate what your tits feel like for me.

I've had quite enough of taking care of myself. I'm so turned on I can barely handle all these people around me. I'll just nudge him in the direction I need him to go. Then once cornered maybe I can get some release. My insides are starting to coil up again, and I need to come. Soon. It's like my body is in this constant state of vibration. A low current runs through me looking for an outlet and when it doesn't get it, it circles back around.

ELLE: My nipples are insanely hard. My hands won't do the job. They need you. I need you to come here and suck them for me.

JOSH: There you go again thinking you're in charge. Nope. Do you even want to orgasm tonight? You're pushing it, Parker. Now get that perfect fucking ass out here, and I'll take care of you here. And bring me a present.

ELLE: What kind of present?

ELLE: Josh?

ELLE: Fine. I'm on my way.

I rack my brain to come up with what to bring him. Would he really withhold an orgasm? He's not that strong to resist me. That doesn't seem very sporting, but I'd rather not find out. This man is confusing my head, and it's annoying. I don't waffle on decisions or get confused. I keep denying our connection to make it all the more palatable. But fuck, I want him. I make a lot of people a lot of money, and I choose what gets done. But I really, really want him to make me come. I decide a Mezcal cocktail might do as a gift. I run to the bartender just as he's about to close his van.

"Are you looking for annihilation or just a suggestion?"

"Strong suggestion. And can you make two?"

"Anything for you, Elle."

I pull out *Roman Holiday,* my Nars shell pink sheer lip color and apply while I wait. I'm feeling very Audrey as I pull my dress and hair back into place. Then suddenly, five staff members from the winery show up to finish cleaning. I give them a couple of instructions and ask them to check on the trolley and the favors. I also mention that maybe if they fold the table clothes in half before stuffing them into the dirty linen bags, then they'll have more room in the bag. I can't help myself. I leave them to do as I've asked and it's killing me not to follow through, but I really want to come.

I'm carrying two exquisite cocktails in long-stemmed plastic wine glasses adorned with tropical flowers. The staff and I wrapped fake leis around the bases of all of the stemware for tonight. Alone and on my way back through the tunnel, I remove my coral thong and wrap it around the base of his glass, then I wrap a similar colored lei on top of it. It's soaked through just thinking about it rubbing against me.

He's in a circle of bros. There's a second circle to their left made up of that film festival girl Meg, a stunning brunette, a striking dark-haired woman, and one distinctively tall woman with a shock of pink hair. The pink hair belongs to Tommi Schroeder. I met her at a dinner with her father, Adrian.

I was told earlier that they were all sons and daughters of the winemakers and vintners and that they grew up together. I got a text earlier that Poppy wasn't going to make it. I see Jims there, but I want to know the rest. There are five families that the parents and kids were all very close growing up. I have finally memorized the families: Aganos, Schroeders, Gelberts, Langerfords, and the Whittiers. I push through a couple of the boys and one whistles. I turn towards this raven-haired man with muddy blue eyes.

"I'm sorry. In this current era, you think a whistle is an appropriate way to tell me you think I'm attractive? How old are you?"

The direct crowd laughs, and the women cheer from just outside the circle.

The whistler speaks, he has a kind look to him, but I'm not so sure he has manners. "I didn't mean anything by it. Whatever." Dark-haired dude rolls his eyes at me. The tall raven-haired woman with stunning golden-brown eyes walks over and punches him in the arm.

"Fucking idiot. Shut up, man. I'm so sorry for my brother. You don't really do things like this, do you?"

The brunette with the coffee-colored eyes and yells, "He's done it to me. But then I kicked him in the balls." Everyone giggles, but I am a stranger in this group.

Josh chimes in. I spin around to look at him as he addresses his friend. I'm in the middle of the circle and directly between the two men. "You did, though. You meant to demean her by whistling at her. Your purpose was to help her remember that women don't matter as much as men. That's she's not worth looking in the eye. You should have told her how utterly stunning and ethereal she looks tonight. Or even if you want to be bold, that you'd like to kiss her or depending on how she reacts, that you'd like to screw her. Or perhaps learn of her considerable business acumen or how she could probably outrun you. All of those are better options than a non-consenting grunt or whistle or even an out-of-date ouyga."

I'm dumbstruck. The rest of the dudes are dumbstruck. And the women laugh heartily and walk away. And then the party begins to applaud him. The whistler looks at me. The man who wants to dominate me just defended feminism and me. But his dominance play has to do with trust, not forcing me to do filthy things in order to demean me.

The thug almost bows to me as he says, "I'm sorry if I offended you. I just wanted to convey how gorgeous you look tonight, and I wouldn't mind getting to know you better."

His tone is sarcastic. "Thank you for the apology, but from your behavior and the way you're standing, I can tell you're not quite man enough for me. But have a great night."

I hear him mutter 'bitch' as I turn my back, and before I know what's happening, Josh is on him as well as two of the other guys. Another one leans forward and pulls me away from the incident. I hear a punch land with a thud. I turn and this teddy bear bearded fellow, who just appeared, takes me out of the strike zone.

"Thank you."

"I'll get him. But you should know..."

"What?"

"I've never seen him defend a woman like that before. And I've known all of them."

The bearded guy breaks it all up and then leads the asshole up and out of the party. Randy puts the music back on, and everyone cheers. I rush to the tasting room to grab ice. I get three bundles of it. I'm not sure how many people threw punches. Josh and one of the other guys are holding their fists. Jims is swilling beer, but there seems to be a mark on his cheek. Some of the women saunter back over.

I ask, "Are you okay?"

Josh looks up with a resolute grin and says, "I am. You know Jims, and this is Baxter Schroeder."

"Thank you, Jims. And it's nice to meet you, Baxter."

Jims air-kisses me and then announces me. "This is Elle Parker, everyone. And I might be in love with her." They all groan and laugh.

Baxter has pure blonde hair and ice-blue eyes and similar coloring to me. His sister, the pink haired Tommi, has the same eyes. He's incredibly fit, and his salmon polo shirt hangs perfectly over what I suspect are some damn chiseled pecs. He's dressed as if he's headed to a yacht party instead of a tiki party. I think maybe his ribbon belt with embroidered grapes might be worn unironically. Jims is a taller, leaner, and shaved version of the teddy bear guy but impeccably dressed in pressed and coordinated tiki garb.

I put my hand out to Baxter as I hand him an ice pack. "The pleasure's mine. Thank you very much for defending my honor. I hope you're not hurt."

I walk to Jims and press on his cheek, he winces. I place my impromptu ice pack on his cheek. Then he swigs his beer again. I wrap the ice around Baxter's hand. I turn to Tommi.

"Glad to have a bit more estrogen around. Becca took her drunk ass brother home, but you'd probably like her. And Tabi just took off for a rando date. She said something about a coconut bra. She wanted you to know that you're a badass." I notice Baxter roll his eyes.

I inquire. "Tabi?"

Josh answers, "Tabitha Aganos, her parents own Stafýlia Winery."

Baxter explains, "She's was the Greek-looking brunette with the copper penny eyes."

Tommi bows to me. "She's not Greek-looking, she's Greek."

"Whatever." Baxter teases back to his sister.

Tommi turns to me, "And if you don't mind me saying so, you look lovely tonight, and I'd like to get to know you better." Laughter breaks out.

"Thank you for that lovely comment. But I think I might be busy tonight." I glance at Josh and he nods.

Tommi says, "Don't deck me, dude." Then she turns back to me. "But you've got a spectacular ass."

More laughter and she walks away. I like her. I step to Josh, and he explains, "Don't worry about David, he can be an ass when he's drunk. Or sober. Always has been. He's a Gelbert. Not the first time we've all beat the shit out of each other, and it won't be the last."

The other two men laugh. I look at Josh and realize he's put ice on his eye. I turn towards him and take the ice pack, looking underneath. There's a slight swelling. I press lightly on his face, and his lips curl as I take care of him.

"It's not so bad, Cosmo. I'm fine. My hand hurts more than anything."

"I'm surprised your head hurts at all, given how hard it is." Then I put my hands on my hips. "I can defend myself."

The bearded man comes bounding around the corner, hearing the end of my statement. He says, "Damn, that bitch's got your number."

I know it's a joke, and I laugh along with everyone else.

Baxter addresses the group, "Wednesday?" They all grunt. "Josh?"

He nods and Baxter hugs him. "Miss Parker, I have to go and check on something. But I assume I'll see you soon."

"Nice to meet you, Baxter." I shake his good hand, and he trots off towards the parking lot.

Tommi and Jims give their goodbyes, and I thank them again. The dirty blonde bearded man with the kind robin-brown eyes stays. I don't want to say this, but he reminds me of Winnie The Pooh. He guides me to the rattan couches I put here for the night. He's in a faded and worn Hawaiian shirt that the buttons pull at the belly a bit. He extends his hand to me.

"Sam Langerford."

"Get out! That's my favorite! I love that Chardonnay!"

"Thank you very much. I'm rather fond of it myself."

"Seriously your Chard is freaking lit. I adore it."

"Hey!" Josh screams as he approaches rapidly. Then he puts the ice pack on his eye. I turn to him, and he looks agitated.

"Yours is good, but I like Langerford's better. There's a vanilla to it and not so much oak. I like the mineral flavor better."

They both laugh. Josh turns to me. "Something you should probably share with our winemaker and not the competition. And when did you develop an actual palate?"

He winks at me. Sam retrieves our cocktails that he took from me in the fray. He hands Josh the one with the blue lei at the base. I lean over and switch them, praying that Sam didn't see my panties draped around the base. It seems to be hidden by the lei, but please on everything holy, let him not have seen it.

"Poisoned one and not the other?" Sam asks.

"I already sipped mine." I quickly make an excuse, so my thong ends up in the right place. Then I turn to Josh and say, "Maybe I'll sit with Alena and share my uneducated palate's opinion."

Josh rolls his eyes at me. "I have no doubt Alena will get an earful."

I slap his arm quickly, and he growls at me. I like it much better than when he's silently judgy.

"Who are you, Sam Langerford? Besides a fantastic vine-yard dynasty family?"

He looks to Josh and says to me, "Reporter? FBI?"

Josh's lips curl up again. Gesturing to Sam, he says, "Sam's my…"

Sam fills in what Josh cannot. "Got your back, guy. If we were women, he'd say bestie."

Josh nods at me. I had no idea he kept in contact with anyone from town. When he's in town, he always seemed to be busy Wednesday nights. I wonder if he was with Sam.

"I'm honored to meet you." I toast him.

We all sit and sip. I sit on the edge of the flowered cushion adorning the Rattan couches gathered on the court-yard. Sam shifts in his seat and sips his beer then turns to me.

"I'm not trying to be rude, but I really don't know your name. Did you tell me and I forgot?"

I quickly extend my hand. "Shit. No. Sorry. I thought you were there when your brother announced me. I'm Noelle Parker. You can call me Elle."

He doubles over with a tremendous soulful joyous laugh. "Don't punch me, Josh. But this is the bitch? The cold New

York bitch? You just laid out Gelbert for calling her that. You punched a guy for someone you've hated. And dude, you've called her way worse."

"Hated? Interesting. Cold hard bitches rarely get a moment to relax or hear the things said about them, so this is nice."

I cross my legs and turn away from him. He takes the ice off his eye and faces me with a suggestive smile. "You cannot tell me you didn't hate me."

"You were of no consequence to me. Hate is too strong of an emotion." He instantly begins to tickle me as Sam watches this unfold before him. "Fine. I hate you. I hate everything about your smug bastard ass."

Sam tips his beer back and nods to us. "Fine line, kids between love and hate." He stands and surveys the courtyard. "Hey, did Serena really leave with Asher?"

He knows Serena. He does share some of his life with someone.

"No clue," Josh says.

I shrug, and Sam's boisterous laugh fills the space around us.

CHAPTER FIFTY-FIVE

JOSH

My mind drifts away from Elle and Sam talking. I push what I must do tomorrow from my mind as well. For once I want to just exist at the moment. I'll deal with the backlash and hope that Elle forgives me for leaving, but I can't walk away from her tonight. I should. If I were a better man, I'd kiss her on her forehead, go to the Farmhouse, jerk off, and go to sleep. I'd leave her confused. But I'd leave her intact. I wish I were a better man.

I sit back and look at the gift she brought me, focusing on what's wrapped around my glass. It's not a just a lei, sweet hell, it's her coral thong. I lift my glass and wave it in front of my nose while she watches. Oh yeah, not going anywhere tonight that doesn't involve this woman.

Not quite lilac and orange blossoms. More of clove, orange, spicy potpourri thing going on. She's so arresting tonight. And I wanted to fucking bury Gelbert for not only calling her a bitch but for the whistle. Don't you whistle at what's mine. All I know is I need to fuck her tonight. I need her to feel me from the inside. She's going to beg me to come.

"I will take my leave of you," Sam says. "It's late, and I need to figure out which one of these ladies wants to be my pumpkin."

Elle leaps up with enthusiasm, almost spilling his beer. He seems caught off guard. That's who she is. She's the 'caught off guard' woman with the sexiest, juiciest ass I've ever seen. Just when you think you know her, she does something that catches you off guard. She puts me off-kilter and off guard. This incredibly sophisticated, cool, and collected, Manhattanite wrapped her sex-soaked thong around my glass. The one who was demure and taking care of me just jumped out of her seat yelling at full volume. Her delicate features and her kicks ass brain. She is all things.

"In the tasting room, there's a girl named Samantha. She goes by Sam. She's this tall willowy slip of a thing that's sweet and funny. The one with the auburn streaks in her hair. She's also a force to be reckoned with so don't fuck with her too much. And you already have an opening, the same name. She's single and just through her break-up mourning period. You have the first crack at her. And you're totally her type."

"Intriguing. I'm rarely someone's type. Usually, I have to convince women of that fact. We can't all just walk into a room like Josh or Bax."

"Fuck off, man. Trust me, I've worked my ass off to convince certain individuals that I'm her type."

She shoots me a look and then her lip curls as she turns back to Sam. Yeah, I'm not a good man. I won't walk away from her tonight.

"She moved here from the city to get away from the world she was in. She's twenty-nine. She wants to be a writer. Nonfiction, I think. Oh! Stay here." She bolts into the tunnel, emerges minutes later with one of our pricer bottles of sparkling.

We do it with Champagne Methode but have to call it sparkling because it's not made in the Champagne region in France. My four times great-grandmother, Emma LaChappelle, the 4G, carried the root for the Chardonnay from her family's Champagne vineyards in a large handbag when she moved here. Her father forbid her from making wine. He told her to be a good wife, so she convinced her winemaking husband to leave and go to California to create their own winery. The Cab, Merlot, Pinot, and the Chardonnay all have some of that original rootstock still a part of their grapes. We've cloned and grafted over the years, but the original French root lives on.

But Emma took special care with the Pinot Meunier, her favorite Champagne grape. She wrapped it in wet burlap because she loved bubbles but hated her parents. She dug it up and cut it herself. The Meunier is just a lab sample stock now. We had a hard time making it grow. But it's a classic ingredient of the perfect Champ.

Our sparking is simply Pinot and Chard these days. I should tell Elle that story. It's a good one. She was the first of the LaChappelles in California and according to legend, a badass. I've been told no one could say no to her and she always got her way. Gee, who else do I know like that? Elle has the balls to expertly open the bottle in front of me, even though we could have sold it tomorrow. Then hands it Sam.

"Tell her it got opened by accident, and I asked you to deliver it to her because it's her favorite. She likes bubbles. Then tell her I said it was okay to go home. But I need her early in the morning to help me with clean up. But go. Take her. Have a great night."

"Elle, who said you could open that?" I say authoritatively.

She turns to me quickly and flashes me a sexy eyebrow raise. I'm going to see my handprint on her ass tonight. And it appears she wants that as well.

Sam turns to me. "This woman. She gets shit done. And that shit includes getting me done."

I shout, "That she does. Always in control. Always a plan. Always finds a way to get what she wants. Every decision weighed and precisely executed. She's always accomplishing things, never a moment to relinquish jurisdiction or dominance."

I purse my lips and do an eyebrow raise of my own. Her knees buckle. I'm wearing her thong around my wrist, and I smell it while she's still staring at me. I enjoy that she seems to be stumbling over her words.

"It's so nice to meet you, Sam. I hope to see you again. But you need to leave now."

"Damn girl, thanks for the hookup."

Sam hugs her, and he gives me the thumbs-up sign over her shoulder. I show him what's around my wrist. He feigns a heart attack. Then we're finally alone again. Well, relatively alone. There are about fifty people still milling about and dancing and drinking. It's one a.m. My mom and dad have gone to bed, and I need to bed this woman soon, or I might explode. My cock needs to pump into her, hard.

"Sit here." I rub a spot on the couch next to me. And miraculously, she obeys. Sitting down very close to me, just missing my hand on the seat. "What am I drinking?"

"It's called a Mezcal Chappelle."

"Cute. It's good, and I like the garnish quite a bit. But I didn't tell you to remove this. Please go put it back on."

She looks at me thoroughly confused.

I continue to explain. "Elle, you may be able to maneuver Sam and Sam's evening, but I need you to lose control. There will be a little punishment for opening that bottle. Surrender. Relinquish. That means doing as I say. Whether you understand it or not. Trust me. I know what you need and I'm going to give it to you. Trust."

I look around. No one is paying any attention to us, and I lean to her ear. I nip, kiss it, then whisper. "Surrender, Cosmo." Her shoulders relax as I begin to taste her neck. I say, "I'm going to drink all of you tonight. I believe I told you how I'd remove these earlier. After you put your panties back on, grab us a bottle of whatever you'd like me to lick off your body tonight."

"In that case, I'll grab two. And I'm not putting that back on." She flings it at my face like a rubber band. Even better. Now, I get to punish her just a little bit more.

CHAPTER FIFTY-SIX

ELLE

I WALK AWAY FROM HIM, KNOWING MY ASS IS BEING STUDIED. I have to regulate my breathing. He's barely done anything to me, and I can hardly breathe with anticipation. I walk to the cooler behind the tasting bar and grab a bottle of Chardonnay. I also slam a bottle of water. I'm grabbing the Chard to make amends for calling it too oaky. And I grab a Malbec as well. I know he likes it. I need to drop these off and find Randy. I need to be responsible for a moment. My phone dings.

JOSH: Is your phone waterproof?

ELLE: Yes. But not sure I'm up for swimming.

Then he appears at the door to the tasting room with my panties in his hand again. He picks up my phone and then does something to it while I begin cutting the foil on the bottles. I pay no attention to him. Then he strides behind the bar and behind me. I continue opening the bottles. He swiftly lifts my dress and smacks my cheek with one loud crack. I groan instantly. It's doing something to me that is unanticipated. I want more. He rubs and caresses the exact spot he just spanked. Damn.

"Oh, god."

"That's for the bottle."

I lean forward on the bar and say, "And for not putting my undies back on?"

And he doesn't disappoint by caressing the slightly red cheek and smacking the other one. I move forward. I realize that I'm kind of controlling this moment. I wonder if he'll notice. He leans over my back, and I feel his erection dig into my back. He squeezes my ass while nipping at my ear. My skin chills up all over, but I'm far from cold. He goes to his knees, and I start to light up. He reaches up and unleashes my hair from the French twist, and it falls forward.

"Better. It's more you. The twist updo thing is too New York Noelle. I just want Elle."

"You've got her. Now, what are you going to do with her?"

"Do you know why I like spanking your ass?"

I look at him and roll my eyes. "Because you like my ass."

He spanks me again lightly, and I push into him. "No. Because in that singular moment, neither of us can think of anything else. It instantly pulls you out of your thought process. It's an impulse reaction, not a calculated one. That I can give you that tiny moment of respite from your over-fucking active brain. You and I are the only ones in those moments." I turn towards him and kiss him deeply. I can think while I kiss him, but he's right; in that split second, it wakes me up.

I turn back around, and he goes down to his knees, lifting my feet. He's physically putting my panties back where they started. He licks my ass cheeks and gives them a promising squeeze. He lifts my dress from the front and then deposits my phone into the tiny pocket in the bottom of my thong.

"Think you can keep that there?"

"What the…" He puts his finger over my mouth.

"Don't question. Now go finish up what you need, and I'm going to get these people the hell out of here."

I have an idea of what he's doing. My phone just feels awkward and cold against the wetness. It's sliding around as I walk, and it doesn't feel sexy at all. Then I catch myself as my phone vibrates. It's a crazy pattern I didn't know existed. Not enough to make me release. The vibration is just intense enough to remind me what's to come. It ends, and I search the courtyard for the demon who's decided to possess me tonight.

Randy's drunk babbling at me. I have a bunch of cars and drivers to take the stragglers home, and tonight that includes Randy. But I can't focus.

"Elle. Elle, you are my best friend. You just are. You don't need that man. He's bad."

"Josh?"

"Jims. It's no big deal. I love you, pretty girl."

I ignore his babble and scan the crowd as I get a series of texts. This time, not knowing when it will stop has me biting my lower lip. He's standing over by the drivers, staring at me with his phone lifted in front of his face. I see him madly type, and the anticipation is high.

Randy's arm is around me as he says, "I have to find my pants."

"Randy. I got them. Trust your best friend."

And now, nothing. I watched Josh type, but he won't push send. He's teasing me. Push send, muthafucker. I want more. But then it all stops. I compose myself.

I escort a group of local moms and dads—who have been out for a kidless drunken night—to the parking lot. I'm sending them home in a car with an extra bottle each. I also had the Basque Boulangerie make up picnic boxes for all the last-minute guests to take with them.

I reach for a box of food for the sweet couple in front of

me, and it's a small shock, but I drop the to-go boxes. I try to bend over, and it pushes the phone into my clit, and the onslaught of vibrations doesn't stop. Each time I think it's done, there's more. I say goodnight to them and walk away looking like I'm having a seizure. I grab the edge of the stone building that houses the tasting room to support me. I need to answer him. No one is in sight, and I yank my sticky phone out of my thong. All the texts are the same except for the last one.

JOSH: Not yet, Cosmo. Not yet. Just wait. Feel this. I didn't tell you that you could remove it.

He's walking the last of the guests towards the parking lot when he spies my phone in my hand. His eyes widen, and he shakes his head. I wipe it clean with some napkins and bottled water.

ELLE: I'm trying.

JOSH: Not hard enough.

ELLE: The question is, are you hard enough?

JOSH: You will not be able to sit down when I'm done with your ass.

ELLE: Promise?

He looks up from his phone, and I disappear.

CHAPTER FIFTY-SEVEN

JOSH

GAMES ARE DONE. IT'S TIME TO FUCK THIS WOMAN INTO NEXT week and let her know she's mine. The last of the guests are sloppily hugging each other and me. They keep calling me Will, and I let them. I pass out her sandwich care packages. I'm stunned she thinks this far ahead to take care of these people's hangovers and late-night munchies. The bags have boxes of baguette sandwiches, chips, cookies. The rest of it contains coconut water, Emergen-C, Advil packets, mini mouthwash, vitamin B, and barf bags.

I'm shoving Randy into a car as he tries to kiss me. It's not the first time. He's a good man but ironically can't handle his wine. Then I hear Jackson Browne over the speakers. It's not my favorite song, but it's for me. She put on music for me. I threatened to redden her ass, and she gets me ice for my eye and Jackson Browne. Caught off guard.

I round the barn, and she's pulled a couple of chairs in the middle of the courtyard. She's wrapped in an LC/W picnic blanket. There's a pile of them sitting on a chair next to hers. She's sipping Chardonnay and has poured me a glass of red.

It's probably Malbec, my favorite, knowing her capacity to hold on to details.

I'm not sure if we're winding up the evening, taking a respite or she's seducing me. I stand at the end of the courtyard before she sees me. Her hair is a bit mussed up from the night but falling delicately over her shoulders. She never put it back up in her business French twist since I made it come cascading down.

She's staring out over the Pinot block that sits just off to the right next to the pond. I can hear the crickets and the breeze through the vines. It appears she's just listening. All these sounds are a part of my soul. I'd just turned the volume down on them. Then she jumps a bit when the owls start chattering. The strung party lights are giving off a soft glow and swaying in the breeze. She looks like a painting. So beautiful and untouchable. It's like my home is helping seduce her as well.

My phone pings, and she looks in my direction.

SAM: Hey, man. Not going to make it to breakfast tomorrow. Thank fucking god. Hopefully, I'll be deep into her muff instead of having muffins with you. Call me on the drive.

JOSH: Cool. Tomorrow then.

SAM: Wait, you're still up?

JOSH: So are you.

SAM: I'm on a date. And about to get laid, are u?

JOSH: We'll see.

SAM: She's good for you, man. Hi, Elle!

JOSH: Fuck off.

I put my phone back in my pocket. She's been watching me and now has a curious smile. I need to be with her now. There's something in that smile I need to know. I don't say a word and take long strides to get to her. I bend down and grab her face and take her lips. It's a sweeter kiss than we've shared tonight, but it quickly ratchets up to where I need it. I can't feel what I was feeling. I don't want to be on a date. I don't want to share or have my breath taken away by her beauty. I want to get back to the lust from earlier.

I command. "Stand up."

She does with a mischievous smile and reaches for my drawstring, and I let her.

CHAPTER FIFTY-EIGHT

ELLE

I UNDO HIS DRAWSTRING, THROW MY HEAD BACK, AND chuckle. "Finally."

He instantly scoops me up. I wrap my legs around his waist. He slants his mouth over mine as he carries me back to the couches towards the shadowy area. He places me on the sofa, and his ridiculous shorts fall down around his ankles as he shuffles along. I can see the outline of him in his gray boxer briefs, and I feel him. He's so hard already. He smiles and removes his shirt while I begin to roll down his waistband. I'm delicate, he is not. He whips his underwear off and falls on top of me before I can get a good look. I've missed that thick fucking root of a cock of his. Gorgeous and huge. He inches my dress up and kisses my thighs and my stomach, then stops to look at me.

He looks so earnest I'm afraid he's going to stop what we're heading towards. Now I begin to panic a bit. I need to this. He's not really going to punish me like that by leaving me hanging for real. He's spent the evening winding me up, and I need to let go. I'll do anything.

He says quietly, "I need to know something."

"Anything. As long as you keep moving down my body. Ask while you do it."

"Can't."

"Oh, god. You really are an asshole, aren't you?"

He smiles that amazing fucking smile at me. He's lit the core of flame inside of me, and then he eases off. I want to smash him in the face if all of this was to get me hot and then leave me hanging. He kisses me intensely, and I am ridiculously confused.

"I need to know what happened with Asher. I have a pretty good palate, and I know you taste sublime. But I need to know if he's sipped at this goblet as well. Or anyone since me."

"Asher? Others? Hmmm, let me think."

He jumps off me and rolls me on my side and gives my ass a smack hard enough to restoke my core of desire. I gasp as he does it. I'm instantly flooded and slippery.

"That was for the phone."

I'm still on my side. He's caressing where the skin just flashed hot. His hand begins to search for my entrance. He plays with the rim for a moment as I moan, his tongue kissing and nipping at my back and trailing down towards my ass. Then he flips me back over. I sit up and face him.

"If I tell you what happened with Asher, are you going to think less of me?" I mean it is embarrassing that he didn't want me enough to get me off.

He pulls me to him. His hands are on either side of my face and get so close and graze my lips softly.

"No. Of course not. You met Serena. Imagine trying to stoke that ice queen's fire? I don't care. I'm just a little jealous if he's tasted what I think is the best vintage. I'd like to think that it's a limited production heritage vine estate elixir just for me." Or maybe it's not my issue at all.

I grin widely. "It is limited. And I'm proud to say after several months here I know what all those words mean."

"Wait. He didn't go down on you?"

Josh sits up and seems genuinely offended by this statement. At least someone shares my indignation.

"Not once." I shake my head.

Josh dances around with his hard dick flapping up and down in the inky night. I pull the red picnic blanket emblazoned with LC/W on it up around me. A morning chill over takes me and I miss the body heat that's dancing around the courtyard.

I stand up and walk towards the other end of the courtyard. "Shhh. Someone's going to hear you. And then they'll come down here, and we won't get to finish."

"Good point. But you did fuck him, right?"

I shrug and then bite the inside of my cheek. He laughs at me then runs back over and whips the blanket off me.

"That may require a little punishment."

"Well, in that case, I also went down on him."

He instantly smacks my ass, and I move into him. "He never got you off with his mouth? He's such a selfish asshole."

"In his defense, I like doing that, and the second time and third time, it was to avoid sex. And he never let me finish."

His smile is huge. "So, he's never filled you with cum, in any way?"

"Nope. Condom each time and not sure why he pulled back on the blow job."

"Surely he'd plow you after you got him to the brink?"

"Not really. Asher's an odd duck. He'd just stop and kiss me on the top of the head and walk away to the bathroom. He never got me off in any way."

His gorgeous naked body pulls me to him. I'm in the shambles of my printed blouson-sleeve wrap dress. I'm glad I've worn it a lot because I don't think it will bounce back from tonight. I may be the idiot who wore white to a wine event. But I'm not the idiot who just ripped open the top to get a glimpse of my matching coral lacy bra. That was the naked idiot in front of me.

He sits down and pulls me in front of him. Then raises my dress up, my ass is at eye level. I'm sure it's still red; my skin is too fair to keep secrets. He begins caressing both cheeks and kissing the little divot at the top of my bubble ass. Arching my back, I moan just a little. He smacks where he's been caressing, and I wince.

My nipples grow to twice their standard size with the sting of his hand. I back up into him just a little. He bends me over at the waist. And without warning, his hands are searching for my clit and ripping my thong from my body. His tongue is on me, discovering just how wet I am. His tongue dips into me, and I gasp loudly, and I move into his fingers and tongue.

All I want is to be laying down for this. But then Josh stops licking and reaches under and rubs me. Then another quick smack and a scream from me as pleasure rips me in half from deep within. My nipples are so hard and stretched that I need to grab them myself, my own touch mixing with his. As he smacks my ass again, I pinch my erect and darkened nipples, the pleasure fighting with the pain and releasing me to a place I've never been. His fingers plunge into me.

"Fuck me. So good. Fuck me." I scream loudly as I shiver with release as I clamp down on his fingers. And now I just want more.

His voice is raspy and deep behind me. "Is that what you want now?"

"Yes, please." I groan loudly.

I lean into his lips, trying to force him down so I can ride this man. He stops me and raises his eyebrow.

"I'm not done, pushy woman."

Then he pulls me onto the couch and places me on my back. He unhooks the eye hooks down the front of my dress, and it opens like a robe exposing all of me. He makes quick work of the matching coral La Perla bra. He probably knows, but I may have to remind him of just how much one of their bras costs. But right now my wardrobe means nothing in comparison to what he's doing to my insides. I need him to fill me with his cock soon, or I might actually die.

Now my tit is in his mouth, and my fingernails are digging into his shoulders. Then I grab the sandy hair that is so soft that my fingers slip through unless I truly take hold. He gently rakes his teeth over my nub, and I moan.

"That fucking sound is the best. I'm so hard just from your noises. I'm going to fuck you so hard. I'm going to tear into that tight cunt of yours. Fuck."

"I'm not usually this vocal, but it's been so long since I had this. And your tongue is magical."

"Why didn't Asher go down on you? You're soaked at the thought of it right now. You would do anything for me right now if I promised to suck and swirl your clit."

"Anything. You can have anything. I'd do anything."

"I told you I would get you to beg, Hellcat."

I'm sincere. "I do like it. I like it a lot. But from you, I think need it."

"You think?" Josh raises an eyebrow. I just came, and it's not enough.

"I'm desperate for you to eat me out."

"I'll taste that generous pour in a minute but answer me. Why didn't Asher make you come most gloriously?" He pinches my nipple. I gasp.

"He said it would ruin his palate for days, and his tongue

is his life. You wouldn't ask a concert pianist to move furniture, was his line."

"He's so fucking wrong. It only enhances it."

Josh dives between my legs, spreading them wide and pulling me to the edge of the couch. He puts the blanket on the ground and gets on his knees. He's tracing my hair with his thumbs. "Blonde. True Blonde. Oh, how I've missed this view."

He leans down, licks my inner thigh. Then quickly finds my clit, using his fingers I'm beyond again. I writhe instantly. He moves down towards my opening. I reach down to my unattended center. His hands grab my arms, holding them down.

"Don't make me tie you up. Nod if you understand."

I nod. There's a flutter deep in my twisting stomach at his threat. I moan loudly for him as his fingers spread my lips again. "This is mine. Don't touch what's mine without asking. I don't need help right now. I'm in control. Can you let go? You said you enjoy giving head. Then you can understand that I am going to make a meal of you. What happened minutes ago was my appetizer, and now it's time to dine. I will enjoy every fucking second of it. I need you to come on my face." I moan again. "Good girl. Just keep making that noise, and I won't stop."

"Don't stop. Do it. Make me come again."

"Then submit to me."

"How?"

His eyes are piercingly blue and shining at me in the approaching dawn. I stare back at him, and every part of me wants to grab him and kiss him. I want to reach down and stroke his granite-hard member. But his eyes let me know I should do as I'm told. A new experience for me. I want him, but I trust him. I trust him enough to let go. I've worked for it my whole life, and now he wants me to do nothing but enjoy. I don't have to convince or take care of things myself. I simply get to enjoy it.

"Don't come until I say you can. Hold back. Hold it off until I tell you when to come crashing into me. I don't want a quiver or a wave of ecstasy until I say so. Do what I say, and you'll come harder than you ever have. And for fuck's sake, keep moaning."

I nod, and he tosses me back down on the couches. I moan loudly as his index finger searches inside me again. His mouth and fingers work in tandem for what seems an eternity of pleasure. I'm struggling not to quiver. I'm pushing down into his face to increase the pressure. He's curling inside of me searching around for that one spot that makes me blush more than anything. I moan again loudly as a second finger enters. He's pulling them in and out, stretching and nipping at me with his teeth. His growl on my body vibrates through me. I'm rolling my nipples in the same rhythm as his tongue.

"Josh. Oh. God. Josh. Please. Let me come. I want to come. I have to. Josh." My breath is short and quick. I need this so badly. The pressure builds. I'm wound so tight. "Josh, I have to. Please. I'll do anything you want. Please let me come."

"Keep playing with your nipples." He watches, and it's so hot I might come from his hooded and lustful stare.

I begin whining and gasping. My head thrashing back and forth as he goes at me at a faster pace. In and out, his fingers fucking me as my clit is on fire. The pressure is built, the blood pounding my ears. I've never been to this place before. I need it. I need him to release me. The tension is so high, and with each touch, I struggle not to come.

"Fuck. You have to let me go. I have to."

"Can you hold out while I do this?"

His tongue enters me and swirls while his fingers pinch

my nipples and clit. I thrash my head again and swallow the orgasm by moaning loudly. His name is on each and every breath. I'm bucking wildly against his head and pulling him into me.

"Josh. Josh. Fuck. Josh. Josh. Please."

"That's good begging. Go. Now. My beauty. Come for me. I'm in control. I've got you. Come undone for me. Surrender control. Crash. Ride it. Do as I say. Let it all go."

He sucks my clit hard, and on command, an intense shiver takes over my entire body. It holds me for one second in wordless suspense and then is quickly replaced with a burning flame. I'm shaking and screaming the moan he's been waiting for. I collapse and black out for a moment.

Then as my breath regulates, I pull his face to mine. I taste me on his lips, and I need more. I reach down, and he's insanely hard. He positions me on the couch and himself on top of me. I need his dick deep inside of me.

I grin and whisper, "More."

"You're a fucking demon, Hellcat. It would be my duty and honor to give you more."

And drunk with pleasure, I blurt out, "I'm *your* fucking demon." He kisses me hard. Then I say a terrible thing, "Condom. I know we did it without but…"

"I agree, Hellcat."

His tongue finds mine again. I wrap my legs around him, hoping to god I can stop myself from just letting this happen. Suddenly he's off me, and I'm hyper-aware that he's not touching me. He bolts naked into the tasting room.

CHAPTER FIFTY-NINE

JOSH

I COULD LISTEN AND WATCH HER COME ALL DAY, EVERY DAY. Gorgeous. Poetic. And insanely sensual. I've never made a woman sound like that. I only hope that I'm the only one that can do that to her. Right now, my dick is rock hard and hurts as I run. The condom will help me not explode into her so quickly. Also, she's right, it's safer. I hold my dick and keep stroking it to stop it from weakening in the chill of the morning. I used to keep condoms in this random vintage LaChappelle wooden wine box up on high shelves of the tasting room.

The box looks dusty. Shit. There were a bunch of us that used to use the supplies and would replenish condoms as needed. We called them barn supplies. Each of the five families had a similar box in their tasting rooms. Sam came up with the idea the summer we all started working our family's tasting rooms. Which coincided with the summer we all started fucking tourists. He may not look it, but Sam got more ass than all of us. I think it's his unassuming nature. We hit on tourists all summer long.

The old tasting room manager always made sure they

weren't expired because we rolled through quite a few
supplies together. I only hope the tradition we started
continues to this day.

There's an eerie light in the place with the moonlight
streaming through the door.

A shadow crosses the floor as I'm climbing naked up the
wine racks like a spider monkey. I glance back, and Elle's
standing there in an LC/W winery blanket. The moonlight
creates a halo around her sexy ravaged golden hair. I can't
see the details of her face, but her angelic figure stirs my
mind, heart, and my dick. Not sure there's more I could ever
need or find. She's fucking perfect. Fuck. Sal. I'm not going.
I'm not leaving. I'm not leaving her. I'm staying right here,
and he can just deal with it.

"Jack-fucking-pot." There's a variety of condoms still in
the box. There's an unopened box of my brand. Who knew I
had a legacy here?

"What is up there? Be careful."

"The key to me deep dicking you so hard you forget your
own name and can only utter mine."

"Really? I've already gotten off twice. Hard. So I'm good."

I leap down and swipe at the blanket to reveal her pearly
skin in the soft light. She gasps under my hand, and I kiss her
neck as she reaches for me laughing. She softly moans
against me as I continue to kiss her and pull her to my chest.
She reaches over to the merchandise area and grabs a small
amount of grapeseed oil from a gift set sample. She rubs her
hands together. Then strokes from shaft to tip, and it's my
turn to gasp loudly.

"Elle. Shit. That's insane. That's...That's…"

"Cat got your tongue?"

She grins as her gorgeous skin glows, and her scent fills
the air around us. Her tits stand at attention for me. My
breath is ragged, and the sensation of her hand caressing me

with the oil makes my need to fill her immediate. She licks my lips. I'd fuck her mouth if I had time too. But right now, there are some pressing issues I need to take care.

"No, Hellcat got my cock."

"Hold up. Do I? Hmm, now, what are we going to do with this huge hard rod of yours? If it were my choice, I have an idea, but as you've told me repeatedly, it's not my choice tonight."

Sexy minx. I scoop her up and carry her back to the couches at the far end of the courtyard. The stars are swirling around with the faint rustling of the vines in the distance. They're completing the perfect backdrop to having her completely. My hand clutching her ass as she kisses my neck and my dick bouncing against her back, make this an insanely erotic moment.

I put her down and reach for her swollen and pencil-eraser hard nipples. She pushes me down and mounts me. Kissing down my body.

With my voice desperate and pointed, I say, "I'm going to fuck you now."

She pouts a bit and says in a sticky-sweet voice. "I know I don't have control. And you want to fuck me right now, but may I suggest I get some of that oil off? I mean, we don't want the condom to shred."

I growl at her and push her head towards my cock. She grins madly, eyes flashing, and I realize this was her plan all along. She always gets what she wants. She did say she likes it. She takes my balls in her slightly cold hand, and I suck air in quickly. They are rock hard and tight to my body. She licks from the base of my shaft and pauses just before the tip. This goddess is driving me crazy. "Mmmm. Meyer Lemon."

"I don't give a fuck about the flavor of the oil. My cock needs to be in your mouth or your pussy right now. You pick."

"So demanding."

I'm compelled to look at her and let her know some of what I'm feeling. I pull her chin up, so she's looking right in my eyes, those gorgeous eyes. "You're mine. You were always meant to be mine. And I'm yours. All these glorious dirty things you can do are for me only, you get that, right? Neither of us really have control. Not me and not you. This is bigger than us."

Her eyes soften from jungle cat to kitten. As she comes up to my lips, she kisses me gently. Her sparkling green eyes look more lovely at this moment than all the ones that came before now. She whispers to me, "I know."

She doesn't deny this. I mean every fucking word. I cannot be without this woman or have her with anyone else ever again. For the first time in my life, I'm falling in love. That scares the hell out of me. I'm not going anywhere alone. I'm taking her away so we can stay in bed for a week. And then maybe I'll let her out of my sight. I'm staying right by her side.

She's gently stroking my cock and then flicks the tip with her tongue. I let out a massive groan and twist my fingers into her hair. She slides down on my erect and wet cock. Without pretense, she takes in all of my substantial inches into her mouth. I can feel the back of her throat, and she's slowing sucking me in and out of her pink lips. I slam a hand on the end of the couch keeping my other on the top of her head.

"Shit. Suck me harder."

And she does. So ladylike most of the time and this Hellcat sex diva under the surface. Feels so fucking good. I need her to stop, so I don't blow in her mouth. I want to fill her up in a different way. She looks up at me and slowly backs my dick out of her mouth with a sexy pop.

"Delicious." She winks at me.

"Look, there is going to be a time soon, where I'm going to need you to swallow everything I pour down your throat, but right now I need to come inside of you."

I leap on the opportunity to pin her. I slap the condom on and take her in an instant. I knew she'd still be slick for me. I slide in, and I never want to leave. She groans as I enter. I stretch her, and her tight pussy wraps around me, inviting me deeper. We stare at each other, as connected as two people can be. We don't move. Her hand caresses my cheek, and I kiss it. Then she smiles like the Hellcat who ate the canary, and the sweetness is over as she grinds her hips.

We begin moving together, and I am moving slowly, but she begins to set our pace. As much as I want to explode, I also don't want this to end. I hold her hips and force her to slow down. I don't know what tomorrow looks like, but I do know she's mine right now.

"Fuck me harder. Josh. Fuck me harder."

"I will if you moan. Oh god, your perfect tight cunt. So tight. Elle, give me my moan."

She moans. "You're so deep. You're so good. So big and thick and good."

"You're so fucking gorgeous and sexy. Moan, Elle. Moan for me. You're mine."

"Yes. Yes. Yes, I am."

I slam into her, taking her ruthlessly. "I'll wait until you come. Then I'm going to make you feel me. The hot mess from deep in my soul." I pull out and thrust all the way in.

"Josh. Oh, god. Josh. I'm coming. You moving like that, faster. Right there. Uh. I'm..." And then the loudest most prolonged glorious sound accompanies her twitching body, and her cunt grabs me and pulls me deeper.

I have no hope of holding out. I begin to growl.

She screams, "Show me."

I hold out just long enough to get out of her. She rips the

condom off as I spill on her. Shooting ropes of cum all over her perfect tits. I brand them. An invisible mark that will always live on her skin. And then this Hellcat does the sexiest dirtiest thing she can. She rubs the cum on her tits and moans again. I am still semi-hard, and she puts me on top of her clit. We're slick with a combination of us, and she lifts her pelvis into me, I push down, and she roars and shakes again.

I fall down next to her and grab a bottle of water. Then I clean her up with extra t-shirts and bar towels. Our breath regulates. She's magnificent.

Elle says incredulously, "What the fuck was that?"

"I've marked my territory."

"I'm getting that impression. But I've never done anything even remotely like that before." She looks a little embarrassed, and I can't have that.

I kiss her passionately, proud that I can drive her to insanity. I drove her to a place where she loses control and inhibitions. I want to do all the filthy things to her, but I'm exhausted. I sip from the bottle of lukewarm Chard; it is better than the Langerford's. She's fucking crazy. It's a damn good wine.

She takes the bottle from me and sips. Then lightly kisses me. She's laying on top of me, staring into my eyes. Her eyes are sparkling like the brightest emeralds but softened from her multiple orgasms. Her extremely long eyelashes flutter down as she kisses me again. I pull her to me and lay her head on my chest. I tell her the truth.

"Elle, Cosmo, my Hellcat, I've never done anything like that either. Know that what we do together is ours. Don't judge, just be in this with me." She nods.

I've never wanted to control anyone like I want to control and own her. It's as if I need her to complete me. She's not only opened long-dead parts of myself but discovered new things in my heart and soul I didn't know could exist. I don't know how to deal with all of this emotion. But I know I need to be here with her to navigate it all.

I can't feel this much for her. It's too much. To use my favorite word of the night, it's "more." She's "more."

SHE SCAMPERS to the bathroom wrapped in a blanket. She returns to me and takes my damn breath away again. She snuggles into me and asks.

"What now?"

"You really need a plan, don't you?" She giggles and sits up next to me. She pulls my face to hers.

"At least a blueprint. Rough outline. Something to tell me that you're for real. Can you tell me that I'm not insane for wanting you both in and out of me?"

I pull her hair behind her ear and kiss her softly. "Here's what I know. My immediate plans for the foreseeable future are to be as close to you as possible."

"Let me free up my schedule." She probably means it.

"Pencil me in for all of it." I take her face in my hands.

She kisses me with a little more force and then puts her head on my chest. Her voice is small as she says, "And it's okay that I'm scared?"

"Cosmo, if we weren't scared, it wouldn't be worth it."

WE RETREAT to my bedroom just after sunrise. I don't let her wear bottoms, even those damn perfect yoga pants. It will be easier to ravage her later.

She kisses me. "Josh." Then touches my face.

"Yes."

"Goodnight."

"Until later, Cosmo." She's lightly snuffling instantly, and I wrap myself around her warmth. She's everything now, and I know I won't leave her. Sal's idle threats and empty promises loom in my head. He wouldn't dare. I'll call his bluff. I'll sell my piece of my company. If she lets me, I'll stay right here next to my purring Hellcat. I'll tell my parents tomorrow that as long as she's here, I'll be here. Then we can figure out our next steps. I'm tired of hiding and pretending I haven't completely fallen for her. Or that I'm not in love with Sonoma again. Fuck Sal, I'm rooted, immovable. He wouldn't do anything to me. I make him too much money.

CHAPTER SIXTY

ELLE

I TRY TO SLIDE OUT FROM THE WARMTH WRAPPED affectionately around me. I have to get up. But I can't help but snuggle back down as he pulls me to him. His hand snakes down and circles my opening, and I'm instantly wet for him. I hear condom foil and I'm now thoroughly soaked at the thought.

Then he nudges my leg open and pushes in from behind me. He drapes my leg over his to open me further. He goes up on his elbow and looks down at me as I caress my own tits for him. He's thrusting up, and we can barely contain ourselves. I meet his every thrust, and it's all over quickly with a tremendous shudder from both of us.

We've not spoken. He tosses the condom away and pulls me back towards him. Soft kisses to the back of my neck and shoulders then I hear his breathing even out. He's asleep again. I wish I could be. I kiss him sweetly, but he doesn't stir. I have to be responsible and leave this gorgeous muscled man behind for work. His broad pecs and perfect shoulders beckoning me to nestle down on his chest and stay.

I sneak back to my own room to freshen up then down to

the courtyard to clean up the rest of the party. Samantha's supposed to meet me around 9 a.m. I also grab my bag that's packed for my overnight in the city. I kiss his lips, and he semi-responds and rolls over.

I pray Samantha brings coffee and morning buns from the Basque Boulangerie. Those flaky pieces of sugary heaven can't fix all of the world's problems, but it can undoubtedly fix me up this morning.

Josh and I went to bed in full sunlight. It's been about three and a half hours, but I need to soldier through. I'm headed into San Francisco to meet with some potential winery buyers today who have questions. Then a dinner meeting tonight in the city for the winery followed by a full day of meetings tomorrow. I swallow a fistful of Advil and leave the house. I do indeed feel every inch of what he did to me. I wish I didn't have to leave him right now.

We fell asleep on the couches post-coital snuggling. There was lots of talk about the future, and I think I'm good with it in the light of the day. I want him. And he wants me. This incredible man I once doubted proved to me that he wants all of me. I didn't want to fall for him. I fought it hard, but he slowly but surely found his way into my heart. I trust him.

He woke me up to watch the sunrise and then we put on LC/W merch and collected our tattered clothing and headed to the Farmhouse. He insisted I curl into him. I could get used to being told what to do.

Asher will be at the meeting this afternoon and dinner tonight with the Vino Groupies. I assume he'll be there because he missed the dinner last night with all the winery families. So we'll meet with them today. He claims he can speak to both sides of the sale. Will and I are going tonight, but I'm hoping Josh will tag along. I don't really want to go. I don't really want to be out of bed.

As I round the corner to the tasting room and the courtyard, I grin uncontrollably. Even if my entire body is sore with the pleasure aftermath, I can't stop smiling. Thinking about it, I start to dampen my panties again. We talked about future things. Not coupley things, so to speak, but dirty things involving my ass and innocent things like going to my favorite restaurant in Austin. In those conversations, we both felt the promise of tomorrow, even if we didn't flat out say it.

I see Samantha on the couches with a large bakery bag and a large man kissing her. I call out to them so they know I'm here.

"I take it the night went well?"

Sam says, "Well, if it isn't the first lady of cold-hearted bitches."

I raise my hand in a regal wave as he stands up. My friend Sam beams at his friend Sam. He leans down and kisses her, and I hear him say, "Tonight I cook. Any allergies, Sammy?" Sammy. That's so cute. Now I can tell them apart in conversations.

She smiles, "None. Can there be more bubbles?"

"Plan on it." He attacks her again with kisses.

They're adorable. Sam strides over to me in his clothes from last night, and as he does, he points at my chin.

"That's a mighty interesting stubble burn you got going."

"I still hate him." I smirk, knowing I'm lying.

"Fine line, Cosmo. A fine line between love and hate." I nod at Sam, and he squeezes my shoulder and heads out.

"Sammy?"

She giggles, "Shut up. You can't call me that."

"I'm going to need to so that I don't get the two of you mixed up. And just how mixed up did you get last night?"

Sammy and I get to work, and she regales me with tales of last night. It was romantic and wonderful. I tell her I slept well and say nothing about Josh. She probably knows, but decorum stops her from asking for gossip about the bosses' son. We finish, and I hug her as she thanks me for Sam. I feel as if I've done a good thing. As well as some deliciously bad ones in the last twenty-four hours.

———

I'M SITTING with their former branding agency at what was supposed to be a quick Sunday gathering, not a meeting. I'm exhausted and other people's brand meetings suck. This is going WAY too long, and I hate this shit. I'm bored, and my mind keeps drifting back to this morning. My nipples keep getting taut every time I think of him. I want to go back and do it all again right now.

I look forward to more orgasms tomorrow. My phone vibrates, and I wish I were sitting on it.

JOSH: What am I supposed to do with this tree trunk that's lifting the covers looking for you?

ELLE: You're a smart guy, surely you can handle a little wood?

JOSH: Why aren't you here? I need those lips. I didn't say you could leave.

ELLE: Sadly. I'm in a horrible meeting right now with my thong drenched thinking of you. But I'm in the far-off distant land of San Francisco.

JOSH: Fuck. How did you get forty minutes away from me?

ELLE: It was like an hour with freaky Sunday traffic.

JOSH: How are you this responsible? I thought I told you to give up control. I guess it's more jacking off thinking about you.

ELLE: MORE?

JOSH: Let's just say you're a frequent visitor to my fantasies.

ELLE: Pick one out, and I'll make it come true. Soon.

JOSH: You are the perfect woman. Perfectly filthy.

———

MY DAY DRAGS ON, and then Will blows off the Asher dinner. It's going to be pure drudgery listening to Asher go off on his own attributes. I'm almost ready when Josh texts. I take a quick selfie of my cleavage for him.

JOSH: Why aren't you home yet? When can I expect you on my dick?

ELLE: Tomorrow.

JOSH: WHAT? Nope. That was not cleared. That was certainly not approved. Sam's off banging Sammy. I should be banging you.

ELLE: At the dinner your Dad blew off and then have a 7 a.m. breakfast thing. Am staying in San Fran. Come here.

JOSH: Mom wants to talk to me about something. Come home. Then go back early tomorrow.

ELLE: It will be so, so late and so early with traffic. Can't.

JOSH: I don't want you driving late. If I can scoot out of here, I'll try and get to you. I'll text.

ELLE: Kiss your mom for me. Headed to dinner.

THE DINNER IS ESSENTIAL, but I want to be in Sonoma, not in San Fran for the night. I opened the door for substantial corporation interest like Constellation in a medium production but high-end LaChappelle/Whittier. I was dazzling after Asher was boring as hell.

I scoot out of there before Asher can corner me alone. I was cordial, and he did whisper a strange innuendo in my ear. I told him that I was seeing Josh. Hopefully he gets the message.

I'm grabbing one last glass at the hotel bar. There's an insanely tall and muscular man sitting off to the side of me at a table. His dark eyes look familiar. He was in the restaurant at dinner too. He's so distinctive looking. Now that I piece my day together, he was at Starbucks earlier as well. He must live in the neighborhood. He's staring at me, so I nod and smile. He returns my look but no thanks, not interested. I need a long soaking bath and lots of sleep. Before I go upstairs to my hotel room, I text the one person I wish was here.

ELLE: Asher was at dinner.

JOSH: Did you blow him?

ELLE: My jaw was still tired.

JOSH: LOL. I keep replaying so much of last night.

ELLE: Good. Me too.

JOSH: I'm headed out with Sam. I owe him a night. You cool with that, baby?

ELLE: Can I just say that I like when you call me baby. I like that you are a touch possessive.

JOSH: Good. I'll let you be away from me but just for tonight.

ELLE: Just tonight.

JOSH: I need to chat with you about something later. I need you here, under me, over me. Whichever you choose.

ELLE: No, so wiped out. And I'm super sore. Hard to even walk to the car. I can only make it upstairs. Be back noonish tomorrow. Call me when you get up.

JOSH: Shit. I didn't know that. I need your calendar immediately.

ELLE: So, you can cancel my dinners and meetings?

JOSH: If it interferes with fucking you, then yes. Tell you my thing later.

ELLE: Tell me now. Call me now. I'll try to stay awake.

JOSH: At Sonoma Market, picking up late-night ice cream for Mom. Then I'm headed out. What will you do tonight?

ELLE: Same as you. Touch myself thinking of you, come, and then go to sleep.

JOSH: Can you still feel me?

ELLE: Of course, I can. That giant root of yours stretched me out pretty good. Can I say I wish you were here to share my giant hotel bed with me?

JOSH: Ritz?

ELLE: Duh.

JOSH: I want to take you out on a real date tomorrow. Come home to me early.

ELLE: I'll try. But right now, I'm so tired, I think I'm seeing things.

JOSH: Like stars in your eyes when you remember coming so incredibly hard?

ELLE: Ha! There's a guy here who I think I saw at dinner. And at Starbucks this afternoon. But he looks so familiar. Maybe we're on the same schedule.

JOSH: What man? Have you ever seen him before today? I'm calling you.

ELLE: It's nothing. I said I like the possessive thing, but this is ridiculous.

JOSH: Describe him.

ELLE: Fine. He has dark eyes and muscles and looks a bit like a bulldog, but he's like basketball player tall. Jealous?

JOSH: Shit! Get out of there, please.

ELLE: You are jealous! That's cute.

JOSH: Not jealous. Seriously, do me a favor. Pay your bill and go to your room. NOW. Just go. Elle. Get out of there, please.

ELLE: WTF. Calm down. I'm not going to do anything. Uh oh, the mystery man is coming over.

JOSH: FOR JUST ONE FUCKING TIME. DO AS I SAY. GET OUT OF THERE NOW.

My phone rings.

CHAPTER SIXTY-ONE

JOSH

She picks up instantly asking, "What's wrong?"

"Don't say a word. Elle. I swear to god. Please Hellcat, just be quiet. I promise to explain everything later. Just pay your bill. Go to your room, and I'll call you in five. You have to go to the room. Please do this for me, Cosmo." Fuck me. The threats weren't idle. I hang up and immediately text this asshole.

JOSH: Leave her the fuck alone.

SAL: Joshie. Who? This one?

My phone dings and I lose my shit. It's a picture of Elle sipping wine, looking at her phone. Sal's there, not a goon. I know he won't get blood on his hands, but that doesn't make me feel any better.

JOSH: Bax. Are you in the city?

BAXTER: Yes.

JOSH: Get to the Ritz Carlton bar as fast as possible and find Elle from last night. Escort her to her room and make her stay there. I'll explain later.

BAXTER: On my way. I'm only a couple of blocks from there.

JOSH: Thank fucking god.

Bax will get her. He'll make sure she's okay without asking questions. Fucking Sal.

JOSH: Sal, if one hair on her fucking head even gets frizzy, I will end you. I will ruin everything about you.

SAL: You can fucking try. In the meantime, it's time to go home, Joshie. And remember, I'm a ghost. You tell no one about me. Do not explain why you left. Let everyone think you just went home. Not one fucking word to a single soul or you'll see that I don't do empty threats. Do not come to see Blondie. Meet me at Napa Airport- hangar 17 in forty-five minutes. I'll give you a ride home.

JOSH: Do not go near her or my family.

He sends me another picture. It's my mom walking the dogs from earlier today.

JOSH: I'll be there.

SAL: I know that you will.

JOSH: Fuck you. Until the end of time, fuck you, Sal.

SAL: Tick tock, Joshie. 44 minutes left.

He's got my fucking balls in a sling. I call Elle, and there's no answer. Fuck.

BAXTER: She's not here, man.

JOSH: Keep looking. Is there an Italian man in the bar?

BAXTER: No, just some suits. That's it.

JOSH: Thank you. Now get out of there.

BAXTER: Do you want me to go upstairs to her room? You okay?

JOSH: No. No. Thank you, man. Call you tomorrow.

I'm freaking the fuck out. I call and leave another message. Just when I'm almost to the Jeep to break every traffic law in the world and ignore Sal's demands, my phone rings. I exhale.

"What? That's like nine missed calls. Mr. Mysterious," she says exasperated.

"Elle. Where are you?"

"Changing and washing my face in the bathroom of my hotel room. What the hell is going on?"

I vamp. I can't tell her any of this. Sal warned me, and I don't know if my phone is tapped. "I just wanted you alone. I wanted to see if you'd like to…"

"No. Too tired, baby. And I'm too sore, my Josh."

I like being her Josh, but I'm not sure I'll get to keep the title after tomorrow. I need to get off the phone now that I know she's safe. Fuck. There's no way to explain this to her. I'll have to put my faith in our connection. But for now, my Elle, I need to burn it down. Cruel to be kind, I guess. I can't have her chasing me. I can't have her trying to fix the situation. I can't have her on his radar or even in my sphere. Fuck. It's going to destroy me, but I won't put her in danger. She won't understand, but hopefully, in time, she can forgive me.

"Okay. Hellcat. Are you already in bed?"

"Yes. Drifting off thinking of you."

"Elle. Oh God. Sweet, sweet, strong, beautiful, smart Elle. I need for you to keep believing that I'm always thinking of you. Can you do that? Last night was perfect. Perhaps the most perfect night of my life. Don't doubt that. I meant everything I said."

"Hmmm. Yours." She's already drifting off.

It stabs at me that tomorrow I won't be hers. "Sleep well, baby. Get yourself in working order for the next time I see you."

"Goodnight, Suit," she says dreamily, and it's ripping my fucking heart out.

"Until later, Cosmo."

I couldn't bring myself to say the word *tomorrow* because I know she won't take my call.

"GLAD TO SEE you're finally fucking get this. Turns out you *can* listen."

I don't even look at Sal as I board his plane. I take a seat in the back and ring my hands.

"Joshie, talk to me because we need to lay some ground rules."

"You mean in this new hellscape that I'm fucking trapped in. Is this who you are Sal? Was I that fucking wrong about your humanity?"

He leaps from his seat and towers over me. I'm scared for my family and for myself. But I will not show one ounce of fear to this piece of shit.

He roars at me, "This is who I am when I'm at war. This is not who I am in life. And this is certainly not who I want to be but right now it's who I have to be. I've shielded you as best I could Josh but that ends today. I don't have time to fucking separate the two and hold your pussy ass fucking hand. So do as I say and we all get the fuck out of this situation. Don't make me have to handle you too. Don't contact Blondie. Don't contact your friends. Your parents are already traceable but keep it brief with them. You use only this phone to contact me."

"What the fuck?"

"Anyone you contact gets put on list. I won't let your people be used as my liability. Don't doubt that I'll take care of it first. But I need you. There will be a man at your house and office twenty-four-seven. You take on no new clients and no new partners. You don't take a shit without telling me first."

I nod. My balls are a bit tied up for a while. "How long am I your bitch?

"As long as I need. Last uprising was almost a year. So tuck in for a good long fucking time. Josh, I don't want to hurt you. You're the only person I can completely trust right now."

"You know I don't give a shit what you do to me."

"And that's exactly why I need this to matter." He pulls up his phone and shows me a picture of a hotel door. He has someone outside her door. "You and I are the same. It doesn't matter what happens to us, only them." He turns and heads back to his seat. I don't say another word, mostly because there are none.

CHAPTER SIXTY-TWO

ELLE

MY BREAKFAST MEETING BECAME A LUNCH MEETING, AND I'M finally finishing up with the event company that's going to put on an end of summer city event for us. The thought of his touch overwhelms me, and I begin to blush. I just want to be with him now. I think I could fall in love with him. Actually, I think I am falling in love with him.

The man in front of me asks if I'm too warm. Damn this sensitive skin, hides nothing. Nope, not hot, just thinking about Josh again. I'm left alone at the table for a moment, and I text Will to see if he needs anything from the city. I'm a little tingly and nervous at the thought of seeing Josh. Other than his cryptic texts and odd phone call, he's been off the communication grid today. I'm sure he's sleeping. I slept like a rock last night. I hope he's still in bed when I get home.

WILL: I need the chocolate and cheese. Puleeeeze.

ELLE: COME ON! I'm nowhere near that store.

WILL: You work for me.

ELLE: No! I'll pick up Ho's Szechuan green beans on the way out of town if you want.

WILL: Don't bother. I'll just call Della Santina's. Pick it up on the way home. Gnocchi?

ELLE: Sure. Unless Josh wants to split the dorata.

WILL: He's gone.

ELLE: Out with Sam?

WILL: My son's a shit. Contact him. I'm out of this.

I tune back into the meeting long enough to answer some questions but quickly pull up his number. As I have a chill that's overtaking me and that distrustful ball of knots in my stomach seizing up.

ELLE: Where are you?

JOSH: Home.

ELLE: Where?

I hold my breath and pretend to scribble notes in my notebook and check my phone for stats and nod back to the man boring the hell out of me. I can't breathe.

JOSH: Santa Barbara.

ELLE: For how long?

JOSH: A while. Maybe longer.

ELLE: Are you serious?

JOSH: Yes. I had to. Just leave it alone. Elle. I had to go back to work. I had to leave.

I'm numb. I'm crushed. Was I used? Hell, no. There is no fucking way that was a one-night thing. Oh, my god. He left. He left me. And I freaking knew he would, but I fell for him anyway. Shit. The reality is creeping into my system like ice water in my veins.

I'm so embarrassed that I thought this was something else. Josh Whittier will pay for making me feel like this. Asshole idiot for thinking he can make me trust him and then do something like this. And I find out from Will. Asshole. No way you get away with this. He's a coward. Or he totally led me on. What was all that "you're mine" shit? He knew he was going to get lucky. And he knew he was leaving. Why bother making me believe there was more?

There's no way he didn't feel what I was feeling. I was so careful not to believe his bullshit for so long. He shattered any amount of trust he built. Stupid. Stupid Noelle. I gave up control. I'm an idiot. I'm an amazing idiot who went back on the only tenant I try to live my life by. Always know the outcome or know how to manipulate things to go my way.

I control my life, heart, and business. And he fucking weaseled his way under my skin and into my blood. I made stupid decisions based on how my body reacted to him. He opened me up in so many ways that I knew were dangerous, but I couldn't stop myself. Fuck. Oh, dear god, I wiped him all over my breasts. And he spanked me. Dammit. I wish I didn't like that from him. I'm so embarrassed. I hate men. Especially Joshua Lucien LaChappelle Whittier. People are talking in front of me, and I can't pay attention to any of them. I will recommit to this meeting. Concentrate on this and address the Josh issue later.

A man with the yellow shirt just said something important about the Beverage Event Order and I have no idea what it is. When did he leave? Yesterday? This morning? Yes, salmon is great in a puff. That will be fine as an appetizer. Wait.

"I'm concerned about serving fish in the heat during cocktail hour."

And now they blather on. I can't do it. I can't do this meeting. "I'll be right back." I bolt out to the street and pace up the block, trying to calm myself down. Doesn't work.

ELLE: Asshole.

ELLE: Answer me.

ELLE: Josh?

There's no answer. That's something.

ELLE: You're shutting the door on this? I'm trying to under-stand. Maybe I'm not. Just answer me. Call me later. Call me now.

I turn my phone off, walk back inside, and pretend I have an emergency. This is all nothing I want to be a part of. I want to smash something, mostly his face. I leave lots of money on the table and disappear into the winding roads that will take me back to the scene of the grime.

I turn my phone back on at a red light on my way out of the city and fully expect a message explaining all of this. That's it a misunderstanding. That I overreacted. That he's kidding and he's taking me out for that date he talked about tonight. But there's nothing. My phone is eerily silent. I'm left with nothing.

ELLE: Fuck off.

ELLE: Fuck off.

Sitting in the parking lot in front of the Farmhouse, I stare at my phone as if it's going to magically take this pit of pain way. I send my last text. This will be my last contact with him.

ELLE: There's no fixing this. So, I say again: Fuck off, Joshua.

He's tainted it, made it all dirty. What was all that shit about me being his? How stupid am I? Jackass. How can I trust what he said if he doesn't trust me enough to tell me he was leaving or why he left? Be open with me instead of demanding I believe in him. He didn't believe in me. That's apparent. I was fine. Fuck him for making me feel I wasn't alone. Fuck him for making me feel more alone than I ever have before.

He makes me care about him, sleeps with me, then leaves. And screw him because it was the best sex I've ever had. I will dream about and masturbate to that sex for years to come. For every Asher in my future, where I have to take care of myself, it will his stupid face I see as I come.

Tears are stinging the back of my eyes, and I'm struggling to keep them hidden.

I gave up control, and this is what happens. Not only did I let him see my vulnerabilities, but he rejected them. I need to get a hold of myself. I need to wrap up this project and get the hell out of the Whittiers' life and work. I'll get someone to handle the day to day. I need to leave.

I'll never forgive him for ruining this for me. For contaminating every part of this experience for me. Jackass. I can be gone in a month if all goes well. The sale will be set, and I can leave right before harvest. Although I would have liked to be a part of it, I have to remember that I'm Parker and Company, not a LaChappelle/Whittier. I'm not a vintner. I have no real place here. It's time to go back to the life I carefully built and cultivated over the years. I have to retreat to my safe place, out of pain or confusion.

Josh is no part of that. New York remains untainted. There's no reason on earth for me to ever speak to him again. Not to be petty or angry, just a fact. Whatever place he carved out for himself in my world has closed up, or I'll seal it off with a blowtorch. There will be nothing left and no room for him in my heart or life. See ya, Josh.

CHAPTER SIXTY-THREE

JOSH

THE PAIN AND GUILT I FEEL ARE CRUSHING ME. SHE'S SAFE. I can't believe I have to do this to her. I read her texts and I can't breathe. All I want is to be buried inside of her or have my arms wrapped around her. It's killing me. I won't let anything happen to her or my family. If I lose her, there won't be a day that passes that I don't make Salvatore Pietro pay. There won't be a moment that I don't make him suffer at my hands. Both physically and financially. I will find a way get out of this and back to her. I have to get back to her. You want to play dirty, you fucking Capo, let's dance.

I can't lose her. I won't. She's mine.

End of Book One

WHAT'S AHEAD!

Thank you for reading! I'm so excited you're here. I can't believe Josh and Elle are out in the world instead of just living in my head. I sometimes wish I didn't know what was going to happen so I could enjoy their journey for the first time. But trust me, it's sooo good.

Josh and Elle will return in **Rootstock**, Book 2 of the LaChappelle/Whittier Vineyard trilogy. Available for pre-order on Amazon.

Then their story concludes in **Uncorked**, Book 3 of the LaChappelle/Whittier Vineyard trilogy. Pre-order this one too on Amazon.

You can find all kinds of information and silly extras at all the usual suspects: Book Bub: Kelly Kay, Instagram: @kelly_kay_books, Facebook: KellyKayBooks or sign up for my newsletter at KellyKayromance.com

At least visit the website for the Crushing Spotify playlist!

AND coming later in 2020 a new series spin off- Chi Duets. The first set of stories focuses on another sassy Sonoma resident and her path towards her own Happily Ever After.

Shock Mount (Book One of A Lyrical Duet)

Meg Hannah stores memories and feelings in her mind, in a sacred space she calls her Pantheon. She's waited a long time to move past her divorce and is now all packed up and ready to move from California to New York with her long-distance boyfriend, a hot documentary filmmaker. She has one more night to treasure Sonoma and make memories to store away in her Pantheon. Ian Reilly, pop star, interrupts her well-laid plans for the evening.

He's an internationally famous musician with a million fans but seems to only have eyes for the one girl he can't have.

The feel of his hands, the way he looks at her, the way he makes her laugh makes her question her move for a moment. But after that innocent night she tucks him away as a memory, she only hopes that he'll stay there.

Find out if Ian can stay out of Meg's life in Book One of the A Lyrical Duet- **Shock Mount**. Out later this year.

ACKNOWLEDGMENTS

I didn't think I'd ever be in a place to write what I love. Romance, comedy, and a little bit of cheeky content. I'm so grateful for anyone who reads this. And I hold a special place in my heart and soul for all of those people who actively annoyed, pushed, and encouraged me to do it. I'm so freaking grateful.

It doesn't just take a village to raise a child; it takes one to create a novel or three in my case. There are some who have read all my words dating back a decade and pushed me to self-publish years ago, ahem Celia Fleischaker, and I didn't trust them. I do now. Thank you for believing in me when I wasn't ready to do so myself.

I have so many plots and plans and books to come. And the people that I'm about to list are the only reason I'm able to do any of this.

My beta readers and alpha women. I love you and appreciate every gasp, comment, and criticism from all of you. Special shout out to my sister, Allison, my hype woman, friend, my confidant, and my first critic and fan. Cindy, Liz , Wendy G, Emily & Sara I

I am so fucking lucky to have a legion of amazing women and men at my back:

- The Divas- Nancy H & Boyd
- The Librarians- Corie , Sarah W, Mary & Christy
- The OG Mamas- Karen Y, Rene, Dori , Nancy A & Willow
- My sisters from 633 W Jefferson who helped give birth to Kelly Kay, all naming credit to Sally B. Stafford- Karen O, Kim, Leenie & Sal
- And Brooke, Mikki, Billy & Holly for always understanding who I am and celebrating it.

Becki Shunick-Farm who makes me look and feel beautiful every 6 to 8 weeks. Who provided a laptop to format this book and a safe haven to work. I've written some of my favorite chapters sitting in her chair at B. A Salon on Armitage. Thank you.

The Currys who selflessly chatted about ISBN numbers and technical things and shared self-publishing tales. New to my world but I knew instantly they were my tribe.

The Bunker who never doubted that Lanie Abbott, Kelly Kay's beta testing name, had a place in this world. I stand on the shoulders of Negronis (which I hate) and long evenings of substantial chatting and laughing (which I love.) Matt, Jill, Amy & Tim*- thank you. And thanks to the Bunker Jr. for occupying yourselves while we have dinner and one too many Jill created cocktails.

Timothy Muthafucking Papi Hogan gets an asterisk. He designed my covers and gave Kelly Kay a look and feel. He branded her, and I'm eternally grateful for his artistry and encouragement. Or just pouring another glass of bourbon and chatting about the state of the world and music. Thank you my talented friend.

Erin Young, you are an editing goddess. She saw my words and knew exactly what I meant when I got tongue-tied. I will forever be grateful that I found you. We have much work to do together.

Holly Jennings is the one who knew if she just moved a word, a comma or a dash, my writing would sing brighter. She also reminded me that Irish skin would probably burn not tan. Thank you. Thank you. Thank you.

Mom, Babs, thanks for always letting me scribble on the walls and outside the lines. And please, don't read the dirty parts. My brother, Jess, who will always be the one who had my back first. You're not allowed to read the dirty parts either. Nichole, SIL extraordinaire, you can read the dirty parts if you want. Thanks for believing in me.

There's no romance without my husband, Eric. I love you to the ETC. box office and back. And that kid of ours is pretty terrific. Thanks for him too. And for the space and breadth to find my way. (And the wine delivery to the couch.) You keep me awash.

And Charlie, thank you for turning down Teen Titan's Go or serenading me with piano while I was writing in our shared living room space. I love you.

Thank you to Sonoma and all but two people in that beautiful city. It's odd to thank a whole city, but that's what I'm doing. You'll always have my heart and thanks for providing the backdrop and inspiration for these books and the ones yet to come. I'll miss you Landlass.

About a year ago, my sister recommended I read some of the books she loved. She and Cindy Valdes bombarded me with titles and authors. (#teamedward4eva). I've read voraciously ever since. These writers, these women, became my teachers of the genre I wasn't sure I could write. And now I've read their entire canons, become a fangirl, and have learned from the best. **Thank you to Helena Hunting,**

Meghan March, T.K. Leigh, Lili Valente, Aleatha Romig, K.A. Linde, Willow Winters, Lisa Renee Jones, Staci Hart, Laurelin Paige, and Pippa Grant for your words, humor, your wild strong heroines and alphas to drool over.

(Psst, hey readers. While you wait for my next book, which I'm writing as fast as I can, read theirs.)

ABOUT KELLY KAY

I used to create "dreams" with my best friend growing up. We'd each pick a boy we liked, then we'd write a meet-cute that always ended with a happily ever after.

Now I get to dream every day, although it's a little steamier these days. And I've discovered I can and will write anywhere I can. I have photographic proof.

I'm a writer, married to a writer, mom of a creative dynamo of a nine-year-old boy and currently a little sleepy. I'm a klutz and goofball and love lipstick as much as my Chuck Taylors.

Random good things in the world: pepperoni pizza, Flair pens*, road trips, coffee, sidesplitting laughing fits, matinees on a weekday, the Chicago Cubs, a fresh new notebook full of possibilities, bourbon on a cold night, Fantasy Football, gaggles of friends, witty men, local zoo in the rain and that moment when a character clicks in and begins to write their own adventure. I'm just the pen.

Oh, and wine. I like wine. (duh)

*purple is my favorite Flair pen

Made in the USA
Monee, IL
11 May 2020

29960688R00196